PRAISE FOR

LIKE THE RED PANDA

"Like a contemporary *The Catcher in the Rye* in knee socks . . . a fresh, heart-breaking and tragicomic take on life." —*People*

"Stella may be the most mordantly funny teen narrator since Holden Caulfield—and her quirky story as memorable as J. D. Salinger's classic." —*Teen Vogue*

"If you fell for Scarlett Johansson in *Ghost World,* chances are you'll develop a crush on Stella Parrish, the hilariously disaffected heroine of Andrea Seigel's surprising debut."
—*Time Out New York*

"[An] unabashedly honest novel . . . Read this if you feel like commiserating with your present, past or future teenage angst." —*Elle Girl*

"Stella Parrish can't handle life's absurdities. Deciding to end it all, she details the last days of her senior year in her journal as a suicide note. Using biting sarcasm, Stella dissects her world, giving voice to those wickedly funny things that everyone thinks but nobody would dare to say out loud."
—*Seventeen*

"*Like the Red Panda* succeeds because it transcends cliché . . . By artfully evoking the despair, even the hopelessness, of such an endearing character, Seigel reaffirms our own private hope that maybe, after all, life does have meaning."

—*Salon*

"*Like the Red Panda* doesn't fall for easy solutions or banal effects, as our heroine keeps trying for a miracle that will obviate what she has set out to do. I hope this novel finds the widest possible audience." —Joanne Greenberg, author of *I Never Promised You a Rose Garden*

TO FEEL STUFF

ALSO BY ANDREA SEIGEL

Like the Red Panda

TO FEEL STUFF

ANDREA SEIGEL

A Harvest Original • Harcourt, Inc.
Orlando Austin New York San Diego Toronto London

www.HarcourtBooks.com

This is a work of fiction. Although some actual places and organizations are named,
Brown University in particular, any resemblance to actual persons, living or dead;
events; or behaviors is used merely for verisimilitude and is entirely coincidental.

Library of Congress Cataloging-in-Publication Data
Seigel, Andrea.
To feel stuff/Andrea Seigel.—1st ed.
p. cm.
"A Harvest original."
1. College students—Fiction. 2. Brown University—Fiction.
3. Providence (R.I.)—Fiction. 4. Parapsychology—Fiction. I. Title.
PS3619.E424T6 2006
813'.6—dc22 2005030796
ISBN-13: 978-0-15-603150-9 ISBN-10: 0-15-603150-7

Text set in Garamond MT
Designed by Cathy Riggs

Printed in the United States of America

First edition
A C E G I K J H F D B

For my S.F.D., with love

"Because if it's not love then it's the bomb, the
bomb the bomb, the bomb.
The bomb, the bomb
the bomb that will bring us together."

— THE SMITHS

TO FEEL STUFF

CHAPTER 1

THE JOURNAL OF PARAPSYCHOLOGY OCTOBER 2004

E and Me

BY MARK KIRSCHLING, M.D.

Life is unpredictable, even for those of us whose job it is to predict it. Doctors, such as myself, observe symptoms and, from those harbingers, predict what will come next. We see glimpses of our patients' futures. We are, however, lousy fortune-tellers because no matter how far ahead we may try to look, we are inevitably thwarted by the unpredictability of life and its many forms. We are never granted more than glimpses.

Before I began this study, I predicted that I would publish in *The New England Journal of Medicine* a paper full of test results and established diagnoses. Clearly, I failed to predict correctly. I do not intend this as an insult to the readers and contributors of this journal, for which I have more respect than I could have imagined, but because my failure is so integral to the conclusion of the study itself.

I believe I predicted incorrectly because I imposed on those glimpses available to me the only type of future that I could imagine. Or, rather, I imposed on them the only type of future that I, in my chosen profession, had been trained to accept.

I first became acquainted with my subject, E, in October of 2002. My longtime associate, Dr. Smith Wainscott, told me of a female patient who had been admitted to Rhode Island Hospital an unusual number of times over the past thirteen months. He had been her attending doctor for many of these admissions, and her case had become a source of fascination for him.

"I've never seen a short-term medical history like this patient's," Dr. Wainscott told me. "Or even a long-term history. It's not only that she's had such exotic diseases—which, in fact, she's had. But it's that she's had so many, both ordinary and extraordinary."

Wainscott and I walked the downtown streets, discussing this mysterious E. Downtown Providence is a cityscape with a strange aesthetic allure for a doctor. Because the skyscrapers are few, and in most other cities wouldn't even be referred to as skyscrapers, it's an environment that can lead a man to believe that he might accomplish anything. He's never dwarfed, as he might be in other cities. On that night in particular, the scale of the buildings made me feel as if I held my own against my surroundings, which, in turn, made me feel as if I could do the same against this complicated E. I asked Wainscott to tell me everything he could remember about her.

Wainscott began to list the girl's diseases, counting them off on his fingers; when he ran out of fresh fingers, he folded them back into his palm and recycled.

I had been invited to teach at the Brown University School of Medicine because of the pain research I had done in Chicago. My studies had become well known, and the university, in need of a specialist in the field, offered me so many inducements I couldn't refuse. When Wainscott finally arrived at E's lingering fibromyalgia, a diffuse, physical pain that many experts believe to be psychosomatic, my mind was swimming with images of her.

I knew that I wanted to meet E, but that I couldn't compromise Wainscott's ethics. I couldn't show up on her doorstep, introduce myself by saying that my doctor friend had been discussing her multiple illnesses with me, and then ask if I could check her blood pressure. I asked Wainscott, "Do you know how I might run across this E?" I was hoping he'd invite me to observe during one of her inevitable future visits to the hospital.

To my surprise, Wainscott told me, "You can just go to the Brown infirmary. She's living there."

"She's staying there?" I asked.

"She's living there," he reiterated. "Her illnesses have piggybacked one upon another, so that nearly every time she's recuperated, she's been knocked down by something else. I wasn't exaggerating, Kirschling."

I found this incredible, and wanted to know why the girl hadn't been sent home. If she was so ill, why hadn't the school put her on leave?

"If you pay your full tuition and don't make too much noise, it looks as though they let you stay," Wainscott said, smiling.

Later I found out that this wasn't wholly true. Even though E's bills were covered, the administration had been viewing her with an uneasy eye since September. When she briefly returned to a semblance of health in the spring of her freshman year, the registrar had allowed her to enroll for her fall semester sophomore year, believing that she would be able to resume a normal student life. By the end of May, however, E was back in the infirmary, and through the bureaucratic grapevine, I found out that a few meetings had been called among the deans in an attempt to decide what to do with her. Her professors accommodated her illnesses by delivering assignments to the infirmary, administering exams via the nurse practitioners, and holding monthly bedside "office hours." I spoke to one professor under the promise of confidentiality, and he shared with me that "E probably attended class just as often as at least eighty percent of the kids in my lecture. That is, not at all."

The university, however, began to feel it necessary to draw a line that fall while avoiding any sort of discrimination lawsuits. The powers that be were beginning to fear that E would spend another semester, perhaps even another year, inside the infirmary, and wondered how they could defend themselves against the question of whether or not she had had an actual college experience. Among the deans there was reported discomfort surrounding the conditions of her being awarded a diploma, and there was talk about asking her to redo the in-class credits that she had missed as a result of her extended stay in the infirmary.

Luckily, I discovered E through Wainscott at exactly this time.

A week later, I stood in front of Andrews House, otherwise known as Brown University's Health Services. The building is a red brick classical revival with white pillars framing the entryway. It still looks like the private residence that it was at the end of the nineteenth century. There is nothing clinical about the exterior of the building; as a matter of fact, there is very little that is clinical about the ground floor of the interior, either.

I had been inside Health Services before to visit associates and to retrieve records, but had never looked at the environment through the eyes of someone who might, in this day and age, consider it her residence. Whereas previously my impression of the ground floor had been that it was simply open and inviting, when I set foot in the building that day, I suddenly envisioned it as the parlor that it must have been a hundred or so years ago. I began to interpret things as E might.

On the left side of the floor were chairs and coffee tables, arranged to encourage conversation. From what I've since observed during my time in the building, patients instead tend to be silent, reading magazines and filling out their forms. On the day of my initial meeting with E, a student was having such a bad coughing fit that he exiled himself at the northern windows.

I approached the back stairwell, where a sign directed visitors upstairs and instructed them to follow the lines of colored tape on the floor. The green line led to the pharmacy, the blue line to the waiting room on the second floor, and the yellow line to the lab.

I chose arbitrarily to follow the green tape because there was no colored line designating the route to the infirmary. The green path took me through a corridor with a long, built-in desk, at which a nurse practitioner was entering patient files into the computer. This was Vivian, whom I later came to know well.

I asked Vivian where the infirmary was and she pointed to her right, where I saw a closed door that looked no different from the other closed doors in the hallway. I don't know what I expected—not an entire wing devoted to the school's ill, but maybe at least a plaque. I introduced myself, told Vivian I was a doctor and professor, and asked if I could look in on the facilities.

"Sure," she told me. "We only have one patient right now, and she's out of contagion."

I knew she was speaking about E. I felt an overwhelming sense of anticipation, as if I were about to set eyes on a long-lost love. I don't say this to romanticize the doctor–patient relationship or to suggest that I had anything other than a medical interest in E, but to communicate the magnitude of my feelings about the possibilities of the case.

The infirmary was dim and I had to wait a moment for my eyes to adjust from the brightness of the hallway. Vinyl shades were pulled down over the windows, even though it was the middle of the afternoon. There were translucent curtains over the shades, which I found to be a strange touch, as they seemed to have no utilitarian purpose. It was almost as if they were hung as a joke. I saw six beds with metal frames, all of them empty.

Stepping back out to the nurse's desk, I tapped Vivian on the shoulder and said, "I thought you told me that you currently have a patient."

"We do," she responded.

Then I had a crazy thought: that E had been in the room, and that, for some inexplicable reason, I had not been able to see her. "Could you please show her to me?" I asked. "I'd like to talk with her about her impressions of the infirmary. Her general experience."

Vivian looked at me as if I had insulted her intelligence,

which wasn't my intention. I couldn't tell her, however, that I was finding myself mistrustful of my own eyes.

We approached the infirmary door together, and after Vivian opened it to look inside, she said, "You're right. She's not in here." Vivian gave me an even more insulted look than before, obviously thinking that I had taken her from her work to rub her nose in her error. "She must be down the hallway."

"Down the hallway?" I echoed.

"In the waiting room at the end of the hall. Follow the blue tape on the floor."

I wanted to know if E was waiting to see one of the Health Services doctors. I didn't want to keep her from an appointment.

"She's not waiting for anything. She just sits in there sometimes," Vivian said. I found this odd, but didn't question her further.

I followed the blue tape to the waiting room, a sunny rectangle with wooden chairs lining its perimeter. From the vantage point of the open doorway, I stood and surveyed the four patients who were sitting in the chairs. I knew which one E was right away, not because she looked any sicker than the other patients, but because she looked so at home.

Whereas the other three patients each held a single magazine, novel, or clipboard with an informational form on it, E occupied not only her chair, but the chair to the right of her, the chair to the left of her, and the floor space in front of them. She had books and papers strewn about the chairs and a laptop computer balanced on her thighs. She was using the waiting room as an office of sorts, and she was so busy with her work that she didn't feel my eyes upon her, and thus didn't look up. The other three patients all sensed my presence and stared at me, wondering why the man in the doorway was watching the young woman with the computer, since he wasn't making any movement toward her. This was when I decided, for propriety's sake, to enter the room and approach E.

E has black hair and white skin, the kind that is so translucent that I could see, even from a few feet away, a blue vein in her right temple. Because she was looking down at her laptop, the only features I could immediately make out were her eyebrows, eyelashes, and eyelids, all of which were heavy and dark. I remember thinking that E's eyebrows were much like those of Brooke Shields in the 1980s. She had blunt bangs that skimmed these eyebrows, and the chin-length hair framing her face was tucked behind her small ears.

I'd expected her to be in a nightgown or a hospital gown, but she wore dark blue jeans and a white thermal top. She was remarkably thin, but the thinness seemed natural on her. She was wearing socks but no shoes, which also told me how comfortable she'd made herself in the building.

I walked over to E and stood in front of her. "Excuse me," I said, "but may I talk to you for a minute?"

She looked up at me and I saw the bow of her upper lip. "Are you a doctor?" she asked in a voice that, strangely, made me think of tinsel.

I was surprised at this question, since I was not wearing any credentials, nor was I wearing my coat. I admitted to E that I was a doctor.

I helped her collect her things from the floor and chairs, and we returned to the infirmary together. At that time E was recovering from a potent mix of pneumonia and strep throat, and she was also weakened by a marrow extraction she'd undergone after the hospital discovered her aplastic anemia. She walked slowly, but declined my arm when I offered it to her.

Once back in the infirmary, I asked if I could pull up the vinyl shades to let in some light, but E ignored my question. Instead she asked me, "What are you here for?"

Seeing that E was not what you'd call a natural-born "people pleaser" and that she didn't have a great deal of patience for me, I knew that I would have to present my offer to her with precision. "I am a doctor and professor in the medical program here," I started, "and I've come with a proposal of benefit to both of us. I expect you know that the administration may force you to leave if you're still sick at the end of the semester?"

E looked at me like an expert poker player. "Yes, I'm aware of that," she said.

"And you do realize that, based on your health record over the past two years, it is highly unlikely that you'll be fully recovered and bouncing around campus by January?"

"I've thought about that," said E.

"If you agree to work with me," I suggested, "I'll tell the university that you've become the subject of my newest study, and that I need easy and indefinite access to you in order to carry out the project. I'll tell them that you're a one-of-a-kind medical anomaly that they're very lucky to have—if they don't know that already—and that the study, if based at Brown, will bring the school widespread acclaim, media attention, and respect. Once convinced that if they let you go, they're letting a prodigious opportunity slip through their hands, the university will put you under my care."

E nodded, taking in my proposal, and leaned forward. "What's in it for you?"

I was surprised again, since I thought that my role in all this was more than obvious. "I'm going to publish a study on you."

"Oh. You're serious about doing that?" E said, laughing for the first time. It was neither a laugh of relief nor of pleasure, but somehow a laugh at my expense. I respected that she distrusted me.

"Well, yes," I said. "This isn't a charade for the sake of the university. I'm really going to do this."

"What's the time commitment I have to make to you?" E asked.

I told her, "Until you get better or until you graduate. Whichever comes first."

"How many hours a week?" she asked.

"I'd like two hours every week regardless, and then additionally scheduled meetings when necessary." Realizing that I should cover all my bases, I added, "Should you contract something especially violent or bizarre, I think we'd need to adjust our time accordingly."

After this, E stared at me for a while, and I couldn't begin to tell what she was thinking. I realized this study would be so much more than an exercise in observation, documentation, and analysis. This girl was what my father likes to call a "tough cookie," and if I was going to make any notable progress, I was going to have to establish a high level of intimacy with her. Although I could monitor E as closely as humanely (and technologically) possible, the success of the study and the eventual book I planned to write about my experience would depend on complete access to her mindset and worldview.

That day, though, I felt so unnerved by our first encounter that I could only deal in surface details.

"I'll agree to it," said E.

I drew the contract out of my briefcase and put a handheld tape recorder on the bed. That recorder has since been present at all meetings between E and myself. All conversations that follow are reported verbatim.

E signed the contract, age nineteen at the time, and afterward I did a cursory physical. I checked her vitals and took a family history, although I now know that I was asking the wrong questions about her family. We were wasting time, and neither of us knew it, but then again, E and I would waste a lot of time over the next year or so.

We monitored her serial illnesses closely. These included her first bout of tuberculosis; a brief return of her freshman-year encephalitis; the resulting seizure disorder from the encephalitis; the mumps; aspergillosis; symptoms that highly resembled those of a malarial patient, except E never developed a full-blown case of malaria; a second bout of chicken pox even though she'd had them as a child; flus, and uncommon colds. Even with the most serious illnesses, E would suffer only during the incubation period, then begin to recover slowly but completely. Her afflictions never left her with permanent damage—there were no memory problems, no organ impairment, no paralysis. I found this remarkable. The parade of illnesses was incessant, yet E bore them as if they were minor allergies. The only exception was the fibromyalgia, which produced a widespread muscular pain that plagued her constantly.

During our initial acquaintance, E was a fascinating patient to watch, but a difficult patient to read. For all our hours together, all I had to show for my effort was, essentially, a list of illnesses. E remained silent during most of our meetings, answering questions when I asked them but rarely offering more. I felt that I needed to get inside of E, but she saw me as her academic meal ticket, so to speak, and we had trouble moving beyond that perception.

Many nights I went home frustrated and nervous because I knew I had to deliver a progress report to the deans in December of 2003. E's spring-semester registration was contingent on what I had to say, and my reputation was in danger. I knew that I couldn't go into that meeting with a report that any nurse could offer. Not only were the deans expecting better of me, I had also counted upon being able to publish something about E for the wider medical community, and I didn't yet have a single hypothesis as to why this young woman was so dramatically and repeatedly sick.

I was about to give up when I received a call from E one afternoon in November of 2003. I'd given her all my numbers at the beginning of our relationship, but she'd never used them. If she needed to cancel one of our meetings, she had one of the nurse practitioners let me know.

At home my caller ID showed a number at Rhode Island Hospital, and I picked up, thinking it would be Wainscott. Instead, it was E, who had spent the afternoon in the emergency room.

E wanted to know if I could meet her at the hospital. She said she had something important to tell me, that she had experienced a troubling symptom and it had alarmed her so greatly that she wanted my help. She placed this phone call the day she met a new patient in the Brown infirmary. I'll refer to this patient as C.

CHAPTER 2

PAXIL CR • Get back to being you

I never let you know that before I loved you, I hated your voice. Sorry about that.

I had already met some of the kids who'd been attacked. If you remember the junior who got shot in the neck while chewing a Pizza Bite outside Josiah's, I met him first. He stayed here a few nights because the stitches got infected and then he got a fever. When his voice returned, he told me—he gasped—that when he was in the hospital, they gave him a wipey board to communicate. He wrote, "The irony of this situation is that hours before the shooting, I had been performing a drive-by myself."

The doctor standing at his head had asked, "What do you mean? Is this a confession?"

The guy, Ben, had dashed off, "It's slang, doctor. When you repeatedly drive past the apartment of a girl you're interested in to see if she's home, you're said to be doing a 'drive-by.' Jessica Norman. I thought I loved her, and I was on her street five times that night." Ben remembered going back and putting the quotation marks in last, "like the pen had just become too heavy to hold." He said his strokes were slow and tragic, and so I told him that I thought he liked the experience of getting shot. He stroked his sideburns, which looked like rats stapled to his cheeks, and then he agreed.

I also met the freshman held at gunpoint while he withdrew his last three hundred dollars from the Bank of Boston ATM on Angell. He wasn't hurt, but he didn't want to sleep alone for a few nights, so he slept here. I met the senior pelted with rocks as she exited Dunkin' Donuts. She came here because of some lingering headaches. Also, I spent some time with that graduate student who was almost kidnapped, except she screamed at her three attackers, "My mom just died last week. Please stop. I'm human," and surprisingly, they did. She didn't want to sleep alone for a while either.

I heard, through the nurse practitioners, about a RISD woman who was bludgeoned over the head with a brick as she walked through their sculpture garden and about some other people I never met.

I was jealous of them because their injuries seemed manageable and finite. They got stitches. They got some medication. They left. I met them and never saw them again.

And then I met you. But, first, I heard you.

I was standing at the infirmary window, and I heard all of you singing. Each of your voices tunneled separately through the holes of the screen, and I swear, you were the loudest. You were singing, "Oh-ay-oh-ay-oh," and I recognized the song from a mouthwash commercial that I saw in the mid-'nineties. It had computer-animated bottles swinging through the jungle on vines, and, listening to you, I thought, "This guy is throwing his voice through the air in the same way, just flinging it out."

I imagined what you looked like because I wanted an

image to direct my pissed-offness toward. I pictured your mouth opened unnaturally wide, so that when you made the "ay" sounds, it pulled back into a desperate boomerang shape. I pictured your eyes so wide that the cold slapped at them.

You went into your second round of jungle calls, and I pictured you tearing up, your sight going blurry. I began to call you "A Cappella Guy" in my head. You sang so hard that it was like your jungle song was a prayer that had to get out to the world. (I still know the words: *"I'm far away from nowhere/On my own like Tarzan Boy."*) You were singing so loud that it seemed like the campus wasn't enough acreage for you. Like you had to sing beyond Brown, beyond Providence, beyond Rhode Island, because there were clinically depressed people in Boise and starving children in actual jungles that could be moved by your voice.

I can tell you now that I remember thinking, "Oh you motherfucker, I'll get you." Although you weren't in any danger from me because it would have been too much trouble to get outside anyway.

Before you guys broke into song, I'd been having a good time at the window. Freezing air had been coming in through the screen, turning itself into thousands of invisible needles and poking me in each pore. This felt great. When extreme temperatures pricked me from the outside, the inside of me hurt less.

I remember there were snowflakes coating the trees, which looked like icy fishing nets. I smelled fire. It was burning all over Providence in people's fireplaces and sometimes beyond their fireplaces, all throughout their houses. Vivian told me about a family she'd seen on the news whose house had just burned down a few days before I met you. She had liked and deliberately remembered what the mom had said to the newscaster: "I know what they mean now, when they say that the pits of hell are full of fire and pitch black at the exact same time." The family's house had burned down because of a short from a bad heater. Vivian said it was the dogs and toddlers who never got out in time (or who were never gotten out in time).

I never found out what kind of fire I smelled that night—that of human/animal misfortune or that of chestnuts roasting. I breathed in the smell, though, and felt like the fuzz in my nose was being singed. I also felt like the tuberculosis was being crowded out, which is why I was doing all this deep breathing.

At that point in time I had been picturing the inside of my lungs as a Navajo sweat lodge. I pictured the TB as some loser who wore Tibetan prayer beads and believed in wearing "I believe in whirled peas" shirts. He'd come into the tent to plumb the depths of his theories about himself, but he wasn't welcome. He was an alien there. I had a fantasy that if I could breathe in enough smoke, I'd get rid of him. So I breathed in as much as I could, but my chest kicked back.

I remember seeing some white and getting confused that I had magically landed outside in the snow. The white, however, was all in my head, and when the color passed, I was on the floor.

My forehead hurt, and I realized that I'd hit it on the windowsill on the way down. Before you came, I passed out often. That night, while collapsed, I saw the tally marks I'd made near the baseboard, indicating how many days I'd been here. People in jail do this. People on TV on islands do this. For a while I'd been adding a mark every day with a pencil sent from a new anxiety medication, and I kept the pencil on the windowsill. Since I was already down near the tally, I reached up, grabbed the pencil, and marked myself another day. Hello, 622.

Still, your "oh-ay-oh-ay-ohs" were continuing. They barreled their way into the infirmary and found me even when my ears were an inch from the floor.

Sarah entered the room then with a ceramic bowl of macaroni and cheese balanced in her palms. I looked up at her. She sucked in air and flew to my side to help me. Balancing the macaroni and cheese in one hand and pulling back my bangs with her other, she asked, "Which is it?"

Suddenly I felt like my lungs were disintegrating and taking the world with them, so I hunched over.

Sarah: "Tell me. Tell me. Tell me."

Your voices belted out toward the stars. Some of them—but not you—had vibratos so thick that I could feel them shaking in my stomach. It was like I was involuntarily digesting them. They reminded me of how my dad used to read me *Goodnight Moon,* and I had always felt sick at the line "Goodnight mush." There was an illustrated bowl of mush on the page that made me feel even sicker. Whenever I heard that line, I felt like I'd swallowed that shit and it all grew warm inside me like baker's yeast.

This is how I was that night.

"Come on, Elodie. The TB? The anemia? The fibromyalgia? The encephalitis again? The—" Sarah questioned, and I didn't want to make her put in any more time.

"It's the TB," I told her. "And those voices!"

Right then I heard a painful, crunching thwack outside and your voices stopped. After that, wild yelling. In the moment, though, all that registered was the absence of song.

Sarah curled me up into a sitting position and asked, "The voices?" She offered me the macaroni and cheese.

And I wanted to articulate how pissed and sad I felt that you guys had encroached on my territory. How I'd been wishing that someone would really send all of you into a jungle, so I could have my space back. You guys could have sung anywhere—under a fucking canopy—I wanted to explain, but I was the one who couldn't go anywhere else.

The usual thing happened, though, and I found that when I went to open my mouth, all feeling subsided and I was left with nothing to say.

I've never told you that my mom had wanted to name me Melody, and my dad had wanted to name me Ellen (after his grandma), so they'd compromised. You wanted to know this soon after we met, and I was pretending to sleep.

CHAPTER 3

From The Desk of Chester Hunter III

Dear Elodie,

This is a love note, although for a while, it may seem more like a deposition. I'm trying, El, and what more can a person ever do? Maybe I don't know what kind of words should go in this type of letter, so maybe I should just be as obvious as I can. Love. Love. Love. Love. Love. Love. Love. Love. Love.

There.

Okay?

Of course it's not.

You have no idea who I was before I met you. Because when I did finally meet you, it was almost instantaneous, that change in me, so you never understood where I pushed off from. But it only just dawned on me that you have to know what happened. It's the reason for all of this paper, El.

You were up in the infirmary and I was singing with the group. I remember sweat, how sweaty I was because of my thick sweater and because of the fleece scarf that George's mom had embroidered with bears for each of us. I smelled fire and it seemed like it was coming from us guys because it was like we were burning in our sweaters. I thought that there wasn't anything in the world that didn't come back around to me, is what I guess I should be explaining here.

We'd made a half circle underneath Wayland Arch, choosing it because we liked the acoustics, and, even more than that, we liked that there was a certain gravity to those surroundings. We faced the statue of Augustus in Wriston Quadrangle, who, rising above a nice blanket of white snow, seemed very, very proud. He approved, is what it seemed like to us. We sang toward the Ratty and welcomed the symbolic connection between food for the stomach and food for the soul; we'd considered titling our latest CD *Food For the Soul,* by the way. How unbelievably lame that seems now! Behind us, through the arch, freshmen in Keeney opened their windows to listen. It never occurred to me that you were somewhere in back of us, too, and that you were listening to me singing, and that, even more to the point, you weren't enjoying it.

I remember I was in the middle of exhaling between verses, my breath going white into the night, and I saw that this girl in the front row looked like she was gasping it in. She was staring at me while she was doing this. For the sake of honesty I'll admit that I rotated my body, so she'd have to take in my better side. I never told you this because I thought you'd think I was a fucking idiot, but seeing as I have nothing to lose now, I think I look more mysterious from the left. My eyebrow arches upward to a greater degree.

Then the girl began to mouth the words to the song. She was moving her lips like *"Oh-ay-oh-ay-oh."*

This really surprised me. I know that you never attended any of our performances, or any of any other a cappella group's performances, but these shows were definitely not sing-alongs. If you wanted to sing yourself, then you could go to a karaoke bar or you could go in the shower and amuse yourself there. The point being, you didn't show up to hear people who'd been practicing arrangements together all semester sing if you weren't there to watch and listen. When I looked at the girl's throat, I thought I could see her vocal cords working. I remember thinking to myself something like "Wait, is she singing? She's singing with us?"

The young woman smiled at me because she must have thought I was staring because I liked her. My next verse had started and we were singing in tandem now.

While I was puzzling over that girl, a white Honda Civic peeled up to the curb in front of the arch. The ice on the street shrieked, and that's when I first became aware of the car. When it cut through our performance. The passenger-side door opened.

People in the crowd turned around, wanting to see whose car it was. I remember that some of the older members in the crowd, the earmuffed neighbors in glasses who actually came out of their houses for a show, didn't want to grant the careless driver undeserved attention. They kept their gazes forward and concentrated on listening.

Me, though, I really had no choice but to face the car, couldn't help but look, and this was the moment my sense of myself suddenly unraveled.

My whole life had been effortless up until that night. I hope I'm not being patronizing here, but I need to explain that when your life is effortless like mine used to be, you don't realize that there are other ways. It's like when you're lying in bed at night, the rain is coming down, you're comfortable and warm, and all you really think about is how secure you feel. You forget that everyone doesn't have that, and that for some people, it's possible not to feel taken care of.

It was like I'd always been so tied into the world that I didn't really feel it all around me. All the seams were invisible, and so I never realized I was actually sewn to something, if you can understand that.

Yes, I'd read the *Daily Herald* every day in the Ratty while buttering my Texas toast bread, and I'd seen those headlines and taken in those stories. The police theorized gang initiations: "Maim a Brown student. If you can't find one of them, then you can go for a RISD student, but you'll have to give up sleep for three days if you puss out like this." Everyone was talking about how the Johnson and Wales students had been left alone so far, probably because they majored in things like hotel management and culinary arts.

But none of it ever even seemed close to home. Never once, before that night, did I see some presence in the corner of my eye and then whip around as my heart broke itself against my chest because I thought something was coming for me.

So when I was standing underneath Wayland Arch, looking straight ahead, for the first time I understood that the guy springing out of the Civic with the crowbar in his hand had a specific relationship with me. He was sprinting in a straight line, and what's bizarre is that I felt chosen. I'd been chosen for many things in my life, but always being the automatic selection, I'd never really realized that there were other options. Like I was chosen class president during all eight years that I ran, but there was literally never a second when I even considered someone else might win. Everything in my world was like that. Everything was *obvious.* I just didn't process any of it, El.

This guy, though, he was coming at me like a girlfriend who'd been waiting hours for my flight, so happy to see me, and I know it's idiotic, but I remember opening my arms to catch him.

And then the guy fulfilled that contract of togetherness he'd initiated. He lifted the crowbar over his left shoulder and brought the metal down on my kneecaps, I think as hard as he could. I passed out for the first time in my life. It had never even happened while drinking.

CHAPTER 4

PAXIL CR • Get back to being you

In the dark I was lying on my bed, looking at the five other beds in the room, all empty. Police and ambulance lights slid across the ceiling, pink and aqua, and in the window, I remember the tree branches pulsing like neon.

Sarah threw open the door and I craned my neck from the pillow to see her better. She looked like a sexless Eskimo, because she had her puffy winter coat on and her fur-lined hood up.

"I'm going to go talk to the paramedics. I've got to start networking, getting myself out there. They know all the doctors and staff at every hospital," she said.

I know she never told you this, but in the beginning, Sarah had only wanted to work with babies. That's why she was the way she was with us. The Women's and Infants' Hospital especially taunted her since she could see it from her house. Every day there were hundreds of babies on dim monitors, not even technically babies yet. There were babies being spanked and crying for the first time, and babies in incubators like dioramas. And the reason for her baby fever was that Sarah really believed that humans are born innocent. She told me once that this wasn't to be confused with being born clueless. Which babies are. But she believed in a natural innocence with a moral component. For a while she used to talk about wanting to publish papers on this.

I'd heard a lot about this from her. If you were to put a bomb in a baby's arms, Sarah thought, it would instinctively know what the weapon was and the harm it could do. Babies were adamantly opposed to cruelty and pain. Inside of their heads.

When Sarah had first told me about her theory, I'd wanted to know how motor skills fit into this philosophy. Sarah argued, "Babies are pure goodness, and pure goodness is not something that is physical. As a baby starts to move, it transitions into the adult world and its innocence decreases exponentially."

"But the bomb," I'd said. "The baby simply couldn't do anything with it."

Sarah had gulped, excited by the proof in her pocket. "Get this. I put a gun, unloaded, in my nephew's crib one day and he averted his eyes from it. No interest. None."

I'd tucked my chin into my chest and stared at her while opening and closing my jaw.

Every time a nursing position opened up in the maternity or preemie ward at one of the local hospitals, she'd apply. She was always weeded out. After the last rejection, in September, she collapsed onto a bed across the room from me. Half asleep (I think), she started muttering, "Little star, stay still. Don't move. Trust me, I've been working at Brown Health Services for four years and all that's ahead is mono, herpes, and the day you'll puke up the macaroni and cheese I've brought you because your stomach doesn't recognize anything that isn't malt liquor." I think the baby thing was an attempt to freeze a moment in time and put her faith there. She seems to have given up on it since.

By the time you met her, she had become much quieter about this stuff. I guess I also spent less time with her once you came, so I heard less about the babies.

"Networking is a wise decision," I told her, and then I lowered myself back onto my pillow, thinking of myself as Dracula disappearing into his coffin.

"You don't think it's transparent? That they'll know I'm using them?"

I considered this. I gave it serious thought. I saw the answer appear behind my eyelids, typed out. "Don't behave transparently, and then it won't be."

"Oh, come on. There isn't a switch in the middle of my back," Sarah said as she started down the hallway.

To the room I whispered, "Don't ask if you don't want the solution." A minute later, I heard the front door open and close. I was the only one left in the whole building. I got out of bed, went to the top of the stairs, and looked down at the Health Services lobby. I imagined that I wasn't me, but a dead person watching over me.

People who come here for the first time always say, "There's something charming about this place. It's like a manor." They look at the tall wooden doors, the big brass knobs on those doors, all the old windows. They walk into the marble entryway and gaze up at the crown moldings. They admire the high ceilings.

I always knew the school was in on it, this deliberate beautification of sickness.

Have you noticed the women behind the service window work under crystal chandeliers that give out dinner-party light? It's like all the incoming patients should expect to be handed sourdough rolls instead of forms that ask, "Do you smoke? Do you have unprotected sex? Who should we notify in case of emergency?" Visitors just look at the winding staircase like "Christmas garlands!"

Then there's the warmth that you've internalized by now. Your body probably runs a few degrees warmer than it did when you first came here.

I left the top of the staircase and roamed this floor. I went down to the waiting room and looked at some HIV, depression, and exercise pamphlets just for the hell of it. I went to the blood closet and opened and shut some cabinets. I was trying to figure out what to do with myself.

I went to the pharmacy and tried to pick the lock with a needle from the blood closet, to see if they'd gotten any new promotional notepads or pill cases from the drug companies. I was unable to break in. I have no future in burglary.

After I tried ten seconds of barefoot tap dancing, there was nothing to do but go back to the infirmary. I stood in the doorway looking at my two pillows, the way that they retained the shape of my skull because they'd been under my head for so long. It was the same with the down pad covering my mattress. In the places where my blanket was kicked back, I could also see myself in the pad Sarah bought for me at the mall because the coils in the bed had been bruising my back and thighs. I used to wake up every morning feeling like my ass had been kicked. Now it's just some mornings.

I looked at my metal frame and what I had now begun to consider "my planks" on "my floor."

I've always felt that the infirmary looks a lot like a nursery, but maybe that's just because I've felt so babied in it. Maybe it's also those filmy gauze curtains over the windows that I want to burn.

I walked over to the fireplace. You know how visitors still insist on that weird habit of rubbing their hands in front of it, even though it hasn't been lit for years. A doctor from downstairs had just come the day before and dropped a pile of magazines on the mantel because he'd been cleaning out his basement. He patted the pile and said, "There's some good reading in there."

He must not have looked through the pile before he dropped it off because I found a few copies of *Hustler* and *Black Tail* in between the *National Geographic*s and *Newsweek*s.

That night I looked through the girlie mags and generally preferred them, since the pictures I liked best were the ones where a subject looked directly into the camera, regardless of who the subject was. In the *Newsweek*s especially, the people often looked away like they wanted to pretend the camera wasn't even there.

Outside, the sirens were whooping and your voices were crying out, but the hollowness of the building was closer and louder. I felt like something delicate alone in a vault. Then I went to take a shower, so at least I'd be cushioned by white noise.

CHAPTER 5

THE JOURNAL OF PARAPSYCHOLOGY OCTOBER 2004

When I got to the hospital, Wainscott was finishing up with E. She had acquired yet another illness for her résumé, but it was her newfound desire to confide in me that drew me there.

E seemed agitated in a way that I had never witnessed before. I found her behind one of the curtains in the emergency room, twirling a cotton swab between her fingers, her bare legs dangling over the edge of the bed (she was dressed in a customary hospital gown). As soon as she saw me, she pointed the swab at me and asked, "Are you a good doctor?"

"You're asking me this now?" I questioned. "We've been working together over a year."

"I know, but I didn't care before," she said.

I had known that E hadn't been particularly interested in the details of my study, but I'd chalked up her lack of curiosity to denial. It seemed to me that if she became invested in my work, it would mean taking on an almost overwhelming immersion in her health problems. I'd believed E was keeping herself from depression only by creating a mental wall separating her from the reality of her situation.

As it turned out, I discovered in the hospital that E's indifference was the result of her having very low expectations of me.

"I'm an excellent doctor," I told her.

E laid the swab down on the table next to her bed as if it were a sword she'd used to get the truth out of me and, now that she'd achieved her purpose, no longer needed. "Will you help me figure out what's wrong with me?" she asked.

"What do you think I've been doing?" Even though I'm childless, in that moment I knew what it was like to have an ungrateful child.

"This is something new."

"I know. Wainscott told me over the phone," I reminded her.

"No. Something happened last night. You're the first to hear about it."

I sat down.

E had taken a shower the night before, and she began to describe the details of the showering experience to me, including her attempts "to keep the battered side of my face away from the nozzle." She'd hit the side of her face on the windowsill after experiencing an earlier wave of dizziness. As she related this to me, I realized that this was the first time E was talking freely and at length in my presence.

She told me everything she could remember, saying that she needed me to have every available piece of information for my inquiry. She told me that for the past six months, she'd been having the nurse practitioners buy her travel-sized soaps, shampoos, and conditioners at the drugstore. This was so, according to E, she "could feel like at least one aspect of my life is in a state of flux." Although there were only a handful of travel-sized brands to try, as long as the products ran out on a weekly basis, they delivered the impression of change. Because E never used any one item long enough to become accustomed to its particular properties, she was constantly aware of its unique smell on her skin and hair, and this made her seem "slightly vibrant" to herself.

E told me that the previous night, she had used Salon Selectives shampoo, and while I didn't see how this detail could possibly affect my diagnosis, I listened without comment. She seemed to want to talk, and I certainly wasn't going to stop her. "It smells fruity," E informed me. "Like apple candy that doesn't smell like a real apple, but is recognized by people as an apple smell anyway."

E had been working shampoo into her scalp when she noticed a flash of movement between the edge of the plastic curtain and the shower wall. She thought she'd seen a finger brush the rim of the sink.

"Hello?" she called out.

"I'm convinced," a masculine voice answered her.

None of the nurse practitioners were males, and E had been the infirmary's only patient for two weeks at that time. "This was a stranger in the bathroom," she told me.

E had ducked her head out of the spray of the nozzle so she could hear better. The water was too loud on the tiles for her to gauge how close the stranger was to her, and he made no shadow against the white curtain.

"What are you convinced of?" E had asked, wanting to get him to talk again. She described her wet skin to me as "tingling," and I asked her if she thought this extrasensitivity in her nerve endings was an early symptom of her Raynaud's diagnosis. She replied that she thought it was simple "heat and fear."

"That you had to be sick in order to see me," the stranger had replied.

He was directly on the other side of the curtain, his voice muffled by the mist around her. E had leaned forward to peer through the space between the curtain and the wall to see if she "had enough room to run or if I should fling myself out of the shower and attack. Then I'd have the element of surprise on my side."

All that E could make out was the stranger's hand resting on the faucet. She observed that the hand had a bizarre consistency, as though it were made out of mist. She wondered if the steam from the shower was playing games with her vision because from where she stood, "it looked like the hand of a ghost."

Suddenly, the hand drew away from the faucet, and E, scared that the stranger was on the move, decided the time had come to throw aside the shower curtain and pounce.

She clenched her right fist and held up her left hand with her index finger extended, ready to "jab it into an eye." With her left leg she kicked aside the edge of the curtain, only to reveal an empty bathroom. The door remained shut—she had closed it behind her—and her towel, folded on the tile in front of the sink, was still neatly placed there.

E, nude, walked to the door and opened it, peering into the infirmary. She told me that all of the shadows were the familiar ones, that everything appeared calm and empty.

E remembered subsequently being overcome with the uncanny quality of the encounter, and only becoming aware of herself again when she realized that a dollop of shampoo was still in her squeezed palm, "dripping between the cracks of my fingers onto the floor."

This was where E's story ended. She waited for my first question. I could tell that I was in dangerous territory, that her future trust and confidence depended on my response to her experience and the light in which I chose to see it. This was a moment filled with the potential to win her over or alienate her forever.

I asked, "What do you want me to say? Why did you even come to me with this?" I felt it best to appear slightly exasperated with her, so that she would be forced to reveal her hand. I'd make her educate me, fill in the blanks, because I was fearful that if I offered a wrong opinion, she would never offer me the chance to correct myself. This was our showdown, and I believed that if I displayed any weakness at this juncture, she'd shoot me and leave town, so to speak.

When E finally blinked, I knew we'd pushed through to the other side. "Because I need you to weed out all possible medical causes for me."

"E," I said, "if you think there was someone in the bathroom with you last night, then you're probably right. Call the police or tell Vivian."

"We need to do tests, and you need to be thorough," she said.

"I'd be happy to run them," I told her, "but, please consider, if you think there was someone—"

"I don't think there was *someone* in there with me!"

E shouted at me. This was a day of firsts: her first phone call to me, her first request for my help, and the first time I heard her raise her voice.

Stunned by her outburst, I said, "Well, let's start by running a CAT scan."

With the help of Wainscott, we ran all the tests that we could that day. We did the CAT scan, and then, when that showed nothing, followed it up with an MRI to confirm that there was no tumor in E's brain. E reported that she hadn't had any recent morning headaches, vomiting, exceptional lack of coordination, or any other symptoms that might accompany a tumor, so I told her that I felt we could safely dismiss that possibility.

Jokingly, I told her, "Well, you have had a sudden change in personality, so maybe we shouldn't be so hasty."

She looked at me in a quizzical way, not getting my joke, and asked, "What do you mean? How do I seem different?" She seemed unusually worried about this. Her reaction struck me as interesting, since she had never before seemed concerned what I or anyone else thought of her.

"You're being friendly with me," I said.

"Oh," E replied, patting me gently on the shoulder.

To exclude the possibility that E was embarking upon another course of encephalitis, we did an EEG and, covering all our bases, a tomographic scan to rule out a cerebral hematoma. Test after test came back normal. Once we had worked our way through the more insidious options, I examined E for signs of ordinary flu, infection, and allergy, anything that could possibly cause her to hallucinate. We examined the possibility of drug interactions with no luck.

A hospital psychologist interviewed E for signs of psychosis. By the time we were finished, I was certain that, while E still had persistent traces of her current illnesses that we already knew about (including her latest Raynaud's phenomenon prognosis from Wainscott), there was nothing physical impairing her brain.

The sun was starting to set, and I told E that I'd give her a ride back to the infirmary. She was getting dressed behind the curtain. After a period of silence in which I debated whether or not I should push even farther, I finally decided to ask, "Is it possible that someone's stalking you?"

"What are you talking about?" E asked.

"It seems as if there's something very personal about what happened to you last night." I wanted her to know that I was on her side no matter what, as I felt a new bond being constructed between us. "I believe you. Whatever it is, I believe you."

E appeared from behind the curtain, dressed in jeans and a sweater. She looked so exhausted from the tests that I motioned to a passing nurse for a wheelchair. "You know how I said that the stranger's hand was see-through, like a ghost's?"

"Yes," I said.

"I think I've started seeing ghosts," she told me.

I was trapped. I had told her that no matter what she believed, I would believe it, too, and I knew that showing any skepticism about her confession would corrupt the ground that we had broken that day. So, while I may have chosen to be less honest with E at first, my lie forced me to continue the deception until, ultimately, I discovered it was no longer needed.

"Why would you think that you suddenly have the ability to see ghosts?" I asked her, looking out the window so that she couldn't see the fraud in my eyes.

"Because I was supposed to all along," E sighed, then finally told me the family history that I had never thought to uncover.

CHAPTER 6

PAXIL CR • Get back to being you

The day after I heard you, the door to the infirmary opened at the crack of dawn. I saw two men. They were pushing what looked like a casket on wheels into my room.

When I tried to lift my head to see better, a sunbeam zapped me in the eye, so I went back down. The men shifted, scraped against the wooden frame of the threshold, grunted incoherent things. I was too groggy to ascertain the current situation, so I gave the left side of my face a small slap. The unfortunate thing was that I had forgotten about my bruise from the night before. White pain shot through my head. I jerked toward the window. Then white light went into my eyes, and it felt like a corneal stabbing. After that, my whole body recoiled and I snapped into the fetal position, trying not to think about how much that pose sucked for my lungs. They seemed the size and consistency of prunes. Throughout all this I said nothing to the men or to you, but I remember thinking, "Oh, fuck me" to the pain.

I heard wheels roll across the floor and Voice One say, "Let's get him parallel to the bed, and then I'll get his torso and you get his legs. Back up a little, the stretcher's going to catch on—" I heard the sound of metal scraping against metal. "Mike, we need to make the turn wider, so back it up a little."

"All I have to say is, who knows what else can go wrong? I'll tell you now that it wouldn't surprise me if something did; that's not me being pessimistic, and I'm prepared for, for . . . everything bad," said Voice Two. You.

"Do you want me to go around? I can come around on the other side and put my arms out like a second barrier."

I knew that was Sarah, but didn't know where she'd come from.

"You could do that, why not?" added Voice Three.

"So, where do you guys hang out after your shift, anyway?" Sarah asked.

"Well, we either go home and sleep or we go to Dunkin' Donuts."

"Oh, the one on Thayer?"

"Sometimes, I guess. There's three hundred billion of them. We just pick one."

"Well, I'm really hungry this morning. Are you guys hungry? Do you want to go get doughnuts? Doughnut holes?"

My external pain was draining, so I uncurled myself and rolled to face the bed where the sound came from. It was in the shadow of the opposite wall.

That's when I saw you for the first time—in profile, from the left. My first thought about your face was that your eyes were set so deep that they made your nose look like a rebel for sailing out like that. Next I noticed the dimple in the middle of your chin, which is definitely a dimple and not a cleft. I thought you looked like you'd been shot with a BB gun there. The night of beating and snow had left long pieces of your hair plastered across your forehead. And before I even noticed the braces around your knees, I knew you were unfamiliar with the world of the sick. I had this quick flash where I pictured myself initiating you, sticking twenty rectal thermometers in at once.

That was as far as I got with the fantasy because suddenly, you turned your head and noticed me back.

CHAPTER 7

From The Desk of Chester Hunter III

Shit, El, the first time we met you gave me the kind of stare that I imagine biologists use when looking into a microscope at a fresh strain of flu. You seemed vaguely interested but in no way concerned for my health, and definitely, definitely in no way threatened.

You were studying me, and that made me feel bold enough to study you back. You didn't look too unhealthy apart from the shiner on your temple, but I guess I knew that something must be seriously wrong with you because you were staring at me like I'd walked into your backyard and started building a mansion.

Or, I guess that doesn't even cut it, doesn't even begin to describe how instantly nervous I was in your presence. This is closer, though: it was like you were an old-timer, a regular who drank Guinness, and I was this guy who'd walked into your bar like a doof and asked for a Sex on the Beach with a tropical umbrella. The ambulance worker (Mike?) and Sarah walked away, and then suddenly we were the only ones left in the room.

God, I had no idea what I could even say to you, and I remember how unbelievably uncomfortable that silence was because I was racing through my mental log of thoughts, trying to find something acceptable. You, of course, just stared at me, because you're brave like that. When you continued to stare for about thirty seconds straight, I realized that I was going to have to initiate conversation. And then I had to take a moment to mourn the automatic nature of my old existence again, the way I was before the attack. I used to thoughtlessly walk into a party and have something to say to everyone, but now that I think back on it, maybe I just had something to tell everyone about me. The first time I looked at you, I couldn't even begin to guess what you'd want to know.

So even though I was on all those painkillers, I remember saying something very retarded. I said, "I learned tonight, and I don't mean to make this sound too emotional, but I learned that we're never really alone." It took my brain so much effort to release that thought that it still haunts me.

You swung your feet over the side of your bed and leaned forward. "That's not true," you said. "I was alone until about five minutes ago."

Holy shit, I was taken aback by that. I tried to turn onto my side so I could read the expression on your face, to see if you were playing. I couldn't turn, though, because I hadn't learned how to maneuver my legs. "Is that a swipe at me?"

"No, not a swipe. Before you got here I was lying in this room alone. Now I am not alone because you are over there, in one of the other beds. I was making an objective assessment of the situation." You said these things simply and purely, whereas with anyone else, they would have been delivered with sarcasm and bite. Your eyes didn't twinkle, and your mouth didn't curve itself into flirtatious shapes.

Then you asked me, "Were you here last night—in the infirmary?" and I sank even lower, thinking that over the course of one night, I had become so unremarkable that you couldn't tell me apart from another random patient. I told you, "No. I just got here now," and wanted to know who you were confusing me with, and you just told me it was a "long story." I left that alone, but I still think about it now. I always had the sense that there were a lot of "long stories" I never heard.

There was another silence then, and I borrowed some of your comfort with it to take the time to evaluate you. You were so miniature perched on the edge of your bed. Your arms were all bone—I hope you realize that's not an insult—but your face was complete transparency. I thought I could see everything inside of you, everything essential you were made up of, on your face. And then my world, which felt like such a jumble, met with yours, which seemed so clear, and I thought, "If you were mine, I would have a living compass."

"So anyway. Anyway," I said.

You smiled. "Are we moving onto a new topic?"

"We can." I squinted and pointed across the room like—okay, to extend that bar analogy, which seems particularly apt to me—I was that drunk trying to name an actor in a late-night movie while sitting below your small, fuzzy bar TV. I remember asking at some point, "Hey, am I talking coherently? Because I'm on a lot of painkillers, and I can't tell. And I think you might have an unusual accent except I can't tell that either."

"I can understand you perfectly, but I don't have an accent. That might be the drugs affecting you," you suggested.

"Is it?"

"I would have to literally be inside your body to answer that."

That comment killed me, too. "That's really true, you know."

"Do you mind if I ask what happened?"

"Well, this might be hard to believe," I said, "but a man ran out of a car and swung at my knees with a crowbar last night while I was singing Baltimora's 'Tarzan Boy.'"

"Oh, that was you."

"You heard about it?"

"No, I heard the sound of your bones cracking."

You got up from the bed and opened one of the windows as far as it would go. You did this slowly, like a bodybuilder lifting a two-hundred-pound dumbbell. I understood the intense concentration going into the act, and I wanted to go over and put my hands over yours, come up from under you and support the entire weight of your body. Make a ladle of myself and lift the window for you, be a gentleman for once in my life. The day was so sharp and crystalline, or at least it was in my mind.

"You were only struck in the knees?" you asked.

I made woozy brackets of my thumbs and forefingers in front of my face (I was so, so drugged) and peered through the hole like I was watching it happen all over again. "I tried to stop him myself, tried to grab his arms, but he was like an eel. He rushed at me like he was determined. No. Motivated. And time after time I keep coming back to the conclusion that he was after me for a reason, except what could his motive possibly be?"

"Why wouldn't he have struck you in the head?" you asked.

"My head?"

"To punish you for your a capella singing."

"Why would someone purposely want to punish an a capella singer?"

"Oh-ay-oh-ay-oh," you replied quietly, running through the syllables so fast that I thought you said something else.

That's why I said, "Yeah, I don't know either."

And you clarified, "Actually, I said, 'Oh-ay-oh-ay-oh.'"

Then you walked back to your bed, moving in slo-mo, and got down on your knees. I watched the curve of your back while you pulled out a brown canvas suitcase and flipped open the top. In your sea of underwear and bras was your vast collection of cable-knit sweaters, and I can still see you pulling out the pink one and a pair of 501s. You took a long pause before you got back up, like you had to wait for the blood to return to your head. From the floor you asked me, "What's the outlook? Did he get your patellas and popliteals?"

"Did he get my what—what?"

"Sorry. I'm asking if your attacker shattered your knee bones and the arteries that run behind your joints."

"Oh. I guess, if I correctly understand what the doctor said, that I have multiple small fractures, but—"

The door to the infirmary reopened, and I met Vivian for the first time. I thought the drugs were really having a field day with me when she peeked in and a parrot squawked, "Nobody's available right now." I was like, whoa, whoa, whoa, thinking I was having aural hallucinations. And then I started thinking I was having visual hallucinations, too, because Vivian's eyes looked so abnormal to me. You know how they're so big and far apart that they look like they're about to slide off her face? Except once I sobered up, I realized that's just how they are. And she really did have a parrot on her shoulder. And it was just that kind of day, an eye-opening day all around.

You held up your hand and opened and closed your fingers with the speed of an arthritic. "Good morning, Vivian."

"What are you doing up? I was just going to check on how you were sleeping."

"I was talking to—"

You looked at me expectantly.

"Chess," I said, pulling out the last *s* for a long, long while, because it was like I was hearing my name for the first time.

"Chess," you repeated. "He's new."

Vivian and her bird came into the room, Vivian's eyes flicking up and down my legs like laser scanners. Or maybe that memory is a created one. It's nerve-wracking because I'm starting to doubt myself as I write, wondering if I'm getting the truth down or if I'm making it even more distorted. But I guess that's the point of this.

Vivian said, "Hi Chess, nice to meet you. Hey, looks like you might be needing surgery. I hope you're not at Brown on an athletic scholarship."

I was very, very taken aback by her pessimism. "But the doctor at the hospital said he'd have to wait and see before making any decisions and wait and see and wait and see?"

Making an "OK" sign, Vivian said, "And doctors never tell you anything just to keep your spirits up."

"What? What? Let's wait and see," I remember insisting.

C.C. McGaw started to talk over us: "I am a pretty bird . . . Pretty ugly!"

"Why's your bird here?" you asked, and I was relieved that you also thought it was weird.

"There's a huge fire a few doors down from me. I figured if my house goes up in flames, then C.C.'s going to be toast. You should see what's going on in the sky. It's pitch black over my house, except I can see the tips of these bright flames in the air, looks like hell, and . . ." Vivian's voice climbed higher and higher.

At this point my mind began swirling uncontrollably with drugs, so that I couldn't place the point in time where I existed. I was momentarily sure that Vivian was talking about a fire happening right there, right in the room, because as the sun rose higher and higher in the adjacent windows, the glass blurred with the orange it let through. My knees were hot, on fire too, and unfortunately I'd forgotten to do my laundry that week, so I was wearing an old pair of tighty whiteys. I specifically remember my dick sweltering, and I remember that my pubic hair felt like an electric blanket on at full blast. I was forgetting what came before that moment and had no idea what I was supposed to do to prepare for the next one, and time just felt like one gigantic emergency.

"The wind's been blowing ash on my porch. It looks like I'm living next to a crematorium," Vivian said.

Then I became fixated on Vivian's parrot and the red spiky feathers shooting out from its head and the orange ones from its tail, and I started to think that Vivian's shoulder was catching on fire. But I was too transfixed by the sight of the flames to do anything about it, to yell out or warn her or anything, because I was in a fully meditative state.

"I talked to the firefighters this morning and they said,

'No, miss, don't worry, we have it contained,' but then I watched the news and the weather guy said there were going to be winds. One spark jumps a couple houses, catches that one on fire, and then a spark from that new fire jumps, and my house is toast."

I blinked to try to reawaken myself, and I remember reaching above my head to feel the cool of the white walls. Things got better. I brought my arms down and propped myself up on my elbows, since I suddenly felt a strong, mandatory need to stare at you. A voice inside of my mind said, "You must do this." But, since the whole mission at hand is to be truthful, beyond truthful, I have to say that what I was doing was beyond staring. I was boring a hole into the center of your face so that the orange coming from behind you seemed to be coming through you. It was like there was something in you that I knew I had to have, and if I could just focus hard enough, I could get it, El.

"It's in disrepair anyway, so I can't care about it too much, but I brought the pets in anyway," Vivian said. "My kitten's in the supply closet outside."

I was shooting my heart at you like it was a spring-loaded snake from a fake peanut can. Some of the errant heartstrings might have even landed on Vivian, since that day felt like an emergency, and in that emergency all these feelings were firing in panicked, unchecked explosions. I know that all of this sounds very extreme, but you've got to understand how I was working.

"She's meowing her heart out, but I keep asking her, 'Would you rather live in confined quarters for a while or die of smoke inhalation and third-degree burns, you ungrateful little—'" Vivian said this while almost glowing, because it was like she was soaking in the fantasy of awful circumstances and was dragging me there with her. But, still, I couldn't tear my gaze from you.

Sarah appeared in the doorway and said, "Going for doughnuts. Just me and the guys. Me and the boys. Take care, everyone."

"See you tomorrow night," you called out.

The heater was churning, hot air lodging in the back of my throat. The whole room smelled like warm apple. When you left the room later I asked about the smell, and Vivian told me it was the smell of your shampoo. She said the heater always spread the smell of whatever shampoo you'd used that day throughout the infirmary, and I remember thinking, "Please, god, bottle some of that up for me. Elodie included."

Vivian asked, "So do either of you want cereal? Toast?"

"I'll take some toast with grape jelly," you replied, rising from your bed and looking at the clothes in your hands. "After I get dressed."

"Chess, you?"

"Please, Vivian, God, please. Pick up the phone," pleaded the bird. Vivian smiled because C.C. was doing his impression of her boyfriend, who I still think she loved even though we watched her dump him weekly. She just had a messed-up way of showing it, but hey, don't we all?

My daze persisted as you opened a door in the wall that I hadn't even realized existed. You in your white nightgown and me in my drugs—you were the white rabbit and it was like I was in Wonderland. There was a click of the door and another mention of toast—

"Chess, do you want toast? Cereal?"

I had to remind myself of the necessity of real things like eating and drinking.

"What kind of toast?" I asked.

"I can get you rye, wheat, white, Texas. Anything that the Ratty supplies."

"Texas toast bread, then, with some butter, please."

"Juice too?"

"I'd love some juice," I said in the movie in my head.

Then I was left alone in the room, but the magical thing was that I was still feeling attached to you and Vivian, like I'd been drawn and bisected by your departures. I murmured to no one out loud, "I know that maybe this sounds ridiculous, but I already feel like I'm growing as a person because of this incident." I felt that change that I've been writing about taking root, and that change gripped me tight, tight, tight. I truly meant what I said.

"Tarzan Boy" seemed to have been sung so long ago that my childhood memories were crisper in comparison.

Suddenly, the door in the wall clicked (I jumped and wondered if this was what post-traumatic stress was like) and you came out, dressed.

"What's your name?" I asked.

"Elodie," you said.

"Have you been here long? You seem to know everyone well."

You stood at the foot of your bed and brought your upturned palms to breast level, a gesture of wanting to be able to explain more but being unable to. All that you said was "I essentially live here." And I needed to know everything about you, so I asked, "What are you talking about, what's wrong with you?"

CHAPTER 8

PAXIL CR • Get back to being you

If I'd been a big talker, I would have begun with the Bell's palsy and worked my way through my first semester of sickness. Then the second. Then the summer. Then fall semester again, all the way until you were up to date. It would have been a talking marathon, disease after disease after disease, and we would have been there all day.

I couldn't bring myself to have that conversation, though. I remember wanting to play all that down. So I went out to the file cabinet at the nurses' desk, and I got my folder. I was a little embarrassed that it was soft and furry like cotton from so much use, but I brought it back into the room anyway. I figured it was pointless to hide.

Inside, my illnesses were bulleted. They looked like a list of things to do, and I thought you'd be less alarmed by the format.

I handed you my folder, and you thumbed through it, looking up five minutes later with a starry expression. "And your bruise up here," you said, gesturing to your own forehead. "Where'd that come from?"

"I got in a fight." Your unflinching eye contact was confusing me. To avoid it, I concentrated on a lock of your hair that was glued to your forehead from when you went down face first in the snow.

Most people's eyes dart around me. I mean that both ways. They dart around my body when they're trying to see how I'm holding up. And they dart around me, the presence, when they don't want to look.

"You got in a fight?"

"Yes, just like you." I punched into the air for effect.

Then I heard a cry from the hallway, which was Vivian's, and I was relieved to have an excuse to break away. When I got out to the desk, I understood from pieces of her phone conversation that the house next door to hers was on fire. C.C. was walking all over her desk, catching his feet on charts and prescriptions.

"Should I come down there?" she asked. "I know. But . . ."

I could tell that the policeman on the phone was explaining that he was sorry, but there was no point in coming and watching her house burn down. Vivian burst into tears.

"I don't know why I'm crying," she said, and I went over and sat down next to her because I knew she was talking more to me than to him. I hate sympathy, and anything I hate, I never give to anyone else. Vivian looked over at me and nodded, then pressed the phone to her chest. I could hear the policeman's voice buzzing his version of comforting talk.

Vivian said to me, "I can't stop thinking about my boyfriend's reaction. He's going to pull me to him and kiss my head, and then I'm really going to cry hard." I just listened. She returned the phone to her ear and listened, too.

"Yes, I have insurance," she said after a pause. "I wasn't even going to stay there long. The plan was always that I was going to fix it up and rent it out." I knew that by the time she saw her boyfriend tonight, Vivian wanted to be dry-eyed and stoic, since she hated the idea of being a wimp in front of him. That's why she was practicing with the policeman, trying to put some rationality into the loss.

There was a meow from the kitten in the closet. I had heard that animals were supposed to be able to sense earthquakes, but I'd never heard anything about house fires. "And I have my animals," Vivian said, stroking C.C.'s breast with her pointer finger.

Then the Health Services doorbell rang.

"How much time would you give it?" Vivian asked.

The doorbell rang again, the bing which I've always thought sounds like glass, and the bong which I've always thought sounds like copper.

"No. I'm not interested in seeing that," Vivian said.

I hate sympathy, but I can stomach empathy, which I think I, more than most people, am in a realistic position to possess and dish out. But empathy takes weird forms in me. On that day it took the form of me reaching out to press the hang-up button, disconnecting Vivian from the police.

"You seemed like you didn't want to talk anymore," I said.

"My house—" she whispered back.

"I know. I'm sorry."

"They estimate that my porch is going up in two minutes."

"You just painted it that green, too," I said.

"How'd you know I painted it green? I never talked about that here," Vivian said.

"You must have told me," I said. "Do you need to watch your house go down?"

"The police said I couldn't come," Vivian said.

"Fire is public property," I told her. "The house is your private property. You're entitled to watch it either way."

Down the hall, near the blood-drawing closet, I saw a hunched kid with longish black hair shuffle past in a bathrobe. I squinted but couldn't make out his face, and then he disappeared into the room.

"Who's that?" I asked Vivian.

She looked where I was looking, but there was no one left to see. "Who?"

"I just saw a guy in a bathrobe. Is he a new infirmary patient?"

"Not that I know of. Where'd he go?" Vivian asked.

"Into the blood closet."

"He shouldn't be in there," Vivian said, perking up now that she had something new and impersonal to freak out about. "He might be stealing needles. I should go confront him." The doorbell sounded again. I think it was the first time she became aware of it. "Will you get the doorbell?"

"Sure," I said. Now someone was pounding to get in.

I knew that I was taking the staircase like a person five times my age. Or like a zombie fresh out of the ground, reacquainting itself with mobility. But I could bag on myself all I wanted, and it wouldn't make me go any faster. I had to clutch onto the rail with both fists and make my way down while turned toward it.

The rubber soles of my slippers kept sticking to the marble, so I put extra effort into kicking my legs forward. I think the doorbell went off at least three more times, and there were a few more rounds of knocking, too. When I finally reached the front door, I used both hands again to turn the lock, and then to hold the knob and pull on it with everything I had left.

The sunshine I let in was staggering. The day was so brilliant that I almost didn't believe in it.

I saw your friends Marna and David on the doorstep. Marna's stud earrings twinkled in the light like her head was a switchboard. She looked foreign, and I expected to hear a Swedish accent. David's cigarette was dangling from his mouth, and the light at the end of it seemed too bright, like a flare in front of his face.

"Can I help you?" I asked.

"I'm sorry we rang the doorbell so many times," said Marna.

"Why are you apologizing to her?" asked David out of the side of his mouth. "I'm sure part of her job is answering the door." To me he said, "We kept ringing the doorbell because we didn't hear any kind of movement inside."

"You can't hear anything through these doors," I explained. "They're thick. Can I help you?"

"Is this Health Services?" Marna tried to peer inside.

"Yes. Are you sick?"

"Actually, it's our friend. Chess Hunter. He was struck in the knees last night—"

"I know Chess. He's upstairs." I stepped back and pulled the door with me, inviting them in. Marna and David entered tentatively. They looked like kids going into a haunted house. I wondered what I looked like to them.

"When you get to the second floor, make a right and sign in," I told them, and I started to release the door so I could follow them up. Except a breeze hit my cheeks right then. It bent backwards and returned outside, where it belonged, and I felt the force of its leaving like a boomerang taking some of me with it. I felt like a string of tissue was being pulled from my stomach and stretched down the walkway.

Glancing over my shoulder, I watched Marna and David climbing the stairs, talking quietly, but the space bounces voices everywhere:

"I had no idea this was even here," Marna said.

"Me neither," David said. "I've never had more than the flu, and then when I do, I just stay in bed and sleep it off."

"My doctor from home prescribes everything over the phone. I fill it at CVS."

"Same here."

I looked back outside, and the world seemed so interesting. It used to be that I rarely followed a lot of my impulses, but that day, all of a sudden I was on the other side of the door. I was hearing it shut behind me. The feeling I had was that the bulk of the door was pressing on the back of me like a magnet, expelling my north pole from its own.

First I stood and rolled my head in a circle, noting the lack of ceiling above me. After that I grasped onto the iron rail, which was pretty cold, and lowered myself down the steps. Then I let go (I had no choice—the rail ended) at the start of the walkway. Snow took a nose dive into my slippers. My feet were numb and wet by the time I hit the corner of Brown and George, and I was thrilled about that.

I hovered on the curb, realizing that I had to come up with a goal. I needed somewhere to get to before I could feel okay about turning back. In under a second I thought of the V-Dub—all people talked about were the waffles there.

"You can make yourself waffles there," said this girl who was admitted into the infirmary last year for never-ending bloody noses. She'd been bleeding through all her classes and dealing with it, mostly dripping onto linoleum floors and those cheap desk-chair combinations. But when her nose bled out onto this big decorative rug in the reading room at the John Hay Library, the university told her that her situation had gotten out of hand and forced her to take care of it.

Whenever a nurse practitioner offered her toast from the Ratty, she'd say, "I'd give anything to be eating a waffle from the V-Dub. You can make yourself waffles there. The stuff is like crack."

I'd ask, "What, you heat them up yourself?"

Bloody Nose said, "No, there's a gigantic vat of batter and you use a Dixie Cup to pour it into the waffle iron, and then you set the timer on the machine. Lately, I've found that I have a better sense of knowing exactly when my waffle is ready than it does. I'm dying for a waffle. I wonder if the school puts something in the batter, and that's why I want it so bad."

Health Services put Bloody Nose on prescription medication and soon she was Clean Nose. On the morning that she checked out of the infirmary, she told me, "You know where I'm going."

I felt the inertia of my life strongly as she left. I'd liked Bloody Nose. She didn't care what anyone thought of her, and she would have gone on bleeding and sticking tissues up her nose except the university said it would consider her negligent if she didn't look into her problem. They made a phone call to her parents stating their intention to start billing them for damaged property unless she sought help. I could see myself having breakfast with Bloody, whether dripping or clean. I could picture the two of us in a corner, sharing a pitcher of syrup, and I thought I'd love it.

I stepped down into the street and crossed it, eager to make a waffle.

CHAPTER 9

From The Desk of Chester Hunter, III

From right outside the door, I heard David saying, "It's just a hole in the wall? I imagined a wing. This school has no sense of ceremony about it."

Then he pushed open the door and looked at me. I was slumped in bed with my legs splayed out in front of me like two machine guns, the metal on the braces glinting in the light. I felt like I needed accompanying sound effects—*bam-bam-bam-bam-bam-bam*. David's eyes went straight down to my knees, of course, and I saw Marna peeking in over his shoulder, wanting to get her own glimpse.

"Oh, hi. I guess you've come to get a look at these," I said, and I tried to make a sweeping gesture over my knees so we could just all take a moment and address the elephant in the room. I thought that was really the best thing to do, since beating around the bush has never been my personal style. Maybe you're doubtful of that because I was always more unstrung and roundabout with you than with anyone else I've ever met in my life, but you've got to know you're the exception. Anyway, I couldn't make that grand, sweeping gesture, because I wasn't able to bend forward far enough to sweep my hands over my knees. I count this as one of the first times I was conscious of not being able to do something that I'd willed.

David walked in, and I think he was relieved that the only proof of my bodily damage was hidden underneath metal. He seemed like he had been expecting to see something worse, like he thought there'd be lots of torn skin and gore. Marna came in right behind him wearing a smile that is best described as being of the yearbook variety.

"I can't believe it. Look at this. RoboCop." David shook his head.

"David can't believe how great you look," Marna stepped in. "But, hey, I have something for you." She cut past David, came straight to the bed, and sat down next to the pillow that one of the guys from the ambulance had put under my shoulders. When I turned my head to try to look at her, all I could see was a whole bunch of her black skirt. It rustled as she squirmed out of her jacket and reached into one of the pockets. I watched her hand pulling out a folded piece of paper—I remember it was like that hand wasn't even attached to a person—and she gave it to me.

Opening the paper, I saw a faded chart with a whole bunch of dots plotted in its sectors.

"I went online and registered a star in your name," Marna told me while reaching over to try to press the creases out of the chart. "This is just the printed receipt, because it takes two weeks for the real certificate to come. The real thing is much nicer and has colors."

I said nothing.

"You didn't tell me you did that," marveled David.

"It's not your star. Why would you need to know about it?"

"I would have gone in on the star. Chess, I would have gone in on the star."

Marna shrugged and returned her attention to the chart. With her French manicured nail she pointed to an X in the upper left-hand corner of the paper. "Here, this one—this is your star. There's official documentation that says that is the Chess Hunter star, and that it has to be referred to as such."

I'm glad you weren't in the room and didn't know about this until now, because I think, looking back, that I shifted into one of my most impressive asshole modes. I wasn't trying to be an asshole, though. My intentions were genuine, as I felt sincere about what I was saying. "Who's going to do that?" I asked.

"Do what?"

I pulled my body up by pressing down on the mattress and arranged myself into a better sitting position. I remember swinging my head slowly back and forth between David and Marna like a goat. "Who's going to worry about the name of a star?"

Marna started to open her mouth, but stayed silent when I lifted my finger to the ceiling and gazed up at the plaster like I was pretending to see God reaching down from the heavens to touch his digit to mine.

"Who's going to point up into the sky and say, 'Baby, I'd love to talk about that star with you, but I don't know its official name.'"

Taking on the high pitch of a woman's voice, I answered myself. "Can't we just name it ourselves? Why don't we take our names and abbreviate them and put them together? I'm Becky, so we'll take the 'c-k-y' from me, and you're Tom, so—"

Back in my lower register, I said, "Baby, I know my name."

The woman's voice: "I know you do, lover. So we'll take 'Tom' from yours." Then I flapped my wrists, trying to indicate manic, girlish excitement. "I've got it. Keetom! That sounds sort of Native American, doesn't it?"

Lower: "Sounds Chinese to me, sweetheart."

Then I shifted toward a new variation, a weak baritone. I had to lower my chin and really reach for it, making the final result croaky, like when I was a kid and I used to speak from the back of my throat to make my parents laugh. "Excuse me, sir. Miss. I am a park ranger, and I thought I saw you pointing up into the sky. Were you, perhaps, looking at the stars?"

My falsetto replied, "We were, actually."

The park ranger: "Which one?"

Back at my normal level: "Why? Is there a problem?"

"I'm not sure yet. If you'd be so kind as to tell me which one, then I can advise you further."

I tried to soften my body to portray the woman, which was a woman ridiculously unlike you. I actually thought that while I was doing the impression. I pulled my shoulders in and wilted my neck and used a hand to delicately tuck a piece of my hair behind my ear. Looking out from under my lashes, my woman sheepishly said, "We were talking about the bright one up there. The one that's in the middle of all those duller ones."

In my baritone: "I thought so. What were you referring to it as?"

In my normal voice: "Well Becky here just named it Keetom."

"That star has an official name, folks. You can't just go

around naming stars and thinking that they're yours to play around with."

"It has a name?" asked my woman, looking bewildered.

"Absolutely. That's the Chess Hunter star."

I stopped there, only realizing how I sounded once I heard my own name. And I guess I just stared at my friends.

Marna's mouth was opened a little and her two front teeth were showing like they always did, even when she wasn't smiling or talking. The first time I met her I was walking around the top floor of our dorm, and, as I passed her room, I glanced in and saw her standing on a bed with a huge remote control in each hand. She was wearing a baby-blue negligée, and her hair was swept up like she was "Post-sex Barbie."

Tons of people were sitting on her carpet, watching, seriously, the biggest TV I'd ever seen outside of Circuit City. Marna also had two VCRs, a cable box, a surround-sound stereo system, and a DVD player. She noticed me standing in the doorway and invited me in.

The only place left to sit was on her bed, so I climbed over the bodies on the floor and made my way there. I ended up staying through *The Tonight Show* and then through *Late Night with Conan O'Brien,* and after *Conan* the people on the floor started to get up and make plans to snort coke in someone's room down the hall. Anyway, long story short, by three A.M. Marna and I were lying in bed together and talking about numerous things, especially how nervous she was about starting college. Her roommate was out at this Third World Center sleep-over, so we had the room to ourselves.

What I remember most strongly about that night was

how concerned Marna was with my comfort. It's crazy because she had only just met me, and already she was going out of her way to treat me like I was the most important person in her life. We were sharing a pillow and she kept making sure that I had the bulk of it under my head, even though her head would sometimes slip off.

I feel the need to tell you all this now because I know I didn't before, because I unintentionally washed myself of a romantic past when I met you. Being in that infirmary was like getting amnesia, and around you, all I dealt with was what was in front of me. So just bear with me, even though you might not want to read this, and read this. It's important that you know all the things that I left out before, El.

So Marna and I stayed up all night with the lights on, and she confessed to me that she was completely scared she'd never make real friends again. Everyone so far seemed nice and polite, she said, but she couldn't figure out how things were supposed to proceed from there.

"I figure there's so much I'm going to have to go through with someone, and I haven't had to do that for about ten years. My friends in high school were there from a long time ago." Marna slurred her words because she was so sleepy, but I could tell that she needed to have this conversation with me. "I wonder if I've forgotten how to do it. I can't even figure out how we'll ever have time to get to know each other, in between studying and taking classes and trying to be social."

I told her something like "Part of being adult is knowing that everybody turns adult. We stepped into a force field here. It's as if we went to Japan and got off the plane with the latent ability to speak and understand Japanese. Maybe you just haven't gotten your tongue and ears used to it yet. You will. We all grow up and get there."

"What can we do about that?" Marna asked. "I'm not sure I like it."

"One day you'll like it."

"I will?"

"It's like the changing of taste buds. You probably didn't like certain sauces when you were younger, either." As I'm remembering all of this, I'm hating myself. I can see that I was kind of a prick, but learning that is part of this process, so I'll have to face it.

Unbelievably, Marna accepted what I was telling her. "I guess that makes me feel a little better, that you think relationships are just going to be different and not worse. Yesterday was apples, today is oranges."

"*Que sera, sera.* Right," I said.

Then she wanted us to promise that we would be there for each other throughout everything, which I was okay with, was willing to agree to.

"Even if, in a few weeks or semesters, we find out that we don't like each other," she said, "then we'll still be there for each other anyway. We'll have to like each other."

"Why wouldn't I like you? I like you," I told her.

"I like you, too."

"Good. It's settled."

"One more thing: I promise."

I promised. That's how it went down between us. We kissed and she became my first college girlfriend, except we never made it long enough to say "I love you," or share toothbrushes. But, and this is key, the great thing is that we ended up being really, really tight friends, and I think that our relationship is better now than when we were technically in a relationship. Once I asked Marna what she liked about me, why she stuck with me, and she said, "Being with you is like making a right decision. Around you, I know everything's going to be okay."

I don't think she felt that way when she came to visit me in the infirmary, and I know I should have been better to her. But when I was staring at her from my bed, all of a sudden there was this difference I was seeing between the two of us. She was filmy, ethereal. And I know this sounds dramatic, but I was so solid that I'd been cracked, El. Then there was David, near my feet, David who seriously writes his name with a dash in between the 'v' and the 'd' because he says that's his way of illustrating 'that certain men are gods.'"

"What a dickhead," David said about me.

In hindsight, I should have agreed and told them I was sorry, but instead I said, "Neither of you came to my performance last night."

"We meant—" Marna started.

"I can't help it," I apologized. "I want to do this. But I really can't." Then, pushing my back as hard against the wall as it would go, I said, "I'm feeling distant from you."

I looked hard into their faces, and I was figuring the physical space between us like time had suddenly materialized and dropped a chunk of itself into the infirmary. This is the best way I can make you understand what was happening then: I was at the head of the room, and they were near the mantel, and we were two different film frames from two different days, weirdly spliced together to form an optical illusion. I felt like if I tried to talk to Marna and David more, if I tried to explain, my voice would have to travel back twenty-four hours. And my words wouldn't make sense, and when the two of them replied to me, I swear I thought I wouldn't have a clue what they were talking about.

Marna redid the braid in her hair and watched me. I was out of my mind, and I felt so, so watched. David picked up a *National Geographic,* exhaled, and violently flipped through it without even looking down.

Finally, Marna snapped her rubber band and let go. "Do you just want us to leave?"

That's when I opened my mouth—or I guess I should say that's when my mouth opened itself, because that's more what it was like. Anyway, I sang, *"If I stay here with you, girl/ Things just couldn't be the same,"* then stopped.

The heater clicked.

David dropped his magazine on the floor. "'Freebird'? You're singing 'Freebird'?"

"What's wrong with 'Freebird'?" I asked, but I should have known.

"Listen, just because you've decided, for whatever reason, that your respect for us has flown out the window, does not mean that we deserve that disrespect, or that we have to stand around here and take it. You fucking cripple, I hope this is the drugs talking."

"Suddenly 'Freebird' is a sign of disrespect? It's a beautiful song."

"Let's just go," Marna said. She looked scared.

"And it expresses everything I want to get across right now," I went on.

"I know you're going to snap out of this," said David, and he threw one arm up on the wall and tucked his head under it, reminding me of a duck. "And when you do, I hope your apology, long or short or even fucking sung to me, is a good one." Then he turned toward the wall completely and his neck bristled at me.

"Let's leave. He's sick," Marna said, pulling on the hem of David's coat. She wouldn't look at me when she reported, "Your dad will be here this afternoon. Your mom said she'll be calling and updating you on the plans."

"My dad's coming?" I asked.

"He's coming here to get you and take you home."

"Hmm," I said, to cover my own fear. I was thinking about going home and looking at my parents and brothers, and feeling like I wasn't a part of their group either. I knew they'd encourage me, tell me that I was going to recover and that the worst was now over.

What I thought in that moment, though, was that yes, maybe the worst was over, as far as there was a very slim chance of someone racing up to me during the next month and attempting another swipe at my knees. But what was really hurting was that a whole new worldview had taken me over, and that was a different kind of injury.

I glanced over to the other side of the room for you, but all that was there was your empty bed.

"There was a girl, a girl with black hair, and she was probably in the hallway when you came in. Did you see her?" I asked.

"There was a girl that let us in," answered Marna. "She looked like that."

"Why, who is she?" asked David.

"A girl. From here. Do you know where she went? Can you open the door and see if she's out there?"

David swung the door open, still pissed, and looked out into the hallway for me. I guess he just saw Vivian, because he said, "There's only a woman out there now with some animals. If you weren't being such an asshole, I would go and complain for you." Even though, like I said, he was pissed, I was touched right through my druggy haze to hear some tenderness in his voice. "Health Services is no place for fleas and bird shit. It's dangerous."

"Dangerous," I remember saying, and leaning my head back against the wall.

Marna put her coat back on. "Anyway, your dad is coming later."

"Thanks for passing on the message."

"So we'll be seeing you. And. Feel better," she said.

David held the door open for her and put his hand on her back. She passed by him. And then he disappeared.

This is the instant—I can pinpoint it because I felt it precisely as the door clicked shut—when I split from my old life. There were a few seconds when the door was still inches away from being shut, when I could have called out to them, "Come back! Please!" I almost did, with the intention of forcing myself to ease back into our friendship. I had fleeting thoughts about readjustment and temporary effects of trauma, and I swear, I almost cried for them to come back. But something inside me pulled in the opposite direction. And that opposite direction, to put it most directly, was you. And I don't think you'll take it as an insult when I finally acknowledge, on paper, that you're completely incompatible with other lifestyles.

CHAPTER 10

PAXIL CR • Get back to being you

As I went across the main part of campus, I limped with alternating legs. I switched my limp about every three steps. Both legs were tender. For a while I tried a slow gallop, since that movement felt somewhat comfortable. Then I went back to the limping, discovering I'm way too proud to gallop.

Because it was still early in the morning, there were only a handful of people outside—a photographer taking pictures of a snowgirl, a few joggers, and the kind of kids who head for the library as soon as they wake up. Everyone looked at me as I passed, but I don't think that anyone thought I was too unusual. In the spring of my freshman year, when I was out of the infirmary for a short while, I noticed that Brown has a large number of students with leg or foot problems. I was only walking around campus for a few months, but during that time I saw people limping, people stuck in wheelchairs, people with amputations, a girl with a clubfoot, some athletes with major sprains, and two lacrosse players with broken legs. I even met a sophomore who told me that he came back from summer vacation missing two toes. One of them was his big toe, and he was sad that he walked differently now.

It took me a long time to get through the main campus that day. It took me at least five minutes getting past the John Carter Library, and when I got to Wilson, the clock on top of it said seven forty-seven. I gave myself a few minutes to pause for breath in front of Sayles, and by the time I got to Salomon, I realized that I was pretty wet from my feet to my calves. The waffles were my northern star, though.

Because the other side of Brown Street has that slight upward curve, that part of the walk took even longer. I'd be embarrassed to put myself up in a race against an eighty-year-old. I used the low brick wall that runs along the sidewalk to steady myself, and I tried to ignore my shitty lungs and the pounding of my heart by looking down the rows and rows of brownstones on the other side of the street. It helped to focus on the vanishing point where the streets dropped off down the hill.

After about twenty more minutes, I think, I finally reached Meeting Street. Once there I decided to take the descending slope with a sideways shuffle, so gravity wouldn't throw me into an accidental jog. When I got to the bottom, I smiled without even knowing that I was going to smile; I felt somewhat accomplished. A middle-aged woman with a knit turkey sweater reading "Gobble, gobble" in red yarn was going into Emery-Wooley, and she held the door open behind her until I also made it through.

The woman disappeared into the Brown Card Office, but I went farther into the basement. At the soda and candy vending machines I knew I was getting close. Next I came to an open door and stuck my head inside. Because there were wooden tables and plastic chairs and air that smelled like cinnamon, I figured I had done things right.

After stepping into the dining hall, I was stopped by a guy sitting at a folding table.

"Excuse me, I need your card." He had a gigantic chemistry book open on the table and one knee propped up on an orange chair. His hand was upturned in the air, and his thumb and forefinger twitched for me to place something in between them.

"The card," I repeated. During the short periods of time before (and between) my illnesses, I had an ID card like everyone else. I'd forgotten that you needed it to let you into buildings and to eat meals. I couldn't believe how out of touch I'd gotten. I hadn't seen my card for at least a year and a half.

When I didn't reach into my pocket, the card swiper looked at me with an "Are you retarded?" expression. "I need to get it from you. So I can swipe it. So you can eat," he said.

"I don't have a card on me," I told him.

"Well, are you on meal plan?"

"Motherfucking meal plan," I thought. Then I remembered that too—that you signed up for your meals ahead of time. I definitely didn't have a meal plan. "Yes," I said. "It includes breakfast."

"Here's your alternatives. You can pay for your breakfast, and I'll take your SIS number if you know it offhand, and then all you have to do is go to Food Services by the end of the week and file for reimbursement. Or else you can just go back to your room and get your card. If you lost it, the card office is over there." The card swiper pointed out the door.

I looked the opposite way, toward the inside of the dining room. A Hispanic man in a hair net and a chef's uniform was walking toward a table, carrying a thick waffle on a plate. He took a seat and began to spread strawberries across the top of his waffle. Two women joined him, also Hispanic and also carrying waffles. Their hair nets were even like waffles. Their skin was the color of the edges of the waffles. I wasn't hungry at all, just determined to get a waffle.

"I don't have any money on me," I told the card swiper. "What else?"

The card swiper lowered his hand and returned to flipping through his book while shaking his head. "Look, I'm not the breakfast fairy. If you're asking me to let you in for free I can't do it. If you can find someone who will let you use one of their guest credits, then you can do that. Otherwise, you're out of luck."

Three girls who looked like they'd just come from hockey practice came into the V-Dub and handed the swiper their cards. They never stopped their conversation.

"Do you want to share a cab to the airport?" one asked.

"What time is your flight? It's not worth it for me to be sitting there for ten hours," said another. They all had ponytails and the roots of their hair were stiff from dried sweat.

"Eleven twenty."

"That's not bad. I can have breakfast there, I guess, or study. What are you doing, Becca?"

"Train tonight," the third said.

For only a second I thought about asking the girls not if I could borrow a guest credit—because I didn't want to be beholden to them—but if any of them knew a girl who used to get bloody noses all the time.

More people were coming into the dining hall, none of them familiar. A delivery guy for the *Brown Daily Herald* showed up and dropped a pile of papers into the metal rack. You were the headline. I picked up a copy to see if it would tell me something personal about you, but the article was only a fancified police report.

Suddenly, the card swiper switched from glaring at me to flipping out. "You can't stand there all morning! Do you think if you wear me down or something I'll let you in?"

"I'm figuring out what I'm going to do," I told him. I was considering swapping out goals, wondering if my brain would let me do that or if I'd feel disappointed no matter what. Going somewhere else seemed impossible.

"There's nothing you can do. You don't have your card, you don't have money, and it looks like you don't have friends," the card swiper said, his face as orange as his chair.

"I know. I know."

His mouth was open, even in the pauses between his words. "You can't stand there! You're making me nervous, standing there."

To that my left middle finger rose, seemingly on its own. My mom had a hypnotist friend who came over one time and tried to tell me that a big balloon was tied to my finger, and that I should let my finger go where the balloon wanted to take it. My finger had done nothing that day. But in the V-Dub, my finger rose. I stared at the tip of it, wondering why it was so white. The white was startling, especially considering that it was white even against the extreme whiteness of my normal skin.

"Fuck you, I'm just doing my job. This is how I pay for my books," said the card swiper.

The white resembled the white of a blister. It was iridescent and pulsing like it had pus underneath it. When

I opened up the rest of my hand, I saw that my four other fingers looked the same. Then I realized that they all felt the same, too, like I had snow globes inside of each tip. Then I realized that my nose and ears felt the exact same way.

"You flipped me the bird. Great, powerful. Go." The card swiper was still talking.

I turned my hands so that the undersides faced him, and I asked, "Do you see this?"

"Is that the newest insulting hand gesture all the cool kids are tossing around?" The card swiper's eyes were wild, locked on mine, and he was ignoring my fingers. "I don't care! I don't care, okay?" With both arms he pushed himself away from the table and out of his chair, sending a few pages of his book flipping. "I'm getting someone from administration to deal with this. I need to study."

Sighing at the trouble of it all, I wandered back out of the V-Dub and into the hallway. A guy with glasses too big for his face was heading for the door, and I stopped him before he reached it. I held up my fingers.

"Excuse me, do you see how these are whiter than they should be?

Guy With Glasses stopped. From the way he looked at me, it seemed like it had been awhile since a girl had stopped him like this. I could tell he wanted to be helpful. He squinted at the fingers before him. "Yes, the tips of your fingers are discolored. I see it."

I pulled back my hair and leaned forward. "Do my nose and my ears look like that?"

I was breathing lightly in his face and I knew we both were aware of it. "They do, kind of. They're also exceptionally white."

I stepped back to give him some space and kneaded my fingers. "The tingling is starting to go away, but I don't think that's a very good sign. Now they're going numb. I can barely feel them." Then I felt the tip of my nose. "This too. It's also going numb. What could this be?" I asked Guy With Glasses. It was a rhetorical question. I didn't really expect an answer from him.

Guy With Glasses didn't know what to do with his own hands, so he kept making small movements toward me with them. I felt like he wanted to touch me, but he could only do it if he came in at the right angle. "Do you want to sit down? Or maybe you want to eat something?" he asked.

For a split second I forgot my white, tingling problem. I asked him, "Do you have any guest credits left?"

Guy With Glasses shook his head, embarrassed. "My mom and dad insisted on eating at the Ratty when they were here for Parents' Weekend. They took all of mine. I'm sorry. Did you need one?"

"It's fine." I waved the idea away with my right hand, and Guy With Glasses gaped.

"Your fingers are turning blue," he said.

I flipped over my hand and checked. He was right. They were turning blue. "Is there a pay phone around here?"

Still weirded out, Guy With Glasses pointed over my shoulder to the phone near the bathrooms. "In back of you."

"Thanks."

I walked over and dialed 911. While it was ringing, I called out to Guy With Glasses, "My nose, is it blue now, too?"

CHAPTER 11

THE JOURNAL OF PARAPSYCHOLOGY OCTOBER 2004

Once Dr. Wainscott discharged E from the ER, she and I searched for a private place to talk. She didn't want anyone overhearing us—not even strangers, she said—and I wanted a quiet environment so that the recorder would pick up the inflections of her speech. The waiting room was packed with injured adults and crying children, and so we tried the hospital cafeteria. It was surprisingly crowded; a number of staff members and hospital visitors were eating early dinners, and I didn't like the acoustics in the room. The sounds of all the dishes and conversation around us might drown out E's voice.

E suggested that we go to my house. At first I was wary about crossing this doctor–patient boundary. Under normal circumstances, had a patient suggested having a private meeting in my living room, I would have refused. But E was the one who made the request, and because this signified a further display of trust on her part, I accepted her suggestion.

I pulled my car as close to the ambulance entrance as the hospital would allow, then wheeled E to the passenger door. It had begun to snow, so I placed my coat over her head. On the way to my house, I told E that it was crucial that we keep this entry into my private life quiet. I emphasized that this wasn't because our session at my house would be any different from our sessions at Health Services, but because the university was very nervous about this type of cloistered interaction between student and professor.

"Okay. Neither of us will say anything about this to anyone else," E said. "Do you want to cross our hearts?"

I looked over to gauge her seriousness, and I was surprised to see her silently laughing at me.

When I opened the door to my house and ushered E in, I couldn't help but feel like I was bringing a date home for the first time. I was expectant and nervous, although not romantically. E flipped on the lights in the front hallway, as if she'd been there before, and proceeded into my living room, steadying herself by keeping a hand always pressed against the wall.

"Why all the orange and red?" E questioned.

My house is furnished and decorated mostly in shades of these colors.

"I asked the interior decorator to do the house in warm tones. I requested the feeling of 'home.'"

"Oh," E said. I wondered what she was thinking.

"Do you want anything to eat? To drink?"

E sat down on my couch, which, to give readers a mental image, is in the burnt orange family. "I'm really tired," she told me, "so let's get started."

In my notebook, I wrote: "This is how E is—one moment you feel as if you've finally encouraged her to crawl into your palm, and the next you're worried that she's in danger of slipping out." I sat down in the club chair opposite the couch, placed the recorder on the coffee table, and asked E to tell me her family history.

Collapsing back against my pillows, she started with how her mother and father met.

Her mother, A, was an associate's guest at E's father's company Christmas party. She sat down next to E's father and told him that the peanut M&M he was about to eat was missing a peanut, and, when he bit into the candy and the shell caved in, he discovered that this was true.

I wanted to stop E right there, so I could verify she was one hundred percent serious about what I was hearing—that it was a prediction about an M&M that eventually led to her conception. However, I didn't stop her; there was always the fear that if I showed any signs of doubt, she would stop altogether.

"I have feelings about things" is what A told S, E's father.

A discussion followed, in which A revealed to S that she believed she had psychic and supernatural powers, and that this ability was carried through every generation of the women in the family. She also claimed that she was sure her first child was going to be a girl.

Then S apparently delivered the line that became famous in E's household throughout her adolescence. "I can't wait to leave my girlfriend that I feel nothing for and start dating you," he told A.

"Do you know if your father experienced depression during that part of his life?" I asked E.

"Why?" she asked.

"I'm just wondering."

She paused and then said, "Who are we to say?"

I didn't respond. After a few seconds, E told me more about her father's worldview. "No, I don't think it's depression, whatever depression is. I think it's that my mom is my dad's religion," she said.

S, before meeting A, had been living with another woman, who was, from what he told E, someone who only thought about what was "placed in front of her." He worked (and stills works) for a long-distance phone company where he devises new calling plans, and E suspected that he was almost desperate for some kind of momentous event in his life. His meeting with A appeared to have satisfied this need. He proposed to her within months.

I asked E to tell me some stories about the interactions between her parents, so I could better understand their dynamic. She said she had been especially affected by a version of a story that her father had told her in confidence, away from her mother.

One afternoon A had visited S at his office. She entered, out of breath, telling him, "I'm almost sure I saw the heel of a loafer go into the elevator as I turned the corner, but when I got inside it was empty. Guess there was a dead man in there with me."

S shut the door to his office, concerned that his coworkers would overhear this.

S told E that he'd become slightly scared for A because the M&M-type visions had been coming less frequently. A would predict rain when the forecast was for sunshine, and the couple would wake up at sunrise to wait for the storm that "never came," according to E. No worms were found in the apples that A thought would house them. E told me that her favorite failed prediction was the time that A thought that the new neighbors would be black, "and they weren't."

Among these failed predictions were frequent false pregnancies. E knew of two signs that A had brought to S. Once, there had been a squashed baby sparrow on the couple's driveway; later, A had noticed that a worker was always replenishing the nonfat milk cartons when she happened to come down the dairy aisle at the market. Despite these harbingers, A continued to menstruate.

While E related these details to me, I bit the inside of my mouth to keep from making distracting expressions. She relayed all this information without emotion, as if she were speaking about the weather. The only time E revealed a deeper feeling about her mother's predictions was when she told me about the dairy aisle and began to roll her eyes. They flicked up toward her eyelids, but did not come back down for five seconds. Thus, she appeared as if she had only intended to stare at the ceiling.

I had to ask E, "Were you about to roll your eyes?"

"I was about to, but then I stopped."

"Guilt?" I asked, trying to relate to her on a more sympathetic level.

"No," E said. "I stopped because I've heard that if you do that with your eyes enough, they'll stay that way. And I know that's just an old wives' tale. But I've had so many things happen to me that weren't ever supposed to that I've decided to play it safe."

I took this admission to heart, since it lay bare how fearful E had become of her own body's deviations, no matter how casually she tended to regard them.

We returned to that day at the office. S told E that he'd become worried for A, since every time her predictions failed her, she tried even harder to make bigger predictions with bigger payoffs. E felt that "he must have been worried, too, because I believe that he needed my mom to be right."

At S's office, E's parents discussed the "ghost" heel that A had seen in the elevator, and, from what E could deduce, S had ended up believing her. Then A had announced, "But we can figure out why he's haunting the elevator later, because the reason I'm here is that I'm pregnant."

"What did you see? What told you this?" S asked.

According to E, A's answer is also legendary: "A doctor."

They could all laugh about it now, E said, but at the time, it was a significant and humbling admission for her mother.

E had been told the details of the day of her birth, when her parents had encountered a skeptical midwife. A had decided to have a home birth in an inflatable pool, which E described as having "clear walls with plastic fish in them." She added that the family "still has the pool in the garage, which I think is nasty."

The family lives in Arizona, where E was born. E describes the house as a low, sprawling one-story that attempts to marry the "indoors with the outdoors."

E was told that the day of her birth was exceptionally hot, and while S and the midwife were in the kitchen getting ice cubes and cold water for A, the two had a quick discussion.

The midwife alluded to A as being "spaced out," and S assumed that she was talking about A's state during the birthing process. When he suggested to the midwife that he believed this was to be expected, the midwife told S that she meant that A seemed "spaced out in general."

The story in the family is that S almost fired her on the spot, except he did not want to leave A without medical assistance.

Soon after, A went into advanced labor, and E was born within the next hour. She came out head first, but her facial features were indistinct even after she was pulled out of the water.

When E told me that at first it appeared as if she'd been born without a face, I must admit I experienced a quick rush of exhilaration. Here was the real beginning, I felt, of everything that I needed to know about her. Here was the very first instance of abnormality, marking her the moment that she entered the world, pointing toward her later difficulties. "Your features were indistinguishable?" I echoed.

"I was born with a caul."

A caul, for those unfamiliar with the term, is one of the two membranes that protects the fetus in the womb. It is also known as the amnion. Most infants rupture and lose their amnion during the delivery process, but a rare few are born with the veil of skin still covering their faces. There is much superstition surrounding children born with intact amnion, as the uncommonness of this occurrence paves the way for those with magical minds to believe that these children are superior and destined for greatness.

Parents who first see their infants with the caul often believe they have produced a deformed child. I asked E if she knew how her parents had reacted to their first sight of her.

"Yes, I know. They've each told me."

"Go ahead," I said. "We need to get this down for the study."

S had told E that when he first saw her, he tried to convince himself that while it would be difficult to adjust to a daughter missing her eyes, nostrils, and mouth, he could do it. "When I was in sixth grade, he told me," E said, "that when I came out, he began thinking he would just have to alter his perception. He said that he decided when he saw me that slugs and dishtowels had suddenly become the most beautiful things in the world. Because that's what I looked like."

I asked E to describe her mother's reaction.

Apparently, A was thrilled not only about the caul, but also that she had given birth to a girl, as she had always believed she would. A is one of those magical thinkers I've referred to above, and she knew the implications of a child being born with an intact amnion. There had been other female relatives born with the caul, and A regarded her infant as the inheritor of a familial legacy.

The midwife made a comment about how children born with the caul are supposed never to drown and how she thought this was an amusing notion, considering that E was born in a wading pool. A corrected the midwife, alerting her to the more powerful connotation of the caul: this being that the infant was supposed to acquire the gift of second sight.

I began to see how E had arrived at her current position on the subject of the stranger in the bathroom.

The midwife, already believing that A was "spaced out," told her that such beliefs were "ridiculous." She was finally dismissed by S.

"Your parents must have thought that you were very special," I told E.

"It was no fun," E responded. She has an astonishing gift of recall from a very early age—about one and a half. Her memories are spotty, but they have proven to be correct. Her family has confirmed that her images of various toys, locations, and trips have been taken from reality. That night E told me about repeated memories she had of being watched in her crib, and she has come to believe that she wasn't being watched out of curiosity, but out of a stronger need. She felt like she was "a baby born to a family where the older kid is dying of leukemia, and everyone was waiting to see if my bone marrow matched."

When I asked her what she believed that her parents were looking for within her, E told me that they wanted "some kind of sign."

"What was your first word?" I asked her.

"It was 'stop,'" E answered. She still believes that her parents were waiting for her to turn that word into a profound prediction, despite the fact that she wasn't even a toddler yet.

"Give me an example," I said.

E shut her eyes and took a deep breath. "What did they want?" she asked herself, I think, and not me. "Stop, Mom and Dad, I feel . . . in the air. Stop, Mom and Dad, I feel . . . in the air, over there, big things. Stop, Mom and Dad, I feel . . . in the air, over there, big things that are incredibly, incredibly portentous and listen now, for I will reveal them. And don't ask me about certain morbid things because yes, I can predict them, but I won't. But let me tell you that there's a 4.0 earthquake coming in California. And while it will wake everyone up and freak them out a little, there will be minimal damage and no fatalities."

Then E opened her eyes and said, "Like that."

"I'm guessing that your first sentence was a disappointment to them?" I asked.

"Yes."

The story of E's first sentence was also frequently told, although it was wasn't laughed about, despite the passage of time. One evening A pulled E onto her lap to show her tarot cards, and she handed a particular card—the lover—to her baby. E took it from her mother and said, "Stop, these are just cards, Mommy."

A and S froze, disbelieving.

"If you were so skeptical of your mother, even at this young age," I asked, "why the change so late in life?"

"Because I saw a ghost," E said.

"Well, you *think* you saw a ghost." I regretted the words as soon as they left my mouth.

"No. I saw a ghost," E said. "Can you take me back to the infirmary now?"

E reached over to the coffee table and turned off the recorder. We did not speak on the ride back to the infirmary.

At Health Services, I helped her out of the car and up the steps. At the phone next to the front door I wanted to call Lily, the nurse then working the night shift, so she could help E up the stairs. E refused, saying she needed some time to herself, even if that time was only between the front door and the infirmary.

She went inside before I could pin her down on a time for our next session. I wrote in my notes that I wondered if we were still on "intimate speaking terms."

CHAPTER 12

PAXIL CR • Get back to being you

When the ambulance picked me up in front of Emery-Wooley, I didn't have the blue parts to show the paramedics anymore. A few minutes before they came, everything had turned red. Red on a human is less exotic than blue, and when the paramedics put me into the back of their van, they looked bored. I said, "Sorry, guys, I wish I was oozing some pus for you."

When we pulled up to the hospital, the driver paramedic turned around and asked, "Emergency room?" just to make sure I still had to go there.

Dr. Wainscott had been my attending many times before, just through the magic of probability. I could tell he forced a smile when he saw me sitting on the bed, like he was trying to keep his eyes from turning doleful. But he just couldn't resist reaching out to cup my head with his hand. I was relieved that he didn't call me "Little Soldier" that day, as he had one other time.

"Elodie, it's good to see you," he told me. "I'm sorry to see you here, but it's still good."

"Thank you, Dr. Wainscott," I said. "It's good to see you as well." What I meant by this was "It's good to be seeing you, as you are a doctor and I believe I am in need of some form of treatment."

The doctor showed me the preliminary report that the nurse had made about me, since she dotted her i's with open circles. "Funny, don't you think? Every time I pick up one of these workups, I think a seventh-grade girl has left me a secret love note. I tell Nadine that it gets me a little hopeful. I wasn't popular back then." Nadine has also seen me a lot.

I watched the doctor blackening in the dots as he read down the list of symptoms. "So your fingertips, nose, and ears turned bright white, then blue, and then red, and they're back to normal now?"

I held up my hands for him to see.

"Tell me, did they tingle? Go numb?"

"They went both, in that order exactly."

"Elodie," he said, still trying to smile, "have you ever heard of Raynaud's phenomenon?"

I asked him, "What's the treatment?"

"So you've heard of it."

"No, but I can tell I have it from the way you're approaching the subject."

The doctor pulled over his rolling stool and took a seat. He placed the clipboard on his lap, which told me that he was getting down to business.

"What Raynaud's is, basically, in simplest terms, is an abnormal reduction of blood flow to the peripheral arteries and arterioles. This is usually brought on by stress, or cold weather—"

"I'm following," I said.

"And I think, fundamentally, what happened today was that your exposure to the weather caused vasospasms in those parts of your body that went through the color changes, and the changes in sensation—"

"Right."

"And this would make sense because the disease most often affects women and shows itself between puberty and middle age. A little earlier, actually, but you're right in that bracket. But tell me this: have you ever had symptoms like this during the winter before? Even to a lesser degree? Maybe just a slight tingling in your fingers, and you suspected it was just a temporary circulation problem?"

"I've never felt anything like that before," I replied, "but I've also never been outside during the winter."

I watched the doctor's eyebrows dive together. "What do you mean?"

"I've been in bed through every winter I've spent in Providence," I said. "Freshman year I was out for the spring, but the temperature was already in the sixties then. I've been out in the beginning of fall and during various points of the summer, but I've never spent time outside during the winter. Today was the first time I've walked in snow since I was small. Once my parents took me on a vacation to Lake Arrowhead."

"So it's possible," the doctor thought out loud, "that you've been a Raynaud's sufferer for a while, but, because you'd never been exposed to your particular catalyst, the phenomenon never revealed itself before now."

"That seems like it could be true."

"Well, we'll do some tests. I think it's smart if we also check you out thoroughly and make sure you haven't exacerbated any of your other conditions." Looking down at my history, the doctor asked, "The TB was on its way out, wasn't it?"

"I was out of the infectious stage."

"And how do you feel right now?

"This instant?"

"Yes."

"Physically, the same as usual. Doctor Wainscott, how do you treat the Raynaud's? Drugs?"

He stood up from the stool and wouldn't even look at me. "There are some drugs I can give you, but I don't necessarily know that I'm going to prescribe anything since the side effects can give patients more trouble than the Raynaud's itself."

"Can you give me an idea of recovery time?"

He turned his back to me while I changed into a hospital gown. "Well, Elodie, Raynaud's isn't really a disease you recover from."

I started to get naked. I envision you thinking that this was a sexy moment, but it really wasn't. The ER is very unsexy.

"If this is Raynaud's, you're just going to have to watch yourself carefully in cold climates. It might affect where you decide to settle down after college, but I don't think it will ever be as debilitating for you as—"

My jeans fell onto the floor, and they made the sound my remaining enthusiasm would've made if it weren't trapped inside my body. My thoughts went to you then, back in the infirmary. I remember thinking something like "I am always going to be too debilitated to be with someone like that." You showing up was a reminder that I wasn't getting better. On my way to the waffle, I had begun to fantasize about leaving with you when you were discharged.

Putting my arms through the holes in the gown, I said, "I understand." Then I told Dr. Wainscott, "Okay," and he came to me and pressed his stethoscope to my chest.

When he finished his part of the exam, the doctor scribbled on my chart and said, "I'm going to have the nurse come in and do some tests. When we get the results back, we'll have a better idea of exactly what's going on. All right, Elodie?"

"That's fine."

"So, any big plans for the holiday?" the doctor asked, removing his latex gloves.

"The holiday?"

"Thanksgiving. It's on Thursday. Don't tell me you've forgotten about Turkey Day."

I had forgotten. I said, "My days run together."

I can almost guarantee that the doctor wanted to scoop me up into a ball and hold me to him, judging from the face he was making. But he resisted the whim and instead went over to the box of latex gloves. "You're too old for the monkey balloons." He pulled out a white hand. "And probably too old for this, but I can't have you forgetting Thanksgiving." The doctor blew into the glove, then pinched it shut. After he searched around in a drawer near the sink, he found a rubber band and tied off the hole. Then he took out a permanent black marker.

I watched him.

He made eyes on each side of the glove's thumb with the marker, and he drew a beak, too. He drew lines going up the fingers and then diagonal lines shooting off from those original lines. Holding it out, he asked me (in what I think was his impression of a turkey), "Which part of me do you want to eat first?"

I took the rubber bird. I knew I had to say something or this visit would never end. "The wings."

"Hey, I love the wings, too!" He seemed happy.

I asked the doctor to call my regular doctor, Dr. Kirschling, whom I know you've never met, but that's intentional. You know how some people don't like to bring their work home? I've tried not to bring my bullshit home, as much as possible.

All you need to know about Kirschling is that his fantasy is to be the Oliver Sacks of the body. He wants to fill books with stories of patients who are like urban legends, so that's part of why he sees me. When I leave the infirmary every Thursday, he's the one I have those checkups with.

When I came back to Health Services that night, a girl was coming down the stairs right as I was about to go up them. She must have had the last appointment of the day, seeing as how late it was, and she was holding one of the brown bags that the pharmacy hides drugs in. I turned and watched her as she walked out of the building, maybe pretending I was her for a second. Then I climbed the stairs like someone who'd spent the day boating, basketballing, and making shit out of pipe cleaners at summer camp.

Lily was on duty, and when she heard me coming, she ran to the top of the stairs and put her arm around me. She got kind of mad at me for not having called her from the bottom.

"I'm fine," I told her. "Just tired. They drew blood, did some tests. It was a long day."

"You're sure you're fine?"

"I'm sure."

"Do you want to paint each other's nails later, or are you too tired?" Lily asked. I don't think you've seen it that much because you're male, but she has this sleep-over mentality about infirmary nursing. She loves to have her hair brushed and loves to brush hair.

"Sorry, I think I'm too tired," I apologized. I started to go toward the infirmary door, and I realized I was getting nervous about how I'd face you. I thought you'd probably have heard through the grapevine that I'd landed in the hospital, and I didn't want to have to tell you about it. I wanted you to believe I was on the verge of being normal. We could start from there.

When you saw me, you sat up straighter and smiled. "You're back!" you said. The lamp next to your bed was the only light on in the room.

"I'm back," I agreed, and then I flirted with you by falling face first onto my bed. "I'm exhausted," I told my comforter, and that was the last thing I remember before you woke me up.

CHAPTER 13

From The Desk of Chester Hunter III

When you came back to the infirmary, one of the lights from the hallway was shining over your head, and looking at you, I felt like a lost miner who'd just collided with one of my own guys in the darkness. I was that happy to see you, even though we barely knew each other, El. I had the feeling that you were there to save my life. But then you barely even looked at me when you walked to your bed. And then you just collapsed into it, and I saw your back moving from your heavy breaths.

So I waited five minutes. You can't imagine how badly I wanted you to move. I decided to try a little telepathy because I was feeling brand new, and as lame as it sounds, I thought that maybe I had brand-new abilities. So I stared at your pinky finger on your pillow and tried to will it to move. It turned out that I didn't have the patience, though, to actually concentrate and see if I could be telepathically successful. I remember I asked you, "Elodie? How could it be possible that I missed you so much today when I don't even know you, and that I didn't want to see my friends, who I should have been missing?"

I didn't get a response, and Lily came into the room,

holding my macaroni and cheese. I whispered to her, "Can she honestly be sleeping?" We both looked over to you in disbelief. "She came in a second ago, and now she's already knocked out." I could hear the start of alarm in my voice.

Lily tiptoed over to your bed and bent down to check. She stood up and mouthed to me, "Sleeping."

And maybe you'll think I sound like a baby, but I felt your having fallen asleep as a personal loss. I'd been looking forward to your return all afternoon, and god, that sounds whiny, but there were so many things left unfinished.

I beckoned Lily over to my bedside and told her, "I've been sitting in the exact same spot all day. Are there wheelchairs around here? It would be really great if I could just look at the room from a different angle."

Lily went away for a few minutes and came back with a wheelchair, which she helped me get into. You slept through all this, even though we were talking at normal level and my leg braces were hitting up against each other and everything. I could hardly believe your sleeping stamina. After I was settled in the chair, I practiced rolling myself backward and forward with my arms, and Lily seemed really proud.

"Now you can get your own magazines from the mantel," she said.

I asked her, "Who would have thought I'd be so happy about being able to roll ten feet when I could run a thousand yesterday?"

She said she had to go do some paperwork, but if I got bored, I should roll myself to the door and knock, and we could hang out. She never got as far as brushing my hair, but she definitely wanted to throw some dessert in the microwave and shoot the shit.

Once I was alone, I turned myself in a half circle so that I could face you again. You still hadn't moved a muscle, and, well, suffice it to say, I guess I knew I couldn't be passive anymore. So I pulled my elbows back to put as much power into the push-off as possible (I also used my diaphragm training from all my years of singing), and then I flew across the floor and to the foot of your bed. One three-point turn, another push forward, and my nose was seriously only a foot from yours.

And, El, at first I was just going to get a good look at your face. That's it, because I'd been so drugged out before, and you'd been sitting on the opposite side of the room, and your features had been almost bleached by the window's glare. I reached out and placed both my hands underneath your left shoulder, the one that was closer to me. I slightly, slightly lifted your body. By doing this, I was able to bring a little more of your torso into view, but your face was still pressed down into the pillow, and I had to see it.

So then I tried again by lifting your shoulder back with more pressure, and I made sure to move really slowly so that you wouldn't be jarred. I lifted and lifted, and it's both hilarious and embarrassing picturing myself now, how stealthy I was being. If you really want to know how ridiculous I was, I did this for *four minutes.* Finally your chest was opened to me, and I had a look at your profile.

With the utmost care, I removed one of my hands from beneath your shoulder, and I began to work on your hips and legs, adjusting them so that I could get you arranged in a loosened fetal position. Since you balanced yourself that way, I was able to remove my other hand from your shoulder. To anyone else reading this, I must seem like the guy with the most minimal understanding of personal boundaries on the planet. But I knew you were the kind of person who would do the exact same thing, the kind of person who wouldn't stop yourself from obtaining answers when you were painfully curious. Other people never got us and still wouldn't. That I know for sure.

I put one hand up to your exposed cheek, and the other, millimeter by millimeter, I slid under your cheek that was still resting on the bed. Before I even had a full grasp on what I was doing, I was bending down to kiss you. I was thinking that you were such a beautiful sleeper.

When I realized that my lips were pressed to yours, I basically became paralyzed with shock at myself. I was in an alien situation, having no idea what to do, and I guess that's why I just left my mouth there for a few seconds. And then suddenly convinced that I was going to wake you up, and that you'd hate me and never talk to me again, I decided to remove my lips using the same slow process I'd used before. I started to pull away, making the change gradual and jerky like I was a rusty garage door going up. My eyes were open the entire time, and I kept them focused on your fluttering eyelashes.

I had no idea that outside on the curb in front of Health Services, a huge group of my fellow a cappella singers was assembling. I know you probably just thought that it was a big mix of anonymous voices, but that was the Yale Whiffenpoofs, who were visiting Brown for the weekend (they're really good), and they had joined up with the Bear Necessities because of me. We were originally supposed to have a midnight a capella competition against them, but my accident brought everyone together under one cause.

I almost had my lips removed from yours—almost. There was only a tiny bridge between our bottom lips. The room was totally silent. I remember the heater being on a break. Then the Whiffenpoofs/Bear Necessities started singing at full power, and I swear it was like war sirens bleating through the night.

"It used to seem to me—"

At "me," your eyes flew open, and I thought, "Ohhhhhh shit." In my shock I stayed attached to your bottom lip, frozen like I was in the presence of a wild bear.

The Necessities and Whiffenpoofs sang:

"That my life ran on too fast—"

My mind raced to find an apology for you that would sound real and, above all, legitimate. I needed you to know that I had never been so instantly captivated by anyone, and I had never done anything like this before. You surprised me by not moving your face. The only part of you that did move was your eyes, which darted up and down my face.

Down below, the guys were continuing to make promises to me. Channeling Steven Winwood, they were belting, swearing to me that that I'd be "Back in the High Life Again."

Shit, El, I was hoping that they were actually right about me getting better, but even more than that, I *did* want new doors opened to me—yours, specifically. Then, like you knew exactly what I needed, you lifted your head, bit my lower lip, and kissed me.

CHAPTER 14

PAXIL CR • Get back to being you

When those singing guys woke me up, you looked like you were on the verge of either initiating a make-out session or crying. You had the doofiest expression on, and I almost laughed. I think you were scared of what I'd do.

But I was touched by the way you looked, because I knew you'd started something that you were too embarrassed to finish. Once my mom took me to see her hypnotist friend performing at a high school auditorium, and after the student volunteers woke up from acting like chickens, they looked just like you did. I remember thinking, "Who does this? Who brings his face this close to someone who's sleeping?"

For a second I thought that it was the night before again. I thought that I was destined to live in a "Tarzan Boy" world forever. My logic hadn't kicked in yet, and I thought that I would always be at the mercy of loud singers, waiting for them to be quiet.

The difference was you, though. When I opened my eyes and saw you, you were the proof of change. Of time moving forward. I was so overjoyed that I lifted my head to kiss you, and just to make sure that you were real, I bit down on the edge of your lip.

I want to tell you how it felt to kiss you, but it turns out kissing is like sickness in that it exceeds my vocabulary. You'd think that somewhere among all the words I've collected over the course of my life—words from textbooks, words from books read for fun, from magazines, from TV shows, from love songs I've heard, from movies, from rented videos, from Pictionary/Scrabble/Trivial Pursuit, from crossword puzzles, from word searches, from historical quotations summoned for current use, from current quotations, from people talking around me, from people talking to me, from any of the many possible forms of lexicon osmosis—I would have some decent words to describe the kissing. But the only approximation that seems halfway good is that I felt I had minuscule rainbowfish (they're the jumpy, little iridescent fillers in aquariums) darting through my nerves.

After you fell asleep with your mouth still on mine, I realized that I wasn't following you anytime soon. I got out of bed and walked to the window. The street was quiet outside with most everyone having left for the holiday, and soon I saw the security shuttle stop in front of the building, its emergency lights blinking in time with my heart. There was no one to pick up. Kneeling down, I licked my finger and smeared the tally marks underneath the sill. I was declaring a new point of origin.

My junior year of high school I went through a period of insomnia, and during it I became very friendly with the Home Shopping Network. The first time I watched, a host, redheaded Kelly, was showing the lobster clasp on a pearl necklace. The way she was talking intrigued me. She said, "You could wear this, say, if you were going to a dinner party, and you just wanted that one elegant touch. Or, how about a summer vacation? And perhaps you're going on a cruise? Maybe you just love pearls, and you want to put them on with a pair of jeans and wear them when you're running errands? That's fine, too." The clock said that Kelly still had to discuss the pearls for another minute. She just kept coming up with new options. "Or you can give them as a gift. Or you can hold on to them for Mother's Day and give them then." She was impressive.

I was inspired and started to play along. I said, "Or you can twist them and put them in your hair. Or you can wrap them around your wrist and make two bracelets if you don't have a lot of money, but you want to look like you own more jewelry than you do. Or you can put them in the closet, forget about them, find them again a year later, and be completely surprised." It became the late-night game I played with myself when sleep eluded me. I got so good at it that I could not only predict all of the hosts' suggestions, but outdo them with at least ten more of my own.

Looking at you, the lump in my bed, I felt like I did when I used to watch HSN. You were the source of a million possibilities. I sat on the floor, thinking, "Or this. Or that. Or this. Or that," until I was feeling something that approached the start of lovesickness. Incidentally, I don't know why they call it lovesickness, because in my opinion the sensation feels more like an abundance of health. You start to feel like a golden retriever, since you're so frisky it's embarrassing, and if you had a tail you'd chase it, too.

Even though I spent that night wondering about you and me, I didn't want you to wake up. I didn't want to talk to you yet. What I wanted was the chance to be aware of a turn in my life before it happened. I wanted to hover there, allowing all of that hope to shimmer around me, and I didn't want to rush through the phase. I have a lot of experience with waiting. I've waited for doctors who always give me too much time to change into the disposable robe. I've waited for labs that need weeks to process blood and bone marrow samples. I've waited for illnesses that like to take their time moseying through my body. So even though my stomach was jumping, I waited to move until I had given my hope its due. By then I was worn out. I picked myself up from the floor and climbed back into bed with you.

CHAPTER 15

From The Desk of Chester Hunter III

My dad had to call up to the infirmary three times before I finally got in the elevator, and that was because I couldn't tear myself away from you. I'm telling you this now because you were sleeping and had no idea what I was feeling. I'm sure you woke up and thought that I was gigantically fearful of commitment and had run out on you—I don't think we'd ever talked about my going home. In fact, I think we had been too busy being amazed with each other's mouths, and then we passed out.

On the plane I took up two seats, because the braces forced me to sit horizontally. My dad was sitting in one of the seats in the row behind me, and he kept leaning forward to talk to me through the crack between the chair backs.

"How are you holding up?" he asked me for the thousandth time.

"Like a champion," I replied, and I think my dad took this answer seriously because in the past it would have been a serious answer, if that makes sense. I turned my head and looked into my dad's eye there in the crack.

"I'm certainly impressed, proud of the way you've handled this incident. Chess, this shows character."

"Thanks, Dad. But, you see, I don't know that this shows character as much as it builds it. Do you know what I mean?" I asked.

"Mmmm, naturally." My dad rang for the stewardess and she came right away to his seat, since she had only been about two feet away.

"What can I get you, sir?" she asked.

"I'm having a Bloody Mary. Chess?"

I said, "Nothing for me, thanks," and then my dad was there at the crack again, looking at me with his steely eyeball. "A bottled water, then? We're going to have a toast."

The stewardess took a step forward to get a final answer from me—she even bent over me with her big and long breasts. I'm not telling you about them in a sexual way or to say that I was turned on or anything like that, but because I remember them encroaching on my space, and I know you know about encroached space.

"What're you toasting?" she asked. "A handsome guy like you? I bet you just got engaged. All the good ones are always taken!" she laughed mirthlessly. By then, you see, all I was thinking about was you.

• • •

In the car our positions were reversed, with my dad sitting in the front of the Lexus, driving, while I reclined in the back. When we were going through San Jose, my braces kept clicking against each other every time there was an imperfection in the freeway. I was all woozy from the flight, so I was feeling close with the topography of the 280. I told my dad, "My body is equipped with divining rods," and my dad looked in the rearview and asked, "Are you drifting off? I can wake you when we're home."

"No, I'm completely awake, Dad," I said. Feeling suddenly angry, I remember throwing my hands up and drumming out a beat on the car's ceiling.

Since you've never seen my parents' house, I'll make you feel like you have, and that way, you'll be able to understand the logistics of everything I'm telling you. The house is Mediterranean and in one of the nicest neighborhoods in Palo Alto (I have to be honest). It's two stories with a clay tile roof, and there's a long balcony that runs the entire length of the second story. That balcony's divided by stucco pilasters, and behind the balcony there are four windows that are more wide than tall, with shutters on them. There are two picture windows on the front of the first floor that also have the same shutters. Last year my mom put two gigantic pots with miniature cypress trees on either side of the doorway, and the door itself is a little bit sunken inside of a big archway.

Our house is a corner property and so I saw my mom from four blocks away. She was standing out on the balcony, and I thought that she looked like one of those ancient women waiting for a ship to come in. But as soon as we pulled into the driveway, she disappeared into the house and reappeared on the front lawn, when I really was wishing she'd hang back for just a second.

"Chess!" she called through the closed car windows, and, El, her voice sounded the way it used to when she would call to me, underwater, from the edge of the pool. That's when I seriously started getting panicked about this mental distance issue that I was experiencing, since obviously it wasn't stopping before it hit my family.

My dad turned off the ignition and got out of the car. "He's doing fine, Olivia," he said, and went to pop open the trunk.

My mom still had to see for herself, though, and so she opened the rear door near my feet and leaned in. "You're fine? How could that be?" she asked.

"I'm taking it like a champ, Mom," I said. When I was looking at my mom I was thinking that I wanted her to hug me quickly and then let go before I felt the distance creeping between us.

"Nobody's going to fault you if you want to complain, Chess. You don't have to impress me with stoicism."

I nodded.

Behind her, my dad was struggling to unfold the wheelchair, so my mom turned to help him. "I'll hold this part," she told him, "and you push down on that bar there." They started working together to get the wheelchair all set up, and for that brief, brief moment, their attention was off me. Then I heard, "We did it! Success through teamwork."

Even though my parents live in separate bedrooms and have separate phone lines, they work well together and they know it. For about a second, in the early 'nineties when they were talking about divorce, they realized how good they were at living together and that it would be stupid to feel bitter about a failed romance. And they can even laugh about their situation now, which I think is great. Everyone should be able to laugh at themselves. My dad once bought my mom an inside-joke magnet for their "anniversary" that read, "Passion dies," and it's still up on the fridge.

As my parents helped me into my wheelchair, my mom told me, "Your brothers are getting in from the city later today. They can't wait to see you. They were shocked you didn't call them right after the attack. Admittedly, we all were."

"I wasn't trying to worry or insult you," I said. "I just realized, what could you do from over here when I was over there?"

"What a question!" my dad exclaimed, and he gripped me on the shoulder. "For starters, we could have given our love and support."

"Your father's exactly right. But I'm happy you're at least here with me now," my mom said, and she kissed my hand.

• • •

The next afternoon at the Thanksgiving table, everyone else was seated before my mom pushed me in to the table. I was the "guest of honor." But she hadn't calculated the room my extended legs needed, so my metal footrests slammed into the metal base of our dining table.

The scraping sound of the two like elements was really, truly horrible. I know it sent shivers up my spine, as I'm sure it did everyone else's. My whole body rebounded from the impact—my back hit my chair's pad, and my head flew into my mom's stomach.

My two older brothers, Seth and Mitchell (whom you never met), got up and tried to help.

"Mom," yelled Mitchell, "pull him back out! Maybe you should get him away from the table."

All the voices around me rattled in my ears like beans in a can. No, that doesn't even do it. They were plentiful like that, like a whole bunch of beans, but even louder. They were bombastic beans. I was hoping to quiet them, so I said,

"Hey, I took a shitload of painkillers this morning. I barely feel a thing, everyone."

"Chess, we've got guests here," my dad reminded me. "Some with sensitive ears, so please." And then, "Glad that didn't hurt too much, though. Olivia, you've got to be delicate with him right now."

"I know. You're right, without a doubt." My mom backed my wheelchair up with extreme cautiousness. "You're really fine?" she asked me.

"I'm fine, Mom. In that way."

"That's unbelievable," she said. My parents have always been my biggest cheerleaders, and I'm not being facetious. They were famous for being even louder than the real cheerleaders at my high school when I used to play lacrosse. My mom asked my dad, "Well, Chester, how are we going to do this?"

They decided to put me at the head of the table so I'd have enough legroom, but my mom was worried that I'd be sitting sideways.

"He can turn his head. It wouldn't be too hard to turn your head, would it, Chess?" my dad asked.

"Not at all," I said. "I didn't get struck in the neck."

Not to be a total dick, I kept my head turned in the direction of the table for the first five minutes of the meal. I was watching my little cousin Bella putting olives on her fingertips.

"Mommy, look. I'm sick. My fingers are sick and gross," she said.

Bella's dad, my uncle Trevor, licked his finger and ran it across his right eyebrow, which is a nervous tic that he's never been able to shake, even though he knows he does it.

"Honey, when we have real sick people at a table, that's not a nice thing to say," he told her.

My great-aunt Linda piped in, all insulted. "I'm not sick."

"No one said you were, Aunt Linda." Uncle Trevor was going crazy on his eyebrow. "Julia has warts on her hands, and she's very sensitive about them." I knew he was covering, trying to draw attention away from my knees by targeting his wife instead.

"Do you really have to remind everyone, especially while we're at the table?" whispered my aunt Julia, getting really mad at him.

Honestly, I just didn't have patience for family drama, so I gave up, returned my head to its natural position, and watched our front yard turn purple as the night started to come down.

"Chess!" called Seth from the other side of the cornucopia centerpiece that my mom fills every year with orchids, which, by the way, I don't think are traditional Thanksgiving flora. "Tell us about the bashing o' the knees. Was it, without question, the most painful thing you've ever experienced?"

"This is Thanksgiving," my dad said, trying to put the kibosh on.

"He's right," nodded my mom. "If you're going to talk about it, you have to start your story with 'I'm thankful for,' even if the rest of it ends badly."

Mitchell tried to be funny by saying, "I'm thankful for the swipe to the knees, which hurt, but probably not as much as a swipe to the balls." And then all the guys at the table made a big show out of clutching their hands to their nuts and groaning—even my cousin Paul, who told me once, when he was drunk, that he sometimes pays women to wear spike heels and step on his package.

Aunt Julia put her hands over Bella's ears and raised her eyebrows at Mitchell.

He said, "Aunt Julia, don't worry. She doesn't know what 'balls' are. She thinks you dodge them at recess."

"If nobody's disturbed by talking about the incident, then I suppose it's allowed," my dad told the table.

"Thank you, Master," my mom said, in some sort of Chinese-British-Jamaican slave-girl accent. At this point, I wanted so, so badly just to roll out of the room and wheel myself all the way back to Providence.

"If you want to know the truth," I answered, and the whole table got quiet, "I barely remember it hurting at all. There was the first quick jolt, like a flash of lightning, but it felt more like a burst of energy, like energy being transferred, than a burst of pain. And then, after that, I have to say that I really felt nothing."

"You must have instantly gone into shock," my mom said, making her distressed face. "The only reason I can bear to hear this now is because I can look at you and see for myself that you're all in one piece."

"Not shock, Mom," I said. "A nurse told me it's officially called 'the grace period.' There was almost a full hour where I was feeling fine, and I couldn't even understand why I was in the emergency room. I even told them I could get up and walk out. I swear, I was pure grace."

"Isn't it nice how the body automatically knows how to protect you from the worst?" my mom asked.

"The grace period, hmmm," my dad mused. "That is a very nice function of the body."

"We're elegant creatures," said Uncle Trevor while licking his finger and wiping it across his eyebrow again, which I thought mostly cancelled out his personal elegance.

After dinner I was rolled into the living room for some holiday social time. I kept spacing out on one of the tapestries hanging on the wall near the fireplace—it shows these very fat peacocks that are wading through vines, but their stomachs hang so low that I've always thought that in real life, they probably couldn't move. So I just rested there in my wheelchair, backed against the picture window, and I listened to everyone talk without understanding them.

I was almost asleep when my mom's hands came down on my shoulders. "Chess? Chess?"

I'd forgotten where I was, and so what I said was "Elodie?"

"Who?" my mom asked.

"Oh, not Elodie," I said.

"It's me. Are you too tired for a conversation?"

"What kind of conversation?"

"Your father and I want to have a talk with you. And it's late, I know. We hadn't planned on doing it tonight. The fact is, we weren't going to do it for months, but now neither of us can wait."

"This sounds a little ominous, Mom," I told her.

"It's not. I promise."

When my mom had pushed me to the doorway of the study, my dad was already there, pitched forward all businesslike on the couch. "Come in. Come in," he called, but my mom was already moving me toward him, so I said, "Looks like I'm heading toward you anyway."

"Chess," started my dad, "you've been a constant source

of pride for us. I don't think we could express what a pleasure it's been to watch you grow into the young man that you've become."

"I still feel that this is ominous, Mom," I said.

"You have nothing to worry about. Just listen to your dad."

"Chess, you have absolutely nothing to worry about." My dad gave me a weird grin like he was suspicious of me for being suspicious of him. "This isn't a bait and switch. I'm speaking to you straightforwardly. Everything I'm saying is true."

"Okay."

"Really, Chess. It is true. You've never been so wary of us before," my mom said.

"You're right," I agreed.

"Then I'll go on," my dad told me, clasping his hands. "As I was saying, your mother and I feel that you've become a very fine man. And even though the measure of a man can't be reduced to dollars and cents, we have the tradition, as you are aware, of making gifts to our sons upon graduation."

Now I relaxed a little because my brain was clicking and saying, "Ohhhhhhh. Oh."

"Seth received his boat, and Mitchell his year traveling through Europe."

I nodded, and just hoped they weren't going to tell me that they'd bought me a platinum wheelchair.

"And we were going to wait to give you your gift in May, except when we found out your knees were bashed by that vandal—" My dad couldn't even finish.

"It's such a tragic thing to have happen in your senior year, Chess, and we're so proud of the way you're carrying yourself. Look at you," my mom said, gesturing toward me with this look of awe like I was juggling grenades instead of just sitting there like a complete invalid.

My dad was reaching into his inside jacket pocket and pulling out some kind of brochure. "So we wanted to present you with a token of our admiration during this trip home. Even though the gift isn't finished yet."

"Isn't finished?" I asked.

"We've put the down payment on a brand-new townhouse."

I absorbed this news for ten seconds, but I don't think it was really affecting me the way that they wanted it to. How could I think ahead to a house that I would live in after graduation when I had only just started living a life of the moment? My mind couldn't even get past the next five minutes, and in those next five minutes all I knew was that I had to talk to you. I felt that you were living on the same scale of time, and I needed someone who made sense right then, right in that frame. I asked my parents, "Can I be excused to go make a phone call?"

They weren't too happy about the request, but they rolled me to the phone anyway. I think they were scared to deny me anything. I called the infirmary, which I've never told you before because you didn't answer. That was all I wanted that night, though, so you know now—to get ahold of you.

CHAPTER 16

PAXIL CR • Get back to being you

Vivian was supposed to be working on Thanksgiving, but the fire at her house changed things. Her boyfriend called in the afternoon, saying she couldn't make her shift because of "a personal crisis," so Health Services called in a rent-a-nurse. Her name was Bethany. I wish you could have seen her.

Bethany had this habit of looking at me sideways from under her hair. This sometimes reminded me of a horse, sometimes of this prematurely mustached guy that I went to high school with, who was a big, big Metallica fan.

The infirmary desk phone kept ringing all night, which was weird for a holiday.

"I don't want to answer the phone," Bethany said to me, sounding nervous.

"No problem," I said. "I'm not expecting any calls."

"They didn't mention anything about phones."

"Don't answer it."

We were eating fried chicken that we got from Food Services. There had been surplus legs left over from everybody else's Tuesday-night dinner.

"Do you want to give thanks?" Bethany asked.

I looked around to figure out if I wanted to, and then I looked back at her. "Not really," I said.

Bethany didn't put up a fight. "Cool."

The two of us went back to eating, but our mouths weren't making chewing noises. We sucked on that chicken. Every once in a while some lumps of snow fell off the windowsill, and it would surprise us because we'd forgotten that the world made significant sounds.

After a long while, I decided to bridge our gap. "So Bethany," I said, "Let's try some dinner conversation. It's so quiet in here, it's making me feel more dead than usual."

Bethany glanced up at me from beneath a chunk of her hair. "Do you want to, like, know something about me?"

"Sure." And I knew automatically what I wanted to hear. "Tell me about why you became a nurse."

Bethany didn't even think about it. "Because I wanted a job where I could stay inside a house."

"This place isn't very houselike," I said. I had to keep spitting small pieces of bone back onto my plate because they were hidden in the meat.

When she was bent over her chicken leg, Bethany looked feral, like she was eating a vulture's leftovers. She didn't look up from her food when she talked. "What I set out to do was in-home care. And I had a job for a while, for this lady with cancer, who used to call me a whore, but I got past that."

"Why'd she call you a whore?" I asked. "Are you a whore?"

"Do you think I'm like a whore?"

"No, but all I have is a first impression."

"Well, I'm not a whore. She was angry, that was part of it, and she said I smelled like sex, which, I don't know,

I don't think I do. Maybe I just have strong pheromones. But she died."

Feeling nauseous from the chicken (not from the cancer-patient story), I threw the leg I'd been holding into the trash can. I made the basket. I thought about going pro. "I just swallowed another piece of cartilage. I'm finished. Sorry to hear about her death, because of your job."

"I thought I would find another cancer patient to take care of," she told me. "But I didn't realize that I'd been lucky. It's harder and harder to find that kind of job, partly because of the economy. People are mostly going into places like hospices and senior condos now. They're cheaper and they offer movement classes."

"What's the other part of it?"

"If you're not going to have more chicken, can I have that leg?" Bethany asked, pointing to the last piece that was sitting on my plate.

"It's all yours."

"Thanks." Bethany took the leg like she had to beat the spring of a trap. "Well, the other part is that people used to want to die alone in their homes. They didn't want prying eyes on them. And I didn't want prying eyes on me. It was the perfect situation."

"And now?"

"People want to pretend they're not dying when they're really dying. Like I said, they want to be in movement classes until the last second. My profession is becoming obsolete."

"When I die," I said, "I want to be alone. No nurse. Nothing." This is good for you to know, just in case.

"Me too."

"Do you hate your job now?"

"They send me to a lot of functions, not houses. I had to go be a nurse at the Providence Girl Scout Olympics this past summer. It was maybe the worst day of my life." Bethany paused, but she didn't make eye contact with me. "I don't know if I should be telling you about all of this. Why do you want to know why I became a nurse?"

"I ask all the nurses that," I told her. "Doctors will always tell you that they went into practice because they wanted to help people, which is generally an oversimplification or a lie. Nurses will usually tell you why they're really there, though, because they don't have so much to lose from the truth."

"I guess you're right. If I get fired, I'm thinking of going into house cleaning."

We were quiet again while Bethany finished her chicken behind her hair, but the silence was friendlier this time. When Bethany finally lifted her head and I saw the bone, it was all pillaged. That's why it made me think of you and your legs.

"Bethany?" I asked.

"Hmm?"

"Do you know how to do girl talk?"

"I don't understand what you mean."

"Here. I'll try to start it," I said. I paused to get over my uneasiness, and then I started. I don't really do this kind of thing ever. I don't really confess it ever, either. This is for you. "If I was thinking about someone when he wasn't in the room, if the idea of him kept returning to my mind, do you think that would mean that I had a crush on him?"

Bethany nodded. This wasn't to show that her answer was an instant yes, but that the question was one she could live with. She stared down at her sweats. "When you're thinking of him, is it good or bad things that you're thinking?"

I looked up to the ceiling and tried to picture you floating there. "When I think about him, I think about how different he is from me. That difference speaks to me. Do I have a crush?"

"Yeah, probably."

"I thought so." I shut my eyes and leaned back against my pillow. I felt like I was in trouble, like I'd been stealing. Stealing from what or whom, I don't know. But you seemed off-limits, and me liking you seemed like a transgression.

"Wait. Before you go to sleep, you need to take your antibiotics." Bethany picked up my cup of pills and cup of water from where she'd put them underneath the bed. She passed them to me.

"Do you feel like you have fever?"

I checked my forehead with my hand. My temperature seemed okay for once. I told Bethany, "No, I'm still cool." I took my medicine.

"Do you want the lights out?" she asked.

"Yeah," I said. "But listen, it's Thanksgiving. If you want to go to sleep, nothing's going to happen to me overnight. I'm sure of it."

"If anyone found out, somehow—" Bethany interjected.

"Who's telling?" I asked. "The cups?" Since they were both empty, I chucked them over to the side of the room, and they hit the window before they fell to the floor. They rolled around in drunken, half-completed circles. The two of us watched them, entranced.

"Worse comes to worst," I added, "you'll go into dusting."

"Okay," Bethany said. She got up from the bed, took off her shoes, then flicked off the overhead lights. I reached over and turned off my private lamp. After the room was dark, I heard Bethany peeling back the covers of the bed next to mine.

"Good night," I said.

"'Night."

In the hallway, the phone started ringing again.

"Just ignore it," I ordered her because I was feeling good thinking about you, my new crush, and I didn't want any bad news coming my way. Maybe you think that's me being paranoid, but doctors have weird lives, driven by weird passions. They work weird hours. They decide to check on lab results at weird times. And I wouldn't put it past one who felt like he had a familiar relationship with one of his frequent patients to put in a phone call on Thanksgiving. There was always that danger.

CHAPTER 17

THE JOURNAL OF PARAPSYCHOLOGY OCTOBER 2004

Thanksgiving 2002 arrived just a month after my first meeting with E. I asked if her family was coming to Providence for the holiday; she was not well enough to leave the infirmary. E said, "I told them that it wasn't worth coming, since I wouldn't be much fun."

Unable to believe that her parents wouldn't insist on visiting, I pressed E. "Are you not close with them?" This was a year before she confided in me the family's supernatural leanings and the resulting tension.

E answered, "We're as close as we can manage."

I dropped the subject that day, but returned to it when Christmas rounded the corner. From what I could gather, E's parents always offered to make the trip, but E declined. E showed me a coffee-table book her mother had sent her for Christmas, comprised of graphic pictures of psychic surgery, practiced mostly in the Philippines and Brazil. While psychic surgery involves no scalpels or traditional incisions—supposedly, the healer gains access to the innards through the use of his or her fingers—the pictures in the book were undeniably gory. There was also a chapter on psychic dentistry. When I expressed surprise at her mother having sent this as a gift, E said she thought it was an indirect way for her mother to express concern about E's health.

"But doesn't she want to see you in person?" I asked.

"There's probably a lot of reasons why she doesn't," E said, failing to elaborate.

Throughout conversations held over the course of our association, I deduced that these reasons included (1) that E's parents chose to err on the side of too much space when it came to E. Ideological differences had strained their relationship, and S and A were fearful of losing more ground with their daughter; (2) that because A and, to a lesser extent, S do not perceive a thick barrier between life and death, they regard illness more casually than most of us; (3) that because A connected E's string of illnesses to her familial legacy, she was not as frightened by E's health problems as a mother with a different background might have been; and (4) that A and S's parenting philosophy included the somewhat antiquated notions that (a) young persons must find their own paths in life without artificial (i.e., undesired) intervention, and (b) separation of child (or, in this case, young adult) and parent is necessary for the child's coming of age. Moreover, the child should control the duration and nature of that separation.

The family spoke on the phone every week or two.

Only six months after I began working with E did I learn that she had a younger sister, J, "who my parents named half after my dead cousin on my dad's side who was hit by a drunk driver, and half after my mom." J was born fifteen years after E. The only thing that E has ever volunteered on the subject of her sister is "We have a good relationship. She's five. You know?"

I thought that E would be alone on Thanksgiving 2003—I didn't consider the required nurse practitioner to be company—and saw the holiday as a perfect opportunity to strengthen our slightly tenuous relationship. We had not spoken since our talk at my home, and I was anxious about E's commitment to our work. I planned to surprise her with McDonald's, keep her company, and reestablish the goodwill that had existed previously between us. On a more personal level, I thought E might like to know that someone was thinking of her. Unfortunately, although I tried calling the infirmary three times that night, there was never an answer. I drove to Health Services to see if the light was on in her room, but the window was dark.

CHAPTER 18

From The Desk of Chester Hunter III

When my plane landed at TF Green, I couldn't wait to get off it and back to you. But what was excruciating was that even walking off the plane was out of the question, so I had to sit and watch while the other Brown kids strolled down the aisle, using their legs. As they were passing me I stared at their knees with what I guess was envy, and I started to feel like one of those old, fat ladies at the beach who stare at the tight nineteen-year-olds in their small bikinis.

After everyone else had deplaned, a steward came back for me with my wheelchair.

"Okay, sir, I'm going to pull your chair to the side here, and hopefully you can use those big guns to lift yourself and slide over into it," he said. He gave me an uneasy smile, and I must not have smiled back, or must not have smiled back convincingly, because he started to look very guilty.

"Oh man, I'm sorry. Guns are arms, you know? You didn't get shot, did you? I'm sorry, sir."

"No, I didn't get shot," I told him.

"Ah, relief, relief. That makes me feel better," he said.

Down near the baggage carousel, a driver wearing a suit and tie was holding up a sign with "CHESS HUNTER" written on it. I didn't want to wait with him at the carousel because I knew I'd be useless, so I hung back near the escalators while he got my suitcase. This made me feel so stupid and outside the normal world that I started humming a few bars from "The Phantom of the Opera," and then I had to laugh at myself because I felt so wrecked.

When we got to the parking lot, I saw that my dad had actually hired a limo. It was black, complete with tinted windows, and it was really embarrassing, El.

"I think a town car would probably have been sufficient," I told the driver.

"Aww, come on," he said, opening his arms like he was demonstrating the sheer mass of my vehicular luck. "We can take an extra spin around campus if you want, show off the car to your buddies. Make them all jealous."

"But I don't have any buddies that I want to show off for."

"Your call. But you might as well enjoy yourself in the back. Make yourself a stiff drink," the driver told me.

After we situated me in the very back seat, the driver got in up front and, making eye contact with me in the rearview mirror, asked, "Do you want to listen to the radio?"

I said, "Yeah, anything popular's fine."

So he turned on the radio and the first thing we heard was Diana Ross's "I'm Coming Out," and then I felt like the limo had suddenly been turned into the saddest disco that had ever existed.

"Do you want the divider down or up? Company or no company?" he asked.

"Please, please don't think I'm rude," I said, "because this in no way reflects on what I think about you, or what kind of person you may be, but—no company. Definitely no company. I feel like I need to be alone right now." So the driver pressed the button on his dashboard and the divider went up.

On the way back to the infirmary, other cars kept adjusting their speeds so that they could try to get a look at who was inside the limo. There was a mirrored treatment on the windows, making seeing in totally impossible, but this didn't seem to sink in, ever. One lady almost rear-ended the car in front of her because she was trying so hard to figure out who I was and if I was worth it, and after a few seconds she rolled down her window and mouthed the words, "Roll down your window!" to me.

"It's futile! It's futile!" I yelled back at her, which was futile on my part because it's not like she could even hear me.

When we got to the corner of Waterman and Brown and Health Services came into view, I saw you. And what else can I say except that I pussied out, El, because I thought I would have more time to mentally prepare myself for our next interaction. So I started begging the driver, and I'm not proud of it at all, "Please, oh shit! Slow down and pull over! Back up and go back around the corner! Stop the limo!" but the divider prevented him from hearing me. The car kept going toward Health Services like I didn't exist. Totally panicked, I poked at all the knobs and buttons that were near me, hoping that one of them activated the speaker system. Some chunks of ice came out of a dispenser and rolled onto the carpet, and a cigarette lighter popped out of a nearby panel. "Stop, stop, stop!" I kept saying this whole time, just in case the microphone had started working.

Realizing I had no time to spare because we'd be in front

of you in seconds, I flung myself off the seat and onto the floor, and I used my arms to drag myself across the length of the limo. When I got to the partition I supported my weight with one fist. Like a maniac, I began pounding on the glass with the other one.

"Stop! Please stop!"

As the limo jerked to a stop, the divider came down. The driver looked completely riled.

"What's wrong?" he yelled. "Did I hurt you?"

"No," I said. "I'm fine. I just need you to stop the car and pull over, please."

"Why? What's wrong? We're like two buildings away."

"You see that girl coming down the walkway?" I asked, and I ducked farther down while I was mentioning you even though I knew you couldn't see me through the windows. But you'd been insanely observant during my first encounters with you, and while I was lying on the floor, I was honestly nervous. I was nervous that somehow you'd be able to figure out that my eyes were on you if I left them there. I was even nervous that you'd know I was thinking about you, that all of your crazy illnesses had left you with the supernatural ability to eavesdrop on my brain waves.

"The older one or the younger one?" the driver asked.

"The younger," I said.

"What, you like her? You're embarrassed about my limo in front of her?"

"Yes, something like that," I said, because it was all too much to explain. "Can we just park for a second and wait until she's gone?"

"Depending on how long this takes, I'm going to have to charge you a waiting fee."

"That's fine."

"Whatever you want," the driver said, and pulled the limo over to the west side of Brown Street. We were on the wrong side of the road, but since it was the end of a holiday weekend, no one was around to stop us.

"Is she still there?" I asked after awhile, because I was still on the floor and couldn't see anything.

"She's getting into a van. Still getting into the van. Still getting into the van. Annnnnnd, they're pulling away."

"Okay," I said. "As soon as they've rounded the corner, let's count to ten to make sure she didn't forget anything, and then we can pull up to Health Services."

"They've rounded the corner," the driver told me while turning the ignition. "Do I really have to count to ten, or can we just ballpark it?"

"Ten, please. Ten." I knew I was being a pain in his ass.

Under his breath, the driver muttered, "One, two, three, four, five, six, seven, eight, nine, ten." Then he raised his voice. "Is now okay? The older one's still out there on the curb."

"Yes," I said. "That's okay."

• • •

When Vivian and I were riding up in the elevator together, I tried to keep my tone as casual as possible. "So where was Elodie going?" I asked, thinking to myself, "You jackass."

"Elodie? She had a follow-up at the hospital for her Raynaud's."

"Oh. Do you think she'll be gone for a while?" I sounded like such a fraud, but people get away with being fake every day and no one calls them on it, so I thought I had a fair chance of pulling it off.

At the second floor Vivian got behind me and pushed me into the hallway, and I was instantly hot. "I think it'll take at least a few hours," she said. "They're running some tests to make sure everything's under control. Why all the questions about Elodie?"

"Just asking," I shrugged.

"Wait a minute. Do you like her?"

"Sure, I like her."

Vivian seemed to be getting worked up about what she was slowly discovering, and I let her discover it, since I figured, you know, the jig was up. "Wait, do you like-like her?"

"Yes," I finally admitted. "I like-like her."

Hearing this really excited Vivian, because she took a step back and slapped her heart and faked some swooning in front of me. "If she likes you back, it'll be just like *General Hospital* up in here."

I said, "Exactly."

It was easier to talk Vivian into going to CVS than I thought it was going to be. I'd predicted that she was going to give me a speech about how she had a responsibility to ensure my safety while under her care, but when I pushed her just a little bit, she stopped saying no. All I had to do was hold onto her knees and say, "I'll only let you go if you agree to go to the drugstore. Otherwise I'm going to hold on tight to you forever, just like this. We'll make your boyfriend so jealous, he'll want to kill me, except he won't be able to kill me because I'll be attached to you, and he'd never want to cause you bodily harm."

"Chess!" Vivian yelled, although she didn't try to pry me from her, so I could tell I was eventually going to win. "I could lose my job. Something catastrophic could happen to you, and then you could sue me."

"Nothing's going to happen to you or me," I said. I was surprised to hear that coming from me and even more surprised to find out that yeah, I actually believed it. The infirmary was doing me good, I thought—not really because of the treatment and care I was being given for my legs, but because it was helping to rebuild my dented confidence.

And I saw that Vivian believed me, too, because she suddenly became calm and told me she'd do it. She asked what kinds of things I needed. I wrote her a list.

Later we went through the bag of purchases on my bed. I'd told her to get me imitation crystal candle holders with white tapers so I could at least pretend to be organizing something slightly classy, but she bought those fat red and green religious candles with Jesus and the Virgin Mary on them instead. She told me that that they'd have the most impact against the white of the infirmary walls. Also, she said she thought they could function as conversation pieces if you and I ran out of things to talk about, but I said no, no, I believed we had tons of hidden things in common.

I was happy with the red plastic tablecloth and the sparkling apple juice, but wished she'd found plastic champagne flutes instead of tumblers. I picked up the can of rose air freshener and asked, "What's this?" Vivian said, "Rose air freshener," and I said, "I mean, why'd you buy it?" and she said, "I thought it would make this room smell more romantic." I liked the way the room smelled, which was like the shampoo you'd used before you left for your appointment. It was like mint gum.

Vivian also got herself some red hair dye, which really seemed to mean a lot to her. "If I want to change on the inside," she said, "wouldn't it make sense that I could force it with some help from the outside?"

I told her, "I don't know about dye, but becoming handicapped definitely works."

We split up the duties, with me doing most of the stuff having to do with the table, since I could roll around it. Vivian handled everything that required heights or extensive mobility. In the middle of all this, Sarah showed up for the overnight shift and looked so bewildered that it seemed like she might quit right then and there.

"What in the world are you guys doing?" she asked.

"Establishing a particular mood," I said.

So she stood in the threshold and watched us for a while.

At 8:02 P.M. the phone rang. I still remember looking at the clock. It was the hospital coordinator telling Vivian that you were on your way back. I caved in to the rose air freshener because I thought you might like it, thought you might think it was funny, and Vivian pushed me across the room while I held down the button on the nozzle.

CHAPTER 19

PAXIL CR • Get back to being you

The day you came back, Vivian and I killed time going through the new promotional gifts from the pharmaceutical companies. She especially liked the clear pen from an antidepressant manufacturer that had a changing rainbow light inside it.

I said, "I guess the point of this pen is that you're supposed to watch it and feel soothed, and then you're supposed to connect that feeling with the medication."

"They'd do better to distribute pens that depressed everyone instead, don't you think?" she asked.

"Pens that have 'WE'RE ALL DOOMED' written across them."

"I'd carry around one of those pens," Vivian said.

I cupped my hands around the pen and peered in through a gap between my thumbs. "This is one hell of a pen," I told her. "Come with me to the blood closet. Let's go see how it looks in the dark."

We sat on stools in the dark closet and watched the rotating colors. We were hypnotized by the moment when red turned to pink, when pink turned to orange. There was a split millisecond between colors, but the eye couldn't catch the switch. This seemed like the visual equivalent of what it was like to be getting sick all the time. I could never distinguish the point in time when the nausea came on or the fever began or the pain started. Or stopped. Because once things stopped, it was already too late to appreciate the relief.

I figured that it was this way with tons of things. People dumped each other and then couldn't remember why they'd ever thought the love died. So then they got back together, and had to dump each other again if the initial sensation returned. People ate a new kind of food, were grossed out, and then decided to order the same food at a different restaurant, thinking it would taste different. People told the same bad joke to a second crowd, thinking that it would go over better than it did on the first one.

Vivian said the pen reminded her of all the nuclear reactors she'd seen in the late-night movies that she'd liked to watch as a teenager.

We both agreed that the pen was cool. But Vivian let me keep it, because she'd taken the acid-reflux yo-yo last week.

"So, you lost your house?" I asked.

Vivian was rubbing her left eye, dragging its corner even closer to her ear. "Yeah. I did."

"Where are you going to live now?"

"Well, I can stay in a hotel until I find something to rent, or—"

"Or what?"

"Shawn asked me to move in with him. He wants to live together. He even wants the pets."

"Are you going to do it?" I asked.

"If I lived with him," Vivian told me, smiling and cringing, "that would mean that I couldn't do that maneuver where I break up with him anymore. Because I wouldn't have anywhere else to go while I waited for him to beg me to return." She threw her head back. "Well, I have the cell phone, and I could walk around somewhere, the mall or something, and ignore his first five calls, and then pick up. But if I just want to be at home, it's going to make things tough."

"Especially in bad weather."

"I know it's my problem," she said, shaking her head. "I know that I've refused to let myself be happy with him. When I retain happiness for an extended period of time, I break up with him, and I go back to my house and wait for the anxiety to come. When it does, and it usually takes about forty-eight hours, I feel like I can go back."

"I'm surprised he keeps taking you back," I said.

"He knows I'm a coward."

"Then why doesn't he leave you?"

"He says it's because he knows that I'm such a wuss about the relationship that he can set it aside, like a quirk," Vivian said.

"I think it sounds like you're planning on moving in with him."

"I'd have to cut the drama." She was rocking on her stool while looking at me. "You know me as well as anyone. Do you think I can do it?"

"That's not for me to say," I answered.

"I thought that's what you'd tell me."

•••

The rest of the day I was lazy, lying in bed and staring out the window. I didn't feel like doing any work, even though finals were around the corner. The phone started ringing again in the afternoon, and I found out that at least two of the calls on Thanksgiving had come from my parents, wanting to tell me about the gas leak they'd discovered when they tried to cook the turkey. Then I got dressed and went down to meet my ride to the hospital because I had a follow-up.

That night when I came back to the infirmary, Vivian was watching me so closely that I knew something was up. She's one of the people who doesn't normally watch me that way.

"What's going on?" I asked.

"Chess got back this afternoon."

"Oh," I said, and I knew I was blinking more than I should, but I couldn't help it. "I'll go say hi."

"Yeah, you go do that."

When I opened the door, I saw you sitting at the table for two behind the row of Jesus candles.

"What's this?" I asked.

"I did it for you." That's what you said, and that's when my heart started pounding. But you couldn't tell that, so I think you got nervous, which must be why you started rambling. "Listen, I know our first kiss was shared under exceptional circumstances, and that we didn't talk about what it meant or how we felt about it afterward," you said. "And you were passed out when I left to go to the airport. But my head, my head won't leave me alone about you, and I just couldn't wait to get back here. All I want is to have dinner with you."

"Wait. Like a romantic dinner?" I asked.

"Yes. I want to have a romantic dinner with you."

"We can do that," I said. I was so awkward. I know it. I didn't have the sort of composure needed for small talk, so

I was only able to say what was in the front of my mind. "I've been thinking about you," I admitted.

"You have? Really? What have you been thinking?"

"I get this sense that you've lived totally opposite from the way I have. When they rolled you in here you had this look on your face—" I tried to re-create it for you, so you could see—"like they'd just dropped you off in the African bush. It was like you couldn't even imagine that a place like this existed."

I'm going to get it all down if it's the last thing I do. Although I do hope, for the record, that it's not the last thing I do. We talked about a lot that night, but there are pockets of time that have stayed clearer than others.

Vivian and Sarah entered with our dinners. They rolled them in on a meds cart with dish covers they'd made out of tin foil, and I was touched.

I remember looking at that round breaded thing on my plate and being puzzled. It was the shape of a potato, but obviously not a potato. And it looked like it was sweating. "What is this?" I asked you.

"It's chicken Kiev," you said. Before you could warn me, I had taken my fork and stabbed into the Kiev because I was curious about its internal consistency. A spurt of butter shot out of the chicken, and I jolted back in my chair to avoid it. I said, "Holy shit!"

"I should have mentioned that you don't want to puncture it too roughly," you told me. "It's filled with butter. That's what makes it Kiev."

At some point we talked about my being sick. You asked me, "Listen, that stuff you were saying about how shocked

I looked when I got here—is it that you've always been sick? Was ending up in here never unexpected for you?"

"I haven't been sick my whole life. This stuff is new, relatively," I told you. "But when I first came to the infirmary, I wasn't all that shocked by it. You, though, your astonishment. It was astonishing."

"I was astonished. You're totally right." You laughed and said, "This is what I imagine it feels like to go to a psychiatrist."

"You've never been to one?"

"No. My parents have taught us to believe in positive thinking. They believe that if you go to someone week after to week to dwell on your problems, you're going to get sucked down farther into them. They've always held that human beings are—this is their phrase—resilient creatures, and that they can find practical solutions to any challenge. That they're able to adapt to any situation without professional help."

"My parents don't believe in psychiatry either," I said.

"So we have something in common?"

I sensed that this was a turning point. In order to answer truthfully, I'd have to share that my parents talk about ghosts the way other families talk about laundry. So I did, for the sake of being honest.

"Different reason, though," I said. "My mom—especially my mom—believes that if you're having bad feelings about something that you're receiving a message from your future self or a knowing presence."

"What does that mean? A knowing presence?" you asked.

"She believes in ghosts. My dad, too, but he came to it later."

I waited for you to make a face at me or to laugh, but instead you told me, "My parents believe in angels."

"Religious ones?"

"Secular ones. But they're kind of like ghosts."

"Barely," I said, wanting to be on the other side of the table with you.

"Why? What's your difference between angels and ghosts?"

"I think most people accept that angels are figurative. But if you're seeing ghosts, that's literal. A literal sign of being disturbed. I think if you tell people you deal with angels, they just think, at worst, that you're dopey. That you're the rainbow and sunflowers and glass half-full type," I said.

"My parents say angels are the sunbeams that look down on us. I guess that proves your point."

"See? When it's a positive feeling, people say an angel has come to see them. When something has scared the shit out of them, that's a ghost."

"I've never thought about that before," you said, and I remember smiling. I was like, "Oh yes, my teeth. There they are."

We also talked about friends.

"What was your life like before you got your knees bashed in?" I asked.

"That's a really big question," you said. "Can you narrow it down a little?"

"Did you have a lot of friends?" I wanted to know.

"I think I did."

"What are they like?"

"My best friends are—were—I don't know." You told me about Marna and David, who I let into the infirmary the day you came. You said that before you came to the infirmary, you guys did almost everything together. I told you that's the way it was with me and the nurse practitioners, if you could count them.

You asked if I'd ever become close with someone who was in here with me, and I could tell that the answer meant a lot to you. I knew that you probably wanted to hear "no," so you could confirm this was a once-in-a-lifetime kind of connection we were experiencing. But I had my own motives. I wanted to show you that I hadn't been a total outcast. That someone else had wanted me. So I told you about Reggie.

I told you that he was a psychology major and that he was in the infirmary because he had a collapsed lung. I told you that we'd gotten kind of close and fooled around. I didn't tell you the whole story.

One night we were playing Operation, which was a good game for Reggie and me because his analness rivaled mine. That made it a solid competition. We treated the Operation man like we could actually hurt him.

While Reggie "operated," he'd say things like, "Hmmm, wouldn't it be great if you had one doctor for everything? Your physician is your psychiatrist is your gynecologist is your surgeon. Imagine having one person that you trusted to take care of everything having to do with your body and mind. Now that's power. I wonder if Brown would let me create a new concentration to reflect interdisciplinary medical interests."

Reggie was going for the Adam's apple, and he hit the

edge of the cavity with the tweezers. The man's nose lit up and the buzzer went "EHHHHHHHH," and I said, "Face it, I won," because I knew I had.

Then, all of a sudden, Reggie was coming at me. It wasn't a very subtle pass. He pushed me back on the bed and spread my legs with his knees. Then he started to grind himself into my underwear, and he whispered into my ear, "Are you angry at the cards you've been dealt?"

I felt like Reggie was going to bust through my underwear, so I wondered if I should just slide them off myself and save us both the trouble. I was thinking about this and so I forgot to answer him. And he said, "Well?"

I asked him, "Should I be angry?" because I genuinely wanted to know the answer. I wanted to know if it was fair to be angry, or if I should be angrier than I was. Because while I wished all the time that I could get better, I was how I was.

Reggie seemed like he wanted to be the one asking the questions. He spread his knees (and my thighs) apart even farther and tried again. "Do you feel like you're being robbed of a vital experience, now that your new beginning at college has been stymied by things out of your control?"

"Well, I don't feel like things are out of my control," I said.

"You don't have to lie to me." He almost had me in the middle splits. "I'm here for you."

"First," I said, "I'm not lying. Second, what are you doing to my underwear?"

Reggie pressed on. Literally. "Don't you think it strange that modern human beings are fully aware of denial as a primary emotional stage in the face of fear or anger, and yet they still can't keep the door shut when it comes knocking?"

"Well," I said as I felt fabric being pushed inside of me, "what I would say to that is I don't think of things as being out of control—" Reggie suddenly kissed me. Then I finished—"but instead as happening. They happen. Then I make my decisions from that point onward."

Reggie released my thighs (which I was half glad about because they were burning) and slid his hands around to my backside. He winced because of his deflated lung, but he still managed to pull himself up and take me with him. I was sitting in his lap then, facing him.

There was a silence as we looked at each other in the moonlight. Because it was moonlight and because I knew that moonlight was an effect that was supposed to fall under the category of "romantic," I started the process of interpreting it that way. The silence, the moonlight, the smell of skin, the cold of the sheets, us about to have sex. I took all these things in and struggled to make something of them.

Reggie reached out and stroked the lashes above my right eye. "You," he said, "you must experience some kind of disconnect between body and mind if you truly hold that worldview. If you aren't in denial at how much you're being kept back by your illnesses."

It was then that I decided to be bad.

"I love you," I told Reggie. This was the first time I'd said "I love you" to someone in a romantic capacity, but I don't think it counted because it wasn't for real.

Reggie stopped the eyelash playing, and I noticed he even stopped breathing for a second. "Did you just come out and tell me that you love me?"

"Sure."

"Why did you say that?"

"Does it change things?" I asked him.

"Wait, why do you love me? What do you mean you love me?"

"Does it change things?" I asked again. What I meant was: Does the room look different to you? Has the air temperature changed? Is the bed softer or harder? Is the sky darker? Are my eyes bigger? Is time going faster or slower? Do you feel the confines of your body more or less strongly? Are you breathing faster or slower? Am I having some kind of effect here?

I just wanted to stir shit up.

Reggie tried to lift my hundred and two pounds off him using only his arms, but his busted lung wouldn't give him the leverage he needed do to this without, as they say, "making a scene."

"I don't know why you're telling me that," he said, placing his arms behind him so he could lean away from me. "I would say that you're misplacing your emotional needs or exaggerating the situation to distract yourself from your recent pattern of illness, but—"

"Do you feel weird now?" I asked.

"No, I feel fine." I didn't believe him. "You're the one I'm worried about. I'm just not understanding why you introduced this bizarre element into the night."

"I didn't mean it."

First Reggie paused. He stared at me for a few seconds. Then he shook his head. "I can tell. That's a very dangerous game you're playing. You had my attention to begin with."

"I wouldn't call it a game so much as an experiment," I said. I stood up on the bed and stepped over his shoulder, went back to my bed, and lay down on my stomach. For something like two hours after that I heard Reggie sucking in breaths and getting ready to start sentences. He kept making this "schwooooo" sound, like there was something he wanted to say to me, but he never did.

The next day I was diagnosed with chicken pox, though Reggie hadn't been a carrier since he was five.

Now you know that story.

You also asked me what I was like in elementary school. I told you, "I was smart. And serious."

"What were your friends like?"

"There were two of them. The teachers called us 'the three widows' behind our backs, but we knew about it after fourth grade," I said.

You blinked. "The three widows?"

"We weren't crazy about playing during recess, so we'd sit in this one part of the field in a horizontal line," I told you. "I found out from my mom after a parent-teacher meeting that the teachers thought when we were sitting on the grass that we looked like we were carrying the weight of the world on our backs. The widows thing came from one of the teachers joking that we looked like we'd survived the deaths of all our other friends and husbands."

"Wow. Are you still in touch with those two friends?" you asked.

"In sixth grade they got into double-dutch."

You thought there was supposed to be more. "And?"

I said, "And I don't really like to bounce."

From there we got on the topic of favorite childhood songs, and I told you about how my mom believed that

Kermit the Frog was psychically connected. You cracked up when I pointed out the line from "The Rainbow Connection":

"And have you heard voices?/I've heard them calling my name—"

I told you how my mom interpreted this to mean that Kermit had access to the "other side." I said, "She thought the Rainbow Connection was a metaphor for describing the portal that exists between us and the afterlife. So the dead were seeking out Kermit because he had the ability to cross it."

And I remember you saying, all of a sudden, "I love the way you are."

"What do you mean?" I asked, my hand flying over my mouth.

"The way you talk. I don't know," you said. "I don't know. It's great. That's all I know."

"I like the way you talk better," I told you. I figured that if we were going to dork out together, we should just fully go for it.

"I—" you said, but didn't finish.

"What?" I asked.

"I—I don't know exactly what I'm trying to say here," you confessed, and you were blushing. "I—"

"Are you in pain?" I asked, because I know that everything in the world that matters shows up as some kind of pain. Or pang. Joy included.

"It's not the knees," you said.

"Are you in pain because of me?" I phrased it badly. What I meant was "Do you feel like I do?" Being with you, it was like I was falling in love with myself, as bad as that sounds. Everybody else seemed to want to give something to me—diagnoses, warnings, advice, instructions, prescriptions, injections, blood tests, meals, fluids, pills before bedtime, psychological readings, good cheer, sympathy, comfort, fame, meaning. But the way you hung on my every word. The way that you kept trying to size me up and the way you kept failing. It was then that I really started to fall for you. Because you wanted to take something from me.

CHAPTER 20

From The Desk of Chester Hunter III

On our "first date," when you asked me if I was in pain, you asked it so calmly. That question came without any of the normal signs of distress that anybody else would show when asking it, and I'm talking about even the slightest alarm in your voice. There was none. It was just like you were waiting for me to own up to the truth that you already knew.

I remember you asking this: "Are you in pain because of me?"

"You?" I asked back, because I was trying to give myself some time to figure out a lie, if I'm going to be honest here.

"Yeah. Is it me? I feel like it might be me," you said.

"No, it's not you." I was caving, caving. "Or, it's not you in a bad way." It was then I realized that I was definitely on the verge of admitting something dangerous, so I put my fingers to my forehead and looked up at you, hoping I wouldn't have to say it.

And then you told me, "I think that you could fall in love with me."

The feeling your comment produced in me was very

similar to the one I had when my mom found a *Barely Legal* under my mattress when I, myself, wasn't even legal yet. "Wait. Wait!" I said. "I'm the one who's supposed to admit that. To you." But I knew you were right. The love was there. I had no idea where it had started.

As a kid I used to go to a bunch of birthday parties at Chuck E. Cheese, and I loved this ride that took your picture by freezing a video image of you riding in Chuck's plastic car. There was a bust of Chuck in the passenger seat. You'd pretend to drive. Some kind of rolling mechanism underneath the car would simulate a hilly road. Anyway, I'd smile for the black box that was mounted on the car hood, and I'd have to hold that smile for the entire ride because there was never any outward indication when the video froze the image. There was no flash or clicking at all. At the end, when I'd climb down from the driver's seat and go get my picture, it was impossible to figure out when it had been snapped. I was smiling. What moment? Where?

That's what I asked myself in that moment with you. "What moment? Where?"

While I'd been thinking, I saw that you'd pushed your plate away from you. And god, I was hit with a gigantic rush of fear because I was convinced that you were going to get up from the table and close yourself off from me for good. So even though we'd met before, obviously, it was like I underwent the pressure of having to make an irresistible first impression. But I could only come up with a distant whisper of how I used to do it in the days before I had to summon effort, even though I know how cavalier that sounds. The method came back, thankfully, kind of like mental bicycle riding. I had to make you feel like you were necessary in the situation, that there was something about you I couldn't live without.

Then the epiphany came. I really did feel like there was something about you that I had to have near me.

I think you mistook the expression on my face for the bad rather than the good kind of bewilderment because you started apologizing, "I'm sorry. That just leapt into my head and I said it without thinking."

I shook my head and for once, decided to be intentionally brave. "Come here, please. I'd come over there, but with maneuvering the chair, it could get ugly."

"Come where?" you asked.

I swept my hand across my side of the table, and said, "Here. In the general vicinity of me."

So you walked around the table until you were standing inches from me, but you looked at me innocently, like you didn't know what was going on.

"Like here?" you asked.

"Yeah. Like here," I said, just wanting to look at you up close again. And then you surprised the shit out of me when all of a sudden you just put yourself down in my lap. I didn't see it coming. But once you were there, I felt like I could die of happiness, El. I put my arms around your arms and held the whole of you tight, pressing my lips into the back of your neck. I put my forehead on the back of your head, and all I could see was the black of your hair. And being like that, it felt like I'd stepped out of the boring, average, mean world.

The memory of French kissing you came back to me so strongly that there was the physical sensation of my tongue getting bigger. This might sound ridiculous, but I swear it started to feel like I was trying to keep my mouth closed around one of those enormous cow tongues you see at a butcher's shop. I had to figure out how to kiss you again.

But you caught me totally off guard. You turned your head and initiated a kiss. Still, I have to remind you that I was the first to start the tongue action. I had to do it because I was under the sincere impression that there just wasn't room enough in my mouth anymore. There was instantaneous relief when your tongue met mine, like contact with you had miraculously turned me back to normal.

I remember putting my hands around your neck because I had this crazy idea that I wanted to pull myself inside of your head. Your hands were locked on my temples, like you were trying to do the same thing except with a different grip. Then I opened my eyes and I saw that yours were open, too, and that was when I first became aware that you were making me incredibly hard.

I knew you obviously knew that I had an erection, since you were sitting on top of it. To distract you, I tried sliding my hand up your sweater. You were braless, but your tiny breasts impressed me. I thought to myself, "She's so compact. She's everything in the world crammed into the smallest space possible."

When you went for the top button of my pants and it dawned on me that we were authentically moving in the direction of sex, I began to worry, to get obsessed with particulars. I'd contemplated asking Vivian to buy me a pack of condoms when she was at CVS, but I'd changed my mind at the last minute because I didn't want to seem presumptuous. And I didn't want her to tell you that I was a presumptuous kind of person. And I didn't want to deal with every single nurse in the infirmary knowing what I felt was only mine and sparkling new.

So now that I needed a condom, I didn't have one. Reading this, you're probably thinking that I just should have said something. But, the truth of the matter is, I didn't want to fuck up the moment, a moment when we were connecting in a way that transcended the usual discussion of safe sex. The simplest way to put it, I guess, is that I really wanted our first time together to be what I believed it was, which was fate.

"But I'm in an infirmary," I reasoned, and I knew that somewhere, *somewhere,* there had to be a stash of free condoms. But how to get to these theoretical condoms? I considered telling you that I'd be right back, but I thought that would leave you alone in the room with nothing but time and solitude to maybe discover how far you were above me. And also, I didn't know how long the search would take, and I needed a reason to be searching in case Sarah found me looking around.

I tried to attempt a voice so sexy that it would make my suggestion seem conventional, but I have to own up to all this now, my true motives behind why I said, "Let's play hide-and-go-seek."

CHAPTER 21

THE JOURNAL OF PARAPSYCHOLOGY — OCTOBER 2004

A pattern started to emerge. Every time I became concerned that I'd lost my patient, I'd receive a harried phone call. E would have a strange incident to report and request that I review it. The Monday following Thanksgiving I received such a call from her, and we made an appointment for the next day. E asked that I come to Health Services to see her, but that we meet in the pharmacy waiting room instead of the infirmary.

When I arrived at the pharmacy the next morning, she was standing with her back to me, looking down at the floor. Joking, I asked her if she'd lost an earring. E didn't respond to the joke, but told me that she'd found us an empty room. She was much more mysterious than usual, and I soon discovered that this was because of her desire to keep our meeting secret from C, her infirmary roommate.

Before we left the pharmacy, she asked me, "Do you feel anything in this room?"

"Like what?" I asked.

"Anything at all."

I said, "Well, I feel pleased to see you again," which received no response. E led me down the hallway to an examination room and, after we entered, made sure that the door was locked behind us.

E did not want to sit on the examination bed, so she took the stool, and I leaned against the counter. I thought it would upset the power dynamic if I took the examination bed myself.

After a pause, E began. "I was playing hide-and-go-seek last night—"

"That's quite a beginning," I said. "Who were you playing with?"

"C," she answered. "It was his suggestion. It was something I haven't done in forever, so it sounded good to me. Maybe I'm a little too young to be trying to reclaim my childhood already. But it sounded good."

"What did you think when C suggested the game?" I asked, wanting to keep her open.

"I thought—" She paused. "What I thought was that I've found someone who can surprise me. And that his ability to surprise me means that he's really, really separate from me. That's not as obvious as it might first seem. Do you know what I mean?"

"I'm not sure exactly," I said. "Please explain it to me."

"Okay. When I was little, I had a rabbit. One day I walked in my room and saw my rabbit just sitting on my dresser. Before that, my rabbit always stayed outside in the backyard. I didn't know how my rabbit got inside, and I didn't know why she chose to sit on my dresser. But I was so surprised to see her there. She was gray and my dresser was black. Suddenly I was struck with this awareness that my rabbit was an original, decisive thing. I was very touched by . . . I guess what I'd call the phenomenon of individuality. Maybe this is easy to take for granted in people, but, as a kid, it was more awe-inspiring in a bunny."

I knew what she meant. How could I not, sitting across from her, the precise embodiment of the concept she was attempting to explain? E produced the same feeling in me—sheer wonder at her individual existence. At no moment was I ever unaware that she was something entirely distinct and alien from myself, and this prospect was moving. This must have been what early explorers felt when they discovered a new culture, a new people. It was the opposite of recognizing a soul mate. It was awe in the face of barely comprehendible difference.

I told her, "Thank you for your explanation. I understand your impressions better now. I take it something happened during the game of hide-and-seek?"

"Yes. I came in contact with the ghost."

"Go ahead," I said.

While C counted, E went to hide. She chose the pharmacy, which was dark for the night. Knowing that her time was draining, E crawled underneath one of the chairs in the waiting room. She figured that "because of C's wheelchair, he'd have trouble seeing me at floor level."

While underneath the chair, E began to feel pain "everywhere," and her fibromyalgia made it difficult for her to hold the position. She remained hidden, longing to successfully play the game. "I didn't want to f—— it up," E explained to me. "It was a game. It was for fun. How sad is it if you can't even play a game right because you hurt too much?"

Within five seconds of getting settled, E heard the infirmary door open and C call out, alerting her that he was beginning the search. Because of the acoustics on the second floor of the building, E was able to aurally follow C's movements. She could tell by the diminishing returns of the echoes that the first room he chose to visit was the main waiting room down the hall.

After a short while, E heard C return to the nurses' station, where he told Sarah, a late-night nurse practitioner, "I'm going downstairs." E then heard the elevator.

Realizing that she would be waiting "longer than I thought" and buckling under the duress of increasing pain, E decided to stretch out. As she was reaching her arms forward, she saw a pair of slippers on the carpet. They were approximately eight feet away from her.

Initially, E believed that she had been caught by C. She assumed that he had pulled a trick on her—pretending to enter the elevator, and then reversing his course. "I did think to myself, though," E noted, "that I probably should have heard him coming."

Then two details registered with E. The first was that the person in the slippers was standing free of a wheelchair. The second was that the "slippers were translucent. I could see the carpet right through them."

At this point, E confessed that, while stunned at the appearance of the slippers, she immediately comprehended the circumstances of them. She "had this automatic feeling that it was the ghost I'd talked to that day in the shower and that I'd seen around the second floor. I knew."

E partially crawled out from underneath the chair. She described seeing "some pale ankles and then pajama bottoms. Blue ones." Crawling out farther, she saw that "he was wearing a robe. And then I saw his hair. It's black and it goes down to his chin, like mine does." She demonstrated by holding her fingers at chin level. "And I understood it was the same guy I'd seen before."

"Did you say anything when you recognized him?" I asked.

"I said, 'You!' Like I was accusing him of being him."

"Did this apparition respond?"

"He laughed." E described the laugh as being somewhat pained, as if the sound had been difficult for the apparition to produce. He then said to her, "Don't make me laugh."

"I didn't," E argued.

E didn't remember the apparition's words verbatim due to her state of shock, but she recalled that his response had something to do with him being on "meds" and being "giddy" because of them. She also remembered a comment that struck her as particularly eerie. While telling E that she wasn't "off the hook" for making him laugh, the apparition said, "I can't be sure that you're not doing that psychic voodoo that you do."

"It was like he knew all about me," E said.

Listening to E speak, I found myself willing to suspend my usual skepticism. Rather, I should say that skepticism seemed an inappropriate tactic in her presence. It was remarkable to watch this patient—this patient who normally presented an extraordinarily composed façade—reposition herself with very few signs of self-consciousness about this supernatural worldview. She inspired a profound trust. She possessed a sober rationality that rivaled that of the colleagues I regularly encounter in my profession.

There was a lull in the conversation between E and the

apparition, during which he did nothing but "stare" at her. He did not move closer. There was movement, however, in his chest. Despite its transparency, E reported that she could see small inflations and deflations of the cavity. Additionally, the apparition blinked every few seconds.

Wishing to provoke action or explanation, E asked, "What are you doing here?" There was no immediate response. It was then that E decided "to test out his consistency." She surveyed the pharmacy's waiting room, searching for a tool. Because she "didn't want to make any drastic movements," she chose from among the objects closest to her, which were health pamphlets.

She laughed for the first time all day as she told me she chose "the gonorrhea pamphlet." It appealed to her because "the girl on it didn't seem that disappointed to have it. She was still hiking." Jokes aside, I believe that this portrait of manageable illness appealed to a specific fantasy within E. Namely, that one day she might be able to incorporate her health problems into a somewhat normal, mobile life.

E folded the pamphlet into a paper airplane. She aimed the plane for the apparition's cranium and released. The plane "flew in a direct line toward the ghost's forehead, and it kept going along that direct line right through his forehead." Apparently, the apparition did not display any awareness of the attack. His blinking did not increase, and he made no movement to escape it. The plane hit the wall on the opposite side of the hallway.

After a period of renewed staring, the apparition's "face clouded." E believed that this expression was too delayed to be in response to the plane.

The apparition suddenly said, "I'm starting to freak out about your teeth."

"What about my teeth?" E asked.

In response, the apparition delivered a bizarre speech. "I'm thinking about how awful they really are. We have bones jutting out of our gums and everyone's aiming to make them even whiter. I say make them grayer and hope that they fade into the background. I'm freaking out that you have bones shooting out of your mouth." E illustrated for me how the apparition brought his fingers up to his translucent teeth to examine them.

E admitted, "Sometimes I also feel that way about teeth. When I start looking at them in a particular light."

"Do you really have thoughts like that?" I asked E.

"Yes."

It made sense that E should have a dysmorphic view of the body and its composition. There was an illusive autonomy about her cells; they seemed to act without regard to the well-being of the greater whole.

"Did the apparition respond?" I asked.

"Now you tell me what you're freaking out about" was the request that the apparition made to E.

Surprised that he was responsive, E asked him whether he could really hear her. The apparition, however, did not respond to this question, but continued along a course of his own inquiry.

"Do you have it yet?" he asked.

"Have what?" E asked, deeply puzzled and astounded. Then, determined to obtain an answer, she took a small step closer to the apparition. She told me that she "half-expected him to squirt me with ectoplasm like in *Ghostbusters*. I'd never met a ghost before. I'm not sure what makes them nervous." Despite her trepidation, E adopted a more rapid interview technique with the apparition. "What are you? Where have you come from? Why are you talking to me? Are you dead? Are you a ghost?" she asked.

Seconds after E finished, the apparition relaxed his stance and pointed straight at her. "That's a good one."

"What is? That you're a ghost?"

"Eyes *are* disturbing. Everyone always says they're the most beautiful features we have, but think of how they're attached to our heads. It's creepy! Creep-ayyyyy!" the apparition exclaimed.

"I couldn't be imagining you. Could I?" E asked him. Then, taking her right hand, she slapped herself across the face.

When E's vision cleared, she saw that the apparition was still present. She told me that her face tingled for a long while afterward, making her feel "like I was transparent, too." At the very least, the pain of the slap confirmed for E that she had not fallen asleep while waiting for C to locate her.

"That went well," the apparition said.

"Are you a ghost?" E repeated.

Again, the apparition failed to respond to E's question, but this was because he began losing "fragments of himself to the dark." E described his disappearance thusly: "Parts of his body would pulse and dim like they were shutting off." In the midst of his disintegration, the apparition shrugged, turned around, and exited the room. He made a left at the hallway, and then he was gone.

This comprised the entirety of their communication in the pharmacy waiting room.

"What did you do then?" I asked.

"I thought," E replied.

Her first thought, E said, was that that her mother's supernatural assertions had been grounded in reality. E had been told unbelievable stories all her life—A had liked to repeat one, in particular, about a ghostly woman who used to show up over E's cradle and attempt to rock her to sleep—and now she instinctively felt they had basis in fact.

E shared that she had always mentally filed items as correct or incorrect when receiving information from her mother. The example she supplied me that afternoon was, "Correct: 'We are out of milk.' Incorrect: 'I am getting the message that this six-pack of 7-Up cans contains the winning entry for the Caribbean sweepstakes. Oh, yes, I feel that it's the third one here. When we get home we'd better start packing our bags.'"

Following these thoughts about her mother, she began to consider other theories for her experience with the apparition. She was attempting, she said, to explore all possible angles.

One she considered was that "there are natural laws that account for weird occurrences." She had once read an article in which the author theorized that pockets of extreme energy could preserve and repeat themselves. These pockets clung to a space even when they no longer made sense there, making an apparition like the one E had witnessed merely an echo in time.

E said that this theory did not wholly satisfy her, however, as she felt that the apparition seemed to have a specific relationship with her. She was under the impression that he had "sought me out," that intentionally he had located her, not simply "a break in the space/time continuum."

Then E expressed concern that it might be her mind and not physics that had been responsible for the apparition. It occurred to her that perhaps she'd summoned herself "a make-believe friend," which she felt was "a pathetic thought." "I get lonely sometimes, but I don't think it's gotten to that bad of a stage yet," E told me. Nonetheless, after the encounter she had worried that the apparition was the result of a fractured psyche, possibly even a schizophrenic manifestation of another, masculine personality within her. She feared that her hidden desire for a kindred soul in the infirmary had inspired her brain to invent one.

Yet the timing contradicted this theory. Since C's arrival in the infirmary and what E described as a rapidly growing bond, she had been less lonely than during previous months. Why would her mind summon a prolonged meeting with the apparition on the night when she was feeling "the least alone that I had in a while"?

E weighed the merits of yet another hypothesis—that it was not her psyche calling the apparition forth, but her entire body. For a moment, she became certain that she must be sick again, "really sick." She imagined a pea-sized tumor growing inside her head, pressing on the part of her brain responsible for distinguishing real-life occurrences from those in her imagination. E had heard stories of patients whose brain tumors caused them to hallucinate, some of those patients coming to believe in the existence of beings that they normally wouldn't.

"We ran scans the other day, though," I reminded her. "We would have seen a tumor."

"I know," E said. "I was trying to think of everything. Everything." She had also considered that her ailment did not have to be as extreme as a brain tumor. She knew that there were a number of diseases that resulted in the swelling of the brain, temporary confusion of the senses, or permanent dementia.

E told me that on a previous afternoon, when extremely bored, she had perused the pamphlets in the pharmacy (including the gonorrhea pamphlet that she had eventually thrown at the apparition). A syphilis pamphlet featured "a guy sitting on a window seat, gazing out on a healthy field. I realized that maybe he was gazing because he was watching a dead kid in a robe running among the wheat. I know that syphilis also causes hallucinations. I thought that maybe I had it."

"Again," I advised her, "syphilis would have shown up on the tests we did. I promise you that we left no stone unturned." I suddenly recognized that I was working with E to disprove alternative theories. I was surprised to find myself helping her narrow her choices to those within the supernatural realm.

"As of last night at that time, I hadn't had sex for a while either, so that's what I figured, too."

"What do you mean 'as of last night at that time'?" I questioned.

"I had sex with C after he found me last night."

"You should have told me that right away." This was crucial information. We needed to take into account any change in E's life if we were to isolate the source of her multiple illnesses. I told her that it was very important that she keep me updated on all of her activities, especially those that involved bodily contact with others.

"I promise that I would have gotten around to it," she said. "This ghost thing is more urgent."

"Did you use protection?" I asked.

"We'll come back to that." She was reluctant to leave the subject of the apparition and quickly returned to her thoughts from the previous night.

Ruling out syphilis, E conjectured that she might be relapsing. The most obvious candidate was the encephalitis from the beginning of freshman year, which had produced brief hallucinatory effects. Although she had not seen apparitions or imaginary persons during that period, she had lost her sense of time and place. Hours and days went by without her awareness of their passing.

"I didn't have the same muddy feeling, though," she explained to me. "When I had the encephalitis, it was like I was in a dream state. I had the sense that something was off. But last night I was clear-headed. I felt sharp."

As with her previous sighting of the apparition, E's ultimate post-reaction was to consult me and obtain my medical opinion. While she believed that she was "starting to see ghosts," she still wanted me to eliminate all medical possibilities.

"Have you told anyone besides myself about what you've seen?" I asked.

E had not. She felt that if she told C or nurse practitioner Sarah what had happened, they would immediately take her to the hospital. She feared that she would be detained for at least twenty-four hours, and that her "window of opportunity would have closed" by the time she returned to the infirmary.

I asked her what this "window of opportunity" was, and E responded that it was the time during which she felt she had the opportunity to connect with C. It was imperative to her that after the game, they be able to return to the infirmary together as two people "on the mend. People with bright futures and no doom up ahead."

Then E remarked, "Oh, but I did tell my mom. I wasn't counting her because she's outside of the infirmary."

"You called her?"

"Yes. She seemed like the best person to ask about this type of thing."

Asking Sarah for privacy, E had used the phone at the nurse's desk after C had fallen asleep. She called A and asked, "What does it feel like when you see a ghost?"

"How it feels?" A echoed. "Like, you mean excited?"

E claimed she could tell that her mother was excited herself that E was asking this. E had never shown interest in the supernatural, and she knew that A had always been saddened by her indifference.

"No, how it feels bodily," E clarified. "Are there any symptoms that you experience when you've been near to a ghost? Like a headache? Or an internal buzzing?" E figured that if her mother experienced a distinct sensation when in the presence of an apparition, then E would have reason to doubt her encounter. Then it would have been "all in her head," if the meeting with the apparition didn't have the correct "accompanying bells and whistles."

"No, I don't feel anything," A told her. "Sometimes my

heart races and I get a hot feeling because I'm excited, but the ghost doesn't cause it. Directly."

E had read before that when one is in the presence of an apparition, there is often a sensation of coldness that fills the room. She questioned A about the source of this rumor.

"It's never happened to me," A answered. "I think that comes from the old wives' tale, that every time you get a shiver, someone's stepping over your grave in the future."

When E heard that, according to A, there was "no feeling" that accompanied a supernatural encounter, she began to believe that "either we both have tumors, or we both see ghosts."

E hung up with her mother without revealing the new link between them. She told me that she felt that admitting her situation to her mother would make her transformation inescapable, and she had spent much of her life secretly fearing that this day would come. While she may have given the impression to her family that she was a firm nonbeliever, E admitted to me that she felt she "couldn't have been so scared of turning out to be like this if I didn't think it was going to happen."

She had been especially scared off by A's reaction to her very first bout of illness. In the middle of freshman orientation, one of E's classmates had noticed that half of E's face was unmoving. The doctor at RIH suspected that the palsy was a serious side effect of herpes simplex 1, a virus commonly passed around on college campuses. He suggested to E that she phone all recent partners with whom she'd had romantic relations; or, in the absence of these partners, anyone whose bodily fluids may have come into contact with hers. The only person that E could think of was J, the summer receptionist at her father's company.

The day before E left for Brown, she had visited the office's supply room to "borrow school supplies." J, with whom who she had only exchanged casual greetings before, suddenly appeared beside her and kissed her. He accidentally bit her tongue in the process, so E had good reason to believe that he was the one who had passed the virus to her—that is, if she did indeed have the virus.

Once E had a chance to phone J, she suggested that he visit his doctor to get himself tested. He called back the following week to say that he was negative. E's tests came back as well, also negative for simplex 1. The doctor could only determine that her palsy was "very mysterious."

Because of complications—E's left eye had rolled up and in toward her tear duct and, due to paralysis, she couldn't chew and needed liquids—the doctor recommended a stay in the Brown infirmary. This was her first.

E's parents, who had come to Providence to help her get settled, were staying at the Biltmore Hotel. When they arrived at the ER, E's doctor informed them about the palsy before he took them to see their daughter, as he was worried that her physical appearance would alarm them. E was wearing a patch over one eye and still lacked movement in half her face.

Once the family was alone, A could finally express her overwhelming enthusiasm. "When she saw me lying there in the bed," E said, "she looked deliriously happy." While this is obviously not the normal reaction one would expect a mother to have at seeing her child in the hospital, A believed that the palsy was merely a minor symptom of a greater change. She told E, "My mom used to get the same way before a major premonition. Some part of her would freeze up." A was convinced that the palsy marked the beginning of E's coming into her supernatural abilities.

I asked E if she had ever discussed this legacy with her grandmother, M. Although M had died when E was six, E did have memories of "lots of talking about ghosts" during the last years of her life.

E remembered a particularly upsetting conversation she'd had with M shortly before her death. A was present and, according to E, well aware that her mother was not long for the world.

M had told her granddaughter, "Even after I leave this world, I'll still come and see you."

Because the topic was frequent in her home, E already understood the mechanics of physical death by this age. M and A had, of course, already been attempting to school her in supernatural matters as well.

"When?" E had asked.

"When? How soon will I show up?"

"No," E said. "At what times? Just at night?"

M replied, "You know that the dead are around us at all times." The family had been telling E this story for years, explaining that apparitions do not feel the need to get out of "our" way as we (we being the "still living") move around. M continued, "You'll be able to see them soon enough, and I'll be there, too."

E had been distressed by this idea. She remembered asking, "All the time? You'll be in my room and at school all the time?" She expressed to her grandmother that this was not something she wanted.

M had begun joking with E (or perhaps she hadn't been joking—this is unclear) that she would be very quiet while doing her haunting.

Only six, E had to tell her grandmother that she enjoyed being alone, and that she wished that M would restrict her otherworldly visits. Even beyond the issue of her grandmother's presence, the larger notion that one day she would "see a never-ending supply of dead people, that they would fill up my space," had already become the cause of enormous dread.

At this point in her narrative, E looked at me with eyes that appeared on the verge of tears. This is the closest that I had ever seen her come to crying. She began to confess. "I think I spent a lot of time back then worrying that if I began to see and hear ghosts like they said I would, I would just be made up of all these other people. All these people talking in my ear. I'd spend my whole life listening to them, trying to figure out what they wanted. And then I'd be this big hole in the middle of it all. I'd have nothing to offer. I'd just be this empty ear for all the dead people."

I was hoping E would continue, as I was only now beginning to realize that my study was going to be far different from what I'd anticipated. Watching it take on a life of its own was more than thrilling. E's story was developing in unpredictable directions, and I was a hostage of her expectations of me. She was telling me all of this because she felt that I could help her, essentially, draw the line between where conventional, explainable territory ended and Promethean, unexplainable territory began. I felt honored to be endowed with that challenge. I resolved to take her perceptions seriously enough to test them.

E requested a fifteen-minute break, during which she left the room. When she returned, her patience appeared to have waned. She was no longer expounding on the questions that I lobbed at her. Soon I understood that I should move on from the topic of her familial legacy.

"I don't want to pry, but I do feel that we need to discuss the . . . latest development that we haven't finished with," I said.

"The ghost?"

"The sexual intercourse."

I was mostly concerned with her bodily reactions during intercourse. I wanted to know what levels of pain she had experienced, and if she had felt lightheaded or particularly "blurry" during coitus. Her lungs were still recovering from the tuberculosis, and this was the most vigorous exercise she had attempted recently.

E admitted to minor dizziness, but she believed that this was a result of her feelings about the interaction and not an effect of illness. Her fibromyalgia had produced the usual painful sensations throughout her back and thighs, but E found that the intercourse distracted her from it.

"Again, I need to ask—did you use protection?" This piece of information was extremely relevant should E develop any new health problems in the coming weeks.

"Yes. We used a glove."

"Is that slang for a condom?" I asked.

It turned out that E and C had used an actual glove. E realized that the hide-and-seek game had been proposed so that C could search the infirmary for a condom. When he located her under the chair, she did not let him know that she was aware of the deception.

C had stretched the latex comprising one of the glove's fingers as far as the material would allow. To be precise, it was the thumb, and the interior of the glove was pre-powdered. Using this digit as a makeshift condom, he and E proceeded, using his saliva as lubrication.

"And the glove did not break?" I asked.

"No. We checked it."

"And how did you feel afterward?"

"I felt healthy. In my mind, I mean." She placed two fingers to each temple, as if she was receiving messages through the air. "Here's what else I've been scared of lately. I've been scared of grasping onto the wrong person. It's scared me that my lack of a normal life might leave me without choices. I've worried that I'd fall in love only because I wanted to fall in love. I'd do it because I had to pretend that my life had forward motion." E looked down at her knees. When she looked back up, the shine in her eyes had returned. "I thought I'd fall in love with what I was projecting onto the other person, not the actual person."

She stopped.

"But with C?" I prompted.

"He's more right than I'll ever be. So I'm relieved. I'm relieved that it's him." Clearly finished with the day's proceedings, E began playing with a canister of cotton balls on the counter. She removed them and lined them up horizontally. She would not make eye contact with me.

"I'm happy that you're happy" was all I could think to say.

"How do we figure out what's going on with me?" E asked, addressing the cotton balls. "How do we prove it to ourselves?"

"I'd like to resume our session in a week. I'll organize a series of tests."

"Medical tests?" E asked.

"No."

She understood the implication. "What do you know about those kinds of tests?"

I told her that I would learn, and she turned and gave me the smallest smile. This, I knew, was her method of granting approval. We'd come far.

• • •

The next day I delved into the field of parapsychology for the first time. Before then, I had not been willing to extend my study to this domain. Once my research had a home, so to speak, I experienced a renewed optimism about the project. I knew that I was taking an academic risk by giving credence to the possibility of supernatural interference. However, I could not help but feel hopeful about taking the study in this new direction. I reminded myself that the human race would be lost today, perhaps even obsolete, had we not continued to explore unknown forces in our world. Progress, I believe, has always demanded significant risk of danger.

Spending the week at the library, I consulted as many scientific texts on supernatural occurrences as were available. When I mentioned the words "scientific" and "supernatural" in the same sentence while talking with Wainscott, he laughed and told me that the two were antithetical. By definition, he said, the supernatural exceeded the natural, and the natural was the basis for all established laws of science. "The field is not scientific," he insisted, "because there is no science to it. It hovers above and beyond. All of that is up there floating around with God, except God has a better chance of making the books."

I was not discouraged. He had not heard E's reports, did not know the mysterious intricacies of her history. Still, I was well aware that anecdotal evidence could not carry this study, so I began organizing experiments as controlled and well designed as possible.

I decided to conduct the experiments in my home. While this might seem unprofessional, I wished to remove E from the infirmary environment. All of her previous encounters with the apparition had occurred within the walls of Health Services, and I was interested to see if she experienced supernatural manifestations outside of the building. Furthermore, I felt that E's concentration might be improved outside of her normal surroundings. She carried a weighty emotional attachment to the infirmary, as it was a constant reminder of her ceaseless illnesses. I also believed that E's recent and growing attachment to C would be an additional distraction. I suspected that she had not told him the extent of our involvement, and I was concerned that her fears about confidentiality would be an additional complication.

In essence, I was hoping that moving the proceedings to my home would help E to forget who she was. If we conducted the experiments in the comfortable environs of a residence, I thought that she might find it easier to clear her mind.

After arranging the appointment with Vivian, I picked up E outside the infirmary at the end of the week. We had both agreed to tell the nurse practitioners that I was accompanying E to a hospital checkup so that we would not have to answer questions.

On her second visit to my home, I noticed a certain ease in E's demeanor. She sat on the couch without first being invited to do so and asked me for a glass of water.

"Where do we start?" she asked.

I shared with her my discovery that the field of parapsychology is divided into two umbrella categories. The first, extrasensory perception (which the average layperson knows by its popular acronym, ESP), encompasses those abilities resulting from exceptional cognitive powers of the mind. While this information was new to me, I am sure that the readers of this publication are familiar with phenomena included in this category such as telepathy, clairvoyance, and precognition. ESP also encompasses all forms of psychic notification, which may exhibit themselves through other senses such as smell, taste, and hearing.

The second category is "anomalous operation." This category describes those phenomena that involve the transference of energies within or between bodies (or objects), including psychokinesis, mediumship, reincarnation, and out-of-body experiences.

While obviously there were specific areas falling under the second category for which I could not test E—reincarnation, for example—I had set up as many tests as were feasible under our restricted circumstances. There were four areas of supernatural ability that I felt I might be able to investigate successfully.

For the first test, telepathy, I explained to E that I would sit six feet away from her while holding a stack of cards.

Each card contained a word, picture, or symbol. I had made sure that the cards were of a very heavy stock, so that their contents would not show through to the other side. While I concentrated heavily on a card's text or image, E would concentrate as well, attempting to read my thoughts.

For the second and third tests, clairvoyance and mediumship, I had convinced an anonymous nurse at RIH to let me borrow one of the personal items of a DOA woman. The hospital had discovered that the patient had no next of kin and no living or locatable family members. Sadly, there was also no one who had come forward to claim the body. The woman died choking on a large piece of carrot, and apparently, she had either grabbed a miniature pewter horse before she'd collapsed or had been holding it all along. (She was alone when she died, so the order of events remains unclear.) Regardless, the horse was still clutched in the body's fist when it reached the ER.

I had heard about this patient through Wainscott, and after much cajoling, the aforementioned nurse loaned me the horse under the condition that I would return it unharmed within twenty-four hours. I told the nurse that the item was needed for an "unconventional scientific experiment." She assumed that I was going to lift skin cells from its surface.

I cleared my dining-room table, leaving it completely bare. I wasn't worried about the table itself, since it was a new, mass-produced piece of furniture from the Pottery Barn without history. I placed the horse on the table so that E could keep whatever energy or information it contained within a semi-controlled area.

"When I try to read the horse, should I hold it or leave it there?" E asked.

"Try both," I said, shrugging. She shrugged back. Even though we were both ambivalent about the tests, there was a nice camaraderie in exploring new frontiers together.

I needed a similarly neutral surface for the fourth test, telekinesis/psychokinesis, and I decided upon a folding card table. I told E that we would try to get her to move two objects using only her powers of concentration. One would be an object without significant meaning to her. I chose an unsharpened Number 2 pencil, straight out of the box. The other would be an object to which she felt connected. For this reason, I had asked E to bring something that meant a lot to her. She chose the very first hospital bracelet she received when she was taken to RIH for Bell's palsy. She had been keeping it in the suitcase under her bed all this time.

Because I had not discovered a method for inducing precognition or psychic activity, I told E that there would an unofficial fifth test. If, at any point during the day's proceedings, she received a strong feeling or message, she was to alert me and I would write it down and note the precise time that it occurred.

I acknowledge that this last test had very abstract parameters. However, I felt it was important to conduct it for my own purposes, even if I could not include it in the final paper.

While I am sure it would be more scientific to catalog E's impressions and behaviors as she moved through each station, in all honesty, nothing remarkable happened. We went through fifty cards together; she did not identify what I was looking at once. In the beginning of the experiment we spent long periods of time trying to connect our brain waves. I would stare at, to give an example, the word "curtain" for sixty seconds, repeating it silently in my mind. After the stopwatch sounded, I would ask E if she had received my messages. Usually, she did not even offer up an answer. She told me that if she was not hearing something "clear and obvious," she did not see the point in guessing. There was only one instance in which she suddenly said, "pizza," although the card I was holding displayed a picture of the moon. Then, she said she realized that she'd only said "pizza" because that was a message sent from her own brain. She was hungry. We called and ordered a medium cheese.

After lunch, E spent half an hour with the pewter horse and grew bored.

At the twenty-seven-minute mark, I asked, "Is the object speaking to you in any way?"

"I heard something soft," E replied.

"What is it?"

E whispered, barely audibly, "Neiiigghhhhhhh."

"Where and when did you get a sense of humor?" I asked her.

We moved on to the pencil. We experimented with placing it at different distances from her body and also with conducting the test both with E's eyes open and closed. I watched the pencil carefully; it never moved. After an hour, we replaced the pencil with the hospital bracelet, but found ourselves with the same result.

The evening was closing down on us. Demoralized, I asked E if she had perhaps received any inexplicable messages during the course of the day. Did any mental images seem particularly insistent? Were there any thoughts that she couldn't explain, yet still visited her with frequency?

Instead of answering directly, E touched my shoulder and said, "You have a lot of patience for this."

"I suppose I have to," I answered.

E told me that she had to use the rest room before we returned to the infirmary. She disappeared down the hallway and I returned the pewter horse to its plastic bag. I also set the pencil and the cards aside in a plastic case.

She was extremely quiet on the drive back to Health Services, but this did not unnerve me the way it had in the past. Although our trials had been disappointing, I was confident that E understood that my investment in her was genuine. She knew that we were partnered. I knew, as I had not known after previous sessions, that we would speak again.

How soon we would speak was a surprise, however. At around eleven o'clock that night, I got into bed. Because I have difficulty falling asleep, I always read for at least an hour and a half before turning out the lights. I do not use bookmarks. When I feel I have reached a point where I can fall asleep, I simply make a mental note of the last page I read and then shut the book.

I had been reading Capote's *In Cold Blood.* I opened to page 144, where I had left off the previous night. The book appeared to open itself to that page, as if that's where the spine naturally parted. In the middle crease I found a folded piece of paper.

Opening the paper, I saw writing that I recognized. The note read, "I WANT TO READ THIS WHEN YOU'RE FINISHED. I'VE HEARD IT'S GOOD. —E."

I was on the phone right away. I used the speaker function so that I could record the conversation. Vivian put me on hold while she went to see if E was still awake. When E came on the line, she did not sound surprised at my calling.

"Hello."

"What is this?" I asked.

"It's a bookmark," she said.

"How did you know what page I was on?" At this point I began to inspect page 144, wanting to see if I had inadvertently left any signs of my place. I checked to see if the corners were folded or if there were any creases on the page. Then I shut the book and examined the way that the page looked among all the others. There was no evidence of 144's importance.

"Someone told me."

"Someone who?" I threw the book up in the air and allowed it to land on the bed, wanting to see where it would naturally fall open. It parted itself at page 96.

"A man. He told me that he was pissed that you stopped reading at 144 last night because he was really getting into it."

"Did you see this man?" I asked, my heart beating faster.

"No, I just heard him."

"Did he identify himself?"

"I couldn't really understand everything he was talking about, but I think he might be an uncle of yours," she said.

"Uncle Chris?" I asked. "Was it Uncle Chris?" My Uncle Chris had been a voracious reader, who had died five years ago in a car accident. We used to trade books with each other and discuss them over monthly dinners.

"I don't know. I didn't catch a name."

"Did he say anything else?"

"He said that the book you were reading was really good. He recommended it."

I sunk onto my bed and took in this information. We had spent almost six hours chasing a supernatural occurrence, and yet here it finally was—a totally haphazard moment. Suddenly, the number 144 seemed poetic. There was no possible way that E could have known my page without some form of uncanny assistance. She had never seen me pick up the book. She had never heard me speak about it. She had never before that day even been in my bedroom. How could I resist believing in her any longer?

"Why didn't you tell me this this afternoon?" I asked. "I could have noted the time and the—"

"Well, I know that secretly you want some glamour," E said. "I thought that leaving a note was much more glamorous."

The next morning I received a phone call from the infirmary. E had been taken back to the hospital, complaining of chills, vomiting, and a rash. By the end of the following week, Dr. Edwards at RIH had diagnosed her with ornithosis, otherwise known as parrot fever. Edwards believed that E had contracted the disease by inhaling the dust from the droppings of an infected bird.

The only bird that E had had direct contact with was Vivian's parrot. Vivian agreed to have him tested for the disease, but he came back clean.

Edwards suggested that perhaps E had become infected by one of the pigeons that sit on the ledge outside the infirmary's windows. It was impossible, however, to narrow down a pigeon for trapping and sending to the lab. Moreover, because E was the only one in the entire Health Services building who caught the fever, Edwards could not even be positive that she had contracted the disease in the infirmary.

Because of her debilitating symptoms, E and I did not hold another session until the week before Christmas. By the holiday break she had gotten past the vomiting, chills, sore throat, and rashes, and was only plagued by a slight cough. She began tetracycline treatment.

There was absolutely no doubt in my mind that E's body was reacting to her burgeoning abilities. It was then that I began to form the theory I would later call "Psychic Puberty."

CHAPTER 22

PAXIL CR • Get back to being you

Christmas was the best in recent memory, and not just because I got an Adderall travel umbrella in my sock hung by the fireplace. And not just because I beat you at dominos three times in a row. You and I lay in bed and did a lot of tucking each other's hair behind ears. Vivian and Shawn paced the hallway arguing happily, and Vivian was saying, "I find it incredible that people feel comfortable announcing no one has ever been in love to the extent that they are. And they know that every other couple on the planet also claims this! How do they manage to feel secure with this tired pronouncement?" And Vivian's boyfriend kept insisting to her, "But that's faith! That's faith!" which seemed like an ideally Christmasy sentiment to me.

New Year's Eve was less joyous. Meeting your parents, I got scared because your mom looked so scared of me. I kept getting the feeling that she was looking at me like a car accident. She wanted to look away, but couldn't. I know I was still kind of clammy-looking from the bird ordeal, but I think it was more that she wasn't used to being around sickness. I know what you're probably thinking right now, but you don't count. You're broken, not sick.

You kept asking your parents, "Isn't she great? Isn't she great?" and I wanted to tell them, "Don't worry, you don't have to answer that," because I could see it all over their faces. They didn't think I was so great. I worried that the look on your mom's face would be infectious. All of a sudden you'd see me the way she saw me, and you'd blink slowly. You'd turn around in a circle saying, "Whoa, where am I?" and everything between us would have to go.

The school brought in those temps for the holidays, and I was hoping to see Bethany, my Thanksgiving nurse. But when we got Lauren and Deondra, I hoped that maybe Bethany had found herself another dying home-care patient. And if that was the case, then I was very happy for her.

Those temps were fearless, because they knew that they couldn't really be fired. I liked it, though, how they had no desire to be accommodating. I felt like we were staying in a hotel with bad service instead of the infirmary. When I went out to the desk to ask them for chairs for your parents, Lauren said, "The only chairs I personally know about are the ones we're sitting on." Then she swiveled in hers.

"Sorry," added Deondra.

I didn't have it in me to go to the pharmacy and drag some chairs over from there. But I remember thinking that I should have at least tried once your parents were sitting on my bed with us like we were all on a small boat together.

I wasn't trying to be rude when your mom asked me about how I'd been in the infirmary "for a while." I know she wanted me to talk about it, and I understand that it's a topic of interest. But the way I was feeling was that a new year was about to break, and I refused, if just for that one night, to spend time looking back. That's why I answered in short bursts. I was all yeses and nos, and I heard in my head how terrible that sounded, but it was really all I could do.

I knew that my shortness was freaking out your mom even more, and I wished I could have told her that it wasn't personal. I thought about saying something to that effect, but that kind of talk just doesn't seem to have a place at a first-time meeting. If it had been our second, maybe I would have explained that being quiet was something I had to stick to for myself. The best thing I could think to do was not drag down the mood, which everyone was trying hard to keep hopeful. Your parents were so excited about you starting physical therapy.

Your mom was talking about the power of a positive attitude, and then suddenly she was asking me, "Don't you think so, Elodie? I would think you've had some experience in the area."

I didn't say this, but I agreed, technically, that the mind has far more power over the body than most people believe. But I also factored in that the mind is harder to reach than most people realize. Though I just answered, "Yes, I agree."

By the time it was almost midnight and your mom started talking about that show she saw on the Discovery Channel featuring a tumor that had a mouth, teeth, and hair, she was only addressing me. We were all pretending to have a group conversation, but she made contact only with my eyes. You were stroking my hair. I don't think you noticed. But I guess that your mom thought I would somehow know about a tumor like that, like maybe she thought I'd had one before. I'd never said that I hadn't.

Your dad asked us, "What do you two do for fun around

here?" and you said, "It's always hard to remember at the end of the day. I'm always looking at Elodie at night and saying, 'What the hell did we do today?' This place has its own time zone, if that makes sense. The hours here don't feel like my old hours. Your hours. So I don't know. We talk—" You looked to me for input. We both knew that we couldn't really tell them what went on in here because it was too hard to explain.

That's why I said, "We read."

I left out the part about how we lie in bed and go through the accidentally donated porn magazines. How we especially love it when we can match a doctor on the mailing label to his fetish. I couldn't tell them about my favorite times with you, which I think are either (1) when we get up very early and go into the waiting room to drink Coke before appointments start. The light's really good there in the morning. Don't take this the wrong way, but seeing you in it makes me care about you even more. I also like getting that hyper in the morning, when I feel like no one else is awake except us (and the nurses). Or (2) when I sit in your lap and you wheel us down the hallway as fast as you can. And we shout at the nurse practitioners, "Out of our fucking way! We're breaking out of here, suckas!"

How could I tell that story to your parents? I don't think they'd love me for it.

Your parents seemed so relieved when the temps invited us to come out to the desk and watch the ball drop on TV with them. Your mom couldn't say "We'd love to" fast enough, and your dad was already breaking out those gold hats he brought. I put on the hat as my one social concession. It was nice to have everyone crowding around

Deondra's tiny TV, focused on that ball. No one was judging anyone for an entire minute.

When everyone shouted, "One!" I realized that this was the first New Year's party I had ever attended, if you could count it as a party. There was silly string and more than one person beside myself, so I'm calling it a party. You pulled me down into your lap for the kiss, and I shut my eyes so I wouldn't have to think about whether or not your parents were looking on and worrying. That kiss made me happy to be alive. It made me feel like I should run out and sign up for a decathlon. In the background I heard people cheering on TV, fireworks blasting in the sky, and Lauren telling Deondra that she was going to sleep with fewer men this year, and "less Italians."

When we went to bed I had the delusion that I'd never be sick again. You and I lay together, saying nothing, and that we didn't have to talk anymore made me feel peaceful. I've always believed that a comfortable silence is something that's earned. It's not the same thing as the silence that comes when people start to take each other for granted. That kind of silence isn't even recognized, because the people involved are too wrapped up in their own problems and their own indifference. They forget that they're not talking. But I think a comfortable silence is an act of love. It's saying to each other, "It's enough for me just to be by you. You don't have to say anything, I adore you anyway." That's what we had on New Year's Eve, and it felt enormous.

After you fell asleep, I got up to call my parents, since I had this feeling of missing them. Or it was more like I had this feeling of wanting to start over with them. Or I could just admit that the whole idea of New Year's was really getting to me, like I was getting carried away with what the rest of the world was up to.

The first holiday I missed was Christmas of freshman year, when the fibromyalgia had just started I was getting over a big case of the flu, and the doctor thought flying was a bad idea. When I called home to break the news to my parents, they didn't really know that I was still getting sick. They wouldn't see the noncovered medical bills until the bursar statement arrived at the end of the year.

"Why, what's wrong?" my dad asked.

"I'm just having too much fun," I lied.

My mom got on the phone and said, "I had a dream about you last night. I saw what you're going to wear at Christmas. I'm not going to tell you what outfit I saw you wearing in the dream, and then I'll see if you choose the same thing. I feel like you will. When are you flying in?"

"Well, as I was just telling Dad, I'm going to stay here over winter break." In the background I could hear my dad repeating the message. It was echoing. We have fantastic acoustics in our house.

"You're really not coming home?"

"I'm going to take a special month-long dance workshop," I told her. Another girl was staying in the infirmary because of her debilitating migraine headaches, but she opened her eyes and looked over at me.

"Dance?" she asked, because she knew I was full of shit.

My mom sighed. "Maybe I had that dream because you weren't coming home. Maybe I already knew because I don't know why, but I feel less shocked that you're not coming than I should." It was two o'clock in the afternoon, but cars had their headlights on. And I watched them from my window, feeling a hundred stories away from anything that moved faster than me. There was the sound of tires rolling through slush, and I swear I could hear the snow falling from the sky. Altogether the effect was that of the world rushing to get away from the point where I stood.

You don't know this, but my parents call once a week to say, "You can come home, no questions asked. We'd love to have you back."

And I always say, "I know. Thank you."

My mom gave up trying to get information from me. I could tell she was refusing to be the kind of mom who had to force her way into her daughter's life. She feels bad about all the years she's spent trying to make me into a ghost hunter. Only once she asked, "Are you sicker than I know, or not that sick at all?" But before I could answer, she cut in and said that I shouldn't say anything. That she had to trust that I knew what I was doing.

On New Year's, she was the one who picked up the phone. I told her about you for the very first time. I said, "I have a boyfriend." She wanted to hear all about you, but I found it difficult to sum you up. I could have said, "He's the most fun I've ever known," except that says nothing about the kind of fun that you are, and it was like that with every description I attempted. So I asked her how her Christmas was instead.

"It was okay."

"What'd you get?"

"Some dresses, some books, some jewelry. The stationery from you. Thanks, by the way. Oh, and I got a new oven."

"So the old one really was leaking?"

"Your dad decided that he should buy me a new one because he didn't trust the old one, even if it was repaired. So, we have a new oven. It has a lot of options on it."

"You don't really cook all that much," I pointed out.

"I know. They say it's the thought that counts, though." I could hear tension in my mom's voice. She was more disappointed by the oven than she'd admit to me. That's why she changed the subject so fast. "There's a picture coming into my head right now," she said. "I think it's a picture of your boyfriend. Does he have black hair and a nose that curves down a little at the end?"

"That must be a picture of someone else. He's a dirty blond."

"Watch," Mom said, "tomorrow I'll run into someone that looks just like that, and then I'll know where the picture came from. The pictures come, but they don't come with captions."

"Well, keep me updated," I said.

When I came back to bed I was feeling so high that I couldn't help but marvel at your face, which meant nothing to me two months ago. Now, all over the place it said "your best friend." I touched your hair and your cheeks. You kept sleeping. Maybe unconsciously I was trying to wake you up. I touched your nose, and then, because I'm sick like that, I decided to lightly stick a finger inside one of your nostrils. I thought to myself, "I know what people are talking about when they say they wish they could climb inside someone else."

CHAPTER 23

THE JOURNAL OF PARAPSYCHOLOGY OCTOBER 2004

E's supernatural encounters began to occur more frequently. I suggested to her that this was because we had opened a mental floodgate—or, to be fair, that *she* had opened a mental floodgate—through all of our explorations and hard work. E felt, however, that perhaps these abilities had been attempting to surface for the past three years, and that this was the first time she was willing to receive them. She remembered "getting messages that had nothing to do with anything" throughout her stay in the infirmary. She had never given them much credence. Now that she was moving toward a state of acceptance, she had become more sensitive to her paranormal abilities.

I told her that this reminded me of the part in *Peter Pan* where children must clap if they believe in fairies in order to save Tinkerbell's life. There was an almost childlike simplicity in her dependency on "believing." One who believed saw. One who didn't believe didn't see. It was that simple. I asked E if she thought that what she'd inherited from her family was simply a genetic capacity for belief. Perhaps the study I should be conducting was the isolation of a strand of heavy-believing DNA. I was mostly joking with her.

E said only, "I don't know."

"You don't know?" I asked. "That's all you have to say?"

E began to clap slowly, raising one eyebrow at me. "Okay?" she asked.

The day after New Year's, we met at the hospital while E was being examined for a bloody nose. It had started that morning. Because the nose had no accompanying symptoms, on an ordinary person it would not have been a cause for concern. Even though E was bleeding only from the anterior epistaxis, she was taken to the ER for an examination. The nurse practitioners did not like to take chances with her.

Now that I believed E's avalanche of illnesses reflected less on her health than on her special faculties, I was not especially worried about her. While I am not claiming that I have any supernatural abilities, I did have a certain "sense" that she was not in physical danger. I no longed believed that she would succumb to disease at an early age.

While we waited for her test results, I took E down to the hospital cafeteria. Surveying the array of foods, she asked me if I thought that they had a Belgian waffle maker. The cafeteria did, indeed, have waffles, although because it was past breakfast time, they weren't available.

"What will it take to get a waffle?" E asked the server behind the counter.

"The iron has been turned off for over two hours," he replied.

"What will it take to get it turned back on?"

"I can't. It's after breakfast hours."

E looked at me.

"Yes?" I asked.

"You're the one who has the money."

"You want me to bribe the cafeteria worker?"

"Yes," she said. "I'm letting you write about me. I don't think it's that much for me to ask you to slip him a twenty."

Finding her reasoning persuasive, I opened my wallet and offered the server a twenty-dollar bill. He accepted it and reheated the waffle iron for us. I asked him to make me one as well, since I had paid for the privilege.

As E and I sat at a table with our waffles, she told me about how she had spent New Year's Eve. After watching a midnight celebration on TV, she had excused herself from the group at the infirmary desk, which included two temporary nurse practitioners, her boyfriend, and her boyfriend's parents. She announced that she had to retrieve her medication from the bathroom. She noted that "they were all talking and blowing noisemakers, and I don't know that they really noticed my leaving. C's parents were encouraging him to set detailed resolutions having to do with his legs. He was into it."

As she was entering the infimary proper, E's attention was diverted to an abnormality near the farthest infirmary window. At first she perceived it only as a "sliver of black." Walking forward to get a better look, E realized that what she was seeing was the apparition (still wearing the robe), standing in the corner of the room. He was partially tucked behind the curtain. What E had seen was a piece of his hair. The apparition had his back to the room.

Stopping approximately ten feet from the window, E attempted to capture his attention. "Hey," she beckoned as softly as she could manage. She "didn't want everybody to hear."

Surprisingly, the apparition immediately turned around and said, "Hey." Even though she had called to him, E told me that she hadn't been expecting a response. She had merely spoken to him because she could not think of a better tactic to take, and she "couldn't really tap him on the shoulder because my finger would go through it."

Because the apparition's response was unexpected, E did not have a follow-up statement prepared. "How's it going?" she asked.

"You know. It's going." She described the smile the apparition gave her as being "very wistful." Then he ran his hands through his hair, pulling the "long pieces back from his forehead like he was worn out." He looked out of the window—or, as E clarified, the "direction of the window," since we could not be sure that he was seeing what she was seeing. Although E and the apparition appeared to be sharing a moment in space and time, we still did not know from whence the apparition came. He might have been looking at an earlier version of the infirmary window; it was possible that he had been a patient in the past. His terry-cloth robe let us know that he was most likely from the twentieth century. Additionally, judging from his chin-length hair, I told E that I believed he had probably come from the 1960s or 1970s.

When the apparition looked back at E, he asked, "How's it going for you?"

"I'm feeling a little bit melancholy. But it's New Year's. I think you're supposed to," she answered.

I cut into her story. "Why were you feeling melancholy?"

"I could tell that C's parents thought I was weird. It was getting me down a little. I considered trying not to act weird."

"Why didn't you?"

"If people already think you're weird and you try to cover it up with behavior that doesn't come naturally, it's been my experience that you come off even weirder than before," E said.

"When you told the apparition you were melancholy, what did he say?" I asked.

"Nothing." The apparition gave her a small nod, as if he understood and agreed with her assessment of the holiday, then returned to staring in the direction of the window.

E decided that she would administer a test herself to determine if another person would have any awareness of the apparition's presence in the room. She instructed him not to move. Giving her a look out of the corner of his eye, the apparition appeared to comply. Backing up while facing him, E, about twelve feet from the doorway, called out to a temporary nurse practitioner, asking her to bring a cup of water.

The nurse practitioner, clearly unenthusiastic about her job, asked E why she couldn't get herself some water from the tap in the bathroom. E lied, saying that she needed cold, bottled water from the outside refrigerator because it helped settle her stomach. She told the practitioner, Deondra, that "the medication makes me nauseous."

At the mention of medication, the apparition chimed in again. "I'm going to stop taking my medication today," he said. "What do you think of that?"

"Fine," Deondra agreed from the hallway.

"I'll tell you what I think of it if you tell me if you're dead," E bartered.

Before the apparition could respond to this offer, Deondra entered the infirmary. E, unwilling to turn her head, could hear the nurse's tennis shoes squeaking on the floor. E asked, without looking over her shoulder, "Quick, Deondra, do you see—?"

Before she could finish her question, the apparition began to disintegrate. E estimated that the time it took for him to disappear was the length of "five blinks." Presently, the corner was blank.

"Do I see what?" asked Deondra. She handed E the bottle of water.

"When you walked in here, did you get a glimpse of anything over there in the far corner?"

"Like what?"

"Like anything," E answered, wanting to remain vague so that if Deondra had seen something, E would know that she hadn't influenced her answer.

"What is it that you think you saw?" insisted the nurse.

"I'm not sure," E said. "I don't know."

"What do you mean, 'You don't know'?"

E described the look that Deondra "shot her" as being "funny." She meant funny in the strange, and not humorous, sense.

Before E could attempt to answer or lie, C entered the infirmary. He told her that his parents were leaving to return to their hotel, and that E should come and say goodbye to them.

E could not examine the corner again for over an hour, since C was present. After C fell asleep, E got out of bed and went to investigate the window, the curtain, and the floor where the apparition had stood. She saw no evidence of his having been there.

I suggested to her that we should try to locate an EMF

(for those readers outside the paranormal research community, this stands for "electromagnetic field") meter in order to take a reading in the corner. Perhaps there were still remnants from the apparition's visit, and the meter might be able to detect residual activity. I had only learned of these meters after my initial research into the field of parapsychology and was eager to utilize some of the tools of the trade.

E, however, was interested in proceeding in a more decidedly low-tech fashion. "Forget the E-meter," she said, and I corrected her.

"E-meters, I believe, are what Scientologists use to electronically evaluate a person's mental state. This is an *EMF* meter. Your mother never talked about them?"

"No. She doesn't use anything like that."

"What does she use?" I asked.

"Sometimes she pulls out crystals. That's it." E, examining a piece of waffle on her fork, remarked, "This is really, really good. I'm now a big fan of the waffle."

"I'm happy if you're happy," I said. On the tape we often sound like an old, married couple. Again, I say this not to imply any sort of inappropriate intimacy with E, but to indicate the close and honest doctor–patient relationship that we developed as a result of our shared time and interests.

"So how do you suggest we continue?" I asked.

"I want you to hire a sketch artist," E said. "I want to sit down with someone and describe the ghost, and then I'm going to give you the drawing. And then you can use it to do research into who he is and maybe fnd out how he died."

"This sounds like work for a detective."

"Maybe you're going to have to expand your job description," E said, clearly amused. It was as if she were imagining me smoking a pipe and sporting a deerstalker hat.

"And where am I supposed to find this expert?" I asked.

"The police station. I'm sure they can give you a good reference. I bet you can even hire an artist straight from them."

I have to admit that I was curious to see the face of the apparition, as I had been having difficulty picturing him in my mind. Moreover, I realized that with a drawing in hand, I would have an encouraging point of origin while combing the school's newspaper archives. Because deaths on campus are not a common occurrence, the number of candidates would be finite.

"I'll find you a sketch artist," I said, "if you'll do something for me in return."

"What?" she asked.

"I'd like you to start carrying around a small tape recorder like the one I have."

E did not understand what good that could possibly do, since she had already determined that those without paranormal abilities could not see the apparition. When the nurse practitioner had walked into the infirmary to bring E the bottle of water, there had been a very short window (no more than a couple of seconds) during which he should have been visible to her. E seriously doubted that it would be different with others being able to hear the apparition's voice.

I reminded her that a recorder works much differently than the human ear, and that if the apparition was comprised of electrical or magnetic energy, his presence might register on tape. "Even if the recording doesn't manage to pick up his words, there's the chance that it will register a disturbance in the room." If we could match static or a defect on the tape to the time of one of the apparition's future appearances, then we would have a key piece of data.

After we finished our meal and checked E out of the hospital, we went to Radio Shack and bought her a recorder identical to mine. Then I returned her to Health Services.

The next day I inquired at the police station about hiring a sketch artist for a personal matter, and a desk sergeant put me in contact with their best, L. For a reasonable fee she would sit down with E and draw the apparition for us. Of course, we did not tell her that she would be drawing an apparition. Instead, E and I agreed that we would not tell L about any aspect of the study. If she asked any questions, we would insist that we were looking for a long-lost relative.

In order to prevent others at Health Services from asking questions as well, I borrowed a ground-floor office from a doctor friend of mine who was away speaking at Harvard.

When I went to pick up E from the second-floor waiting room, I caught a glimpse of C as we were walking toward the stairwell. The infirmary door was cracked, and I saw a male matching the description that E had provided during our previous conversations. He was watching us. I did not inform E about what I had seen, as I knew that she was determined to keep our meetings as secret as possible.

E and L collaborated for approximately two hours. I gave them their privacy and returned only when L called my cell phone. E presented the finished drawing to me, and there was my first glimpse of the apparition's face.

Even in the sketch, his black hair looked as if it were

slightly greasy. It fell in straggly pieces to his jawline. He had deep recesses underneath his eyes, giving the impression that he had difficulty sleeping—a fitting physical characteristic, I thought, for a person who had failed to rest in peace. His forehead was a little longer than average, and his extensive eyebrows slanted toward his thin nose, giving him an air of deep concern. Even without the rest of his body in the drawing, I could tell that the apparition was underweight; this particularly showed in his cheekbones. His mouth was long and his upper lip crooked.

"Are you happy with the likeness?" I asked E.

"It's exactly him," she said.

I thanked L for her help and compensated her. After she left, I used the copy machine in the main office to reproduce the image twice. I gave one of the copies to E, since she had requested it. I secured the original under protective plastic, then placed the second copy in my briefcase. This is the copy I referenced during my research.

During the next week, I not only searched for a matching likeness in the library's microfiches and local records, but also conducted informal questioning. I tracked down members of the university's staff knowledgeable about the school's history and lore. I heard many stories about deaths on campus, and those stories became the catalysts for auxiliary stories about the recent epidemic of near-deaths on campus. There had been a series of anonymous, violent acts committed against Brown students during the past year, and although no one was dead yet, my sources were sure that was "what was around the corner."

I showed them the drawing of the apparition, asking if the young man was familiar in any way. I found no promising leads until I took the drawing to the university's official photographer.

Even though he had held the position for less than a decade, he was in charge of the greater photography library and so was familiar with campus images that dated back forty years. He also professed to have a "photographic memory." Thus, when he saw the drawing and told me that he had seen the apparition "before somewhere," I had high hopes.

When the photographer pulled a sheet of slides from the cabinet, I thought perhaps I should have brought E so that she could be present for the big moment. I began to study the slides on the light table.

While the young man in the photographs had many of the same characteristics as the apparition, I felt that there was something off about the mouth. The photographs had been taken because the subject (interestingly, having attended Brown in the late 1970s) had received a prestigious grant to study architecture in Europe. The *Brown Alumni Magazine* had written a feature on him, and one of the filed images had accompanied the piece.

As I was looking at the young man's mouth under a magnifying glass, the photographer said, "I remembered this guy because he died right before graduation."

"Excuse me?"

"He was in a car accident over spring break. It was a real tragedy. I had to pull his pictures about a year ago because his niece came here and got the same grant, so *BAM* did another piece on the family."

"He's dead?" I echoed.

"Yes. He's dead."

I returned to examining the young man's mouth under

the magnifying glass. I was still troubled by the shape of it, but the fact of his death gave me cause for optimism. Because library visitors were prohibited from removing slides and negatives, I asked the photographer to make prints. They were ready after lunch, and once I had them in my possession, I went straight to Health Services.

Vivian told me that E was napping. I said that I would wait.

Every fifteen minutes, Vivian went into the infirmary to check if E was still asleep. One time I volunteered to go check myself, and I saw E sleeping in a twin bed with C. They were wrapped in each other's arms; on such a small mattress, there was barely room for the two of them. I was hoping that E would wake first. Although I was curious to meet C officially, I knew that E did not want us to cross paths, and, as always, it was in my best interest to keep her comfortable.

Luckily, E wandered out of the infirmary, looking for soda, within the hour. She appeared confused to see me sitting at the desk.

"We need to talk," I said.

Vivian gave me a suspicious look. Since none of the nurse practitioners knew the true nature of my relationship with E, I suppose that they assumed the worst. Those women were very protective of E, having known her for so long and having seen her through so much.

The rest of the students were still on winter vacation, so the hallways were deserted. E and I convened in a corner near the lab. I retrieved the prints from my briefcase and presented them to E with the images face down.

"Take as long as you need with these," I instructed.

E flipped over the first photograph in the pile and without pause, said, "It's not him."

"Give yourself a moment," I said, even though she had only confirmed what I already feared.

"Sorry. It's not him."

Although I am the scientist, accustomed to the repetitive pattern of trial and error, I seemed to take the disappointment harder than E. My excitement about this new field had created in me a heightened desire for discovery. I wanted to take strides, not steps. It was E, strangely enough, who had to remind me that although our first lead had been a disappointment, we should not be discouraged. As with everything, she told me, "it's all just a matter of time."

CHAPTER 24

From The Desk of Chester Hunter III

My parents didn't say anything while they were visiting, but after they got home they called me. I'm not trying to hurt you, El. Sometimes it's like I'm sitting in this chair with my hands on either side of the keyboard, and I've got these invisible things sitting in my palms: cushioning and hurt. I bounce them around to see how they feel, to see which one feels worse, and as I'm writing this letter I'm constantly reevaluating. But I keep returning to the feeling that hurt is the way to go, because while cushioning will remain cushioning, at least the hurt can turn itself into something new. For both of us, I mean.

They called on one of the days that you were having a checkup at the hospital. Right away, I was saying, "She's really special, isn't she?"

And my mom said, "I'm glad you brought Elodie up because we wanted to talk to you about that." My dad was also on the line.

"What do you mean?"

My dad just came out with it. "She struck us as an odd bird."

I told them that they had no idea who you really were.

My mom said, "I want to be fair. Perhaps there's a lot to her we haven't seen yet."

"I also think it's important to remember that one partner in a relationship doesn't have to weigh directly upon the other," my dad said, and I knew he was talking about his own situation. That made me furious, that he could even attempt to correlate our lives. "They aren't one reflection in the mirror."

"I've got to get off the phone," I told them. "I've got a lot of homework to do."

"Chess, wait," my mom said. "I'm going to hold off on passing judgment on Elodie." But I could hear the lie in her voice. She has a habit of denying her judgment of people the way that hippies deny the variety in humans, the fact that there are just some who are impossible to love.

My dad added, "We didn't place this phone call to insult your girlfriend. We simply want to let you know that you'll be fine, whether it's with or without her."

After that, I didn't talk to them for a few weeks. But when I finally got the green light from my doctor to start physical therapy, I began to see that while they were misguided in dragging you into it, they were right about me. For the first time in months, I started to feel sure that I would be fine.

Before I went to my first session, I fully expected to come back and give you all the details. When I was in the middle of it, though, this realization started to build and build and build that my recuperation wasn't something that I should bring home to you. Like I said, for the first time since the accident, I could actually see that I was going to be better one day, that there was a light at the end of this particular tunnel. I mean, I could see that I was literally going to get up and walk out of this injury at some point in the near future. And then my thoughts went to you, and I was wrecked by how there wasn't any doctor or clinic or place that you could go to to get better. That was when I decided that I would be an asshole to tell you all about my day, rubbing it in your face.

I think the extent of my report to you went something like "It went really well. I like my doctor." Now I'll give you the rest.

The morning I met my doctor—Dr. Daly—he was sitting in his office looking at a row of fishbowls. He had six tiny ones that had betta fish in them, but all of the fish were dead and floating upside down. I was the first appointment of the day and he'd just come in and found them like that. Initially, I took the dead fish as a profoundly bad sign, thinking that they were an omen directed toward me by some power in the universe. I'm not saying God or a conscious higher power, but more along the lines of impersonal, unavoidable forces, like fate or karma.

But I started to feel better and better as Dr. Daly gave me his take on the dead fish.

"One of the new night-shift cleaning ladies must have gotten overexcited and fed them, unaware that I give them four pellets every night before I leave," he said. I was totally surprised when he put his bare hand into one of the fishbowls and scooped out the green betta. "I would never harm any of these little guys while they were living, but I've always been curious. I've always believed that when opportunity presents itself, we shouldn't waste it. Do you mind?"

"No," I said, but I wasn't even entirely sure what I was agreeing to. "Go ahead."

Dr. Daly opened the drawer on his desk and took out a scalpel. He put the fish down on his month-at-a-glance calendar, and then he dragged the knife along the fish's stomach and split it open. After that, he held the fish so that his right forefinger was on its head and his right thumb was pressing down on its tail stub, and he squeezed it. The way the fish looked when it opened up reminded me of those free plastic coin carriers that the bank gives you when you sign up for a new savings account.

Dr. Daly looked inside the fish for a few seconds, then asked me, "Do you want to see?"

"I guess. Sure," I said. I looked into the fish. And, El, that's the moment when my day snapped into place. Because looking into that fish, I could see the simplicity of its insides. There wasn't so much going on in there. And then, kaboom. It came unexpectedly rushing back, the feeling that I had instant access to everything in the world, including fish guts, and that I didn't even have to get permission to look where I wanted, go where I wanted. Reading that sentence back to myself, I acknowledge that it makes me seem like an intense prick. But I know you of all people understand how these mysterious flicks of the switches in our brain work. I'll always remember that you described your pain to me like that in your letter—there one instant, gone the next, and you could never see either state coming. All our lives we're taught that personal growth is this process that takes time, but there in that doctor's office, I think I realized that this isn't the case. There's a point where you cross over to a new side. Maybe people count all the time it takes you to get there, but I don't think that's right. All that matters is that little piece of time when something actually clicks.

After looking into the fish, I decided to smell the guts as well. They didn't smell bad like I thought they would, and I told Dr. Daly that. So he also smelled the fish, waving it under his nose like he was sniffing the bouquet of a good wine. "It doesn't smell like much," he said. I nodded.

Dr. Daly told me, "The Indians—I'm referring to the Native American ones—advocate using every part of a dead animal. I'll save the bodies until I think of something to do with them." So he took out each of the fish and put them into a glass bowl that was holding his change. We both looked at those fish lying there for a few seconds, and when we looked back up at each other it was like there was an understanding between us, like we were on the same page and we knew it.

"Let's talk about your legs," Dr. Daly said. "According to your latest x-rays, your knees are mending tremendously. The fractures are almost invisible. Everything's in place for you to regain full mobility."

It wasn't like I thought I would never walk again, but I guess that I hadn't considered that it was something I could be striving for so soon. "You're serious? Really? I can't tell you how great that is to hear," I said, which was a lot less than I had in my heart.

Then everything was being set into motion. "When you start working with Sascha—she'll be your trainer; we call them trainers here—this afternoon, I don't want you to push yourself too hard. She'll tell you this too. It's better to start out slow and work up to your maximum ability than it is to overextend yourself on the first try, and wake up tomorrow feeling like the Tin Man. Your knees will heal. I assure you. They will. So let them. A lot of patients don't feel the results while they're training. Sometimes bodies can be on a delay of sorts. Keep that in mind."

When he was reassuring me that my knees would heal, it was almost like God telling me that. Okay, not God, but someone who knew a lot more than me. "Thanks," I told him. "I will."

Then I met Sascha, and my first thought was that her thighs were like cannons. Huge and thick, and that made me confident about what she could do for my own legs. I mean, just the sight of her made me feel like an Olympian, to receive the personal attention of that caliber of thighs. They were disproportionate to the rest of her. She was like a satyr who'd shaved her legs.

I thought she was going to say something like "You ready to get pumped?" but instead she was surprisingly normal and calm. She asked me, "Have you tried walking at all since the incident?"

"No," I said. I looked down at my knees, like they were going to tell me why I hadn't even tried. I was amazed that the thought hadn't even occurred to me before she suggested it. "I don't know why I haven't, though, now that you ask. I think I assumed that I wasn't supposed to."

"You'll walk," Sascha told me.

We spent hours slowly bending and unbending my knees with different machines and weights, and at the very end of the session, I got on a treadmill with handrails. Sascha put it on a low, low speed, and before I could even grasp the importance of what I was doing, I was walking. I was holding onto the rails and going about ten inches an hour, but still, I was walking. How many things in our lives we take for granted! I looked at Sascha with awe, like I had reached, I don't know, the top of Mount Everest and was viewing the world from a startling height, and I said, "I'm going to be fine."

When I got back to the infirmary, you were sitting in bed, reading a book for class. I thought you looked pale. You heard the door and glanced up.

"Oh my god!" you shouted, because I was on crutches.

Robin, that dehydrated/food-poisoned sophomore who was staying in the infirmary, even said, "Wow!" and she barely knew me.

I hopped into the room, seeing it from my new level, and the first thing I noticed was that the view out the windows was different. Before, from across the room, I'd been looking at branches. Now I could see down to the sidewalk on the other side of the street. I remember on that day there was a group of Brown kids, and I even recognized one of the guys. I'd met him at a party freshman year and we'd gone to Johnny Rockets afterward.

"You look tall to me," you said, and I suddenly realized that you'd never seen me at my full height. And I realized that in a weird way, that meant you, in the physical sense, had never seen me for real.

You asked me what the doctor said, and I basically told you that my right knee was almost completely healed, so I could put pressure on it, and that the left one was coming along. And then I disguised the physical therapy experience in something like one or two casual sentences.

Suddenly, you stood up on your bed because you were actually that excited for me. I was so touched, El. You yelled,

"I'm unbelievably happy for you!" and I remember looking over at Robin, and seeing that she was staring at you like you were a freak.

"Thanks, El," I said. "Your support means the world to me."

"This makes me happy," you told me. "And I'm so happy to feel happy right now. That sounded simple, but I mean it."

"Believe me, baby. I'm also happy," I said.

We had some fun on the crutches that afternoon, and when you told me that you'd never been on crutches before, I was taken aback. I didn't say anything, but I had sort of assumed that throughout your childhood, you had broken or sprained a lot of parts.

But you told me, "I've never broken or sprained anything in my life."

And I said, "That's funny."

And you said, "Well, not funny in a laugh-out-loud way."

While you were messing around on my crutches, Robin tugged on my arm as I was passing by her bed. "I wanted to give you my congratulations, too. So, congratulations."

"Thanks," I replied. "You know, that's really decent of you to say." I felt this instant kinship with her, and over the new few weeks, that feeling spread to the rest of the community around me. I had the sense that everybody was rooting for me. I'd honestly forgotten how good and unpredictably kind people could be.

You suggested that we celebrate, that we should mark the occasion, and you told me that we could do anything I wanted. You even suggested bribing Vivian to go get us some alcohol, when I knew you couldn't have any because of your medication.

I knew exactly what I wanted to do, though. It had been so long—*so long*—since I'd sung.

"A singing night?" you asked.

"A singing night," I confirmed. It occurred to me that just like I hadn't tried to walk in ages, I hadn't tried to sing in ages either. The last time I'd attempted a song was the night of the accident. "I feel like singing, what can I say? I feel even more like watching *you* sing. I want to hear what you sound like."

You weren't thrilled with the idea, but in the end you figured that the day I got the use of my knees back was at least equivalent to a birthday in terms of momentousness, and if it had actually been my birthday, you would have humored me. "I can sing anything I want?" you asked.

"That's part of the beauty of a capella. You can sing anything you want because you don't need accompaniment."

But you said that you'd rather sing with music, which took me aback. You said that you liked the way it filled the space. I didn't want to spend the rest of the night trying to educate you about the superiority of the solo voice, so I was like fine, okay, whatever, but maybe I should have tried to stop you because then I might not have had to see what I did.

When you walked out of the infirmary I had no idea what you were doing, but you came back with a mini boom box from the storage closet. Then you got down on your knees and pulled your suitcase out from under the bed to get your CD.

I practically had to tear myself away from the window because the night looked so alive and the snow so bright it made me want to go sprint into it. I sat down on our bed and told you I couldn't wait to hear your voice. I was probably more excited than you realized, because I think that singing can be more personal than sex. It's like a person's true voice is hidden in everyday speech, and you only hear what's really underneath when they're performing a song.

I thought you were going to start then, but first you unplugged the lamp from our bedside table and moved it over near the fireplace. I said, "What's that for?" and I don't know if you heard me or not, but you didn't answer. When you went and asked Robin if you could borrow the metal IV stand she'd been using, she shot me a glance like I was supposed to know what was going on. I just shrugged, figuring that you knew what you were doing.

You rolled that stand over to the fireplace and said, "Okay. I'm ready," and I think I said something like "Hey, I'm intrigued."

After you pressed "play" on the boom box and turned up the volume, you walked over to the door and turned off all the lights. I sort of recognized the song's bouncy opening chords, since I had heard them somewhere before, but I couldn't place a title or artist. It definitely wasn't a song in my group's repertoire.

Then the lamp on the floor clicked on at the exact same time as the first word of the first verse:

"Girlfriend in a coma."

You were lying on the floor illuminated from below, the light throwing shadows on your features. You looked like you were at a campfire holding a flashlight under your chin. Like you were going to tell us a scary story, and you were trying to look as creepy as possible.

You'd pulled the IV stand down on a diagonal, and you sang into it, your "microphone," like a strung-out junkie collapsed on the floor. I swear, that's the image I thought of when I saw you like that. I guess it was a coincidence that you were wearing your white long johns that night, but that outfit made you look even skinnier than usual. You looked like you were all one piece except for your hair. In that light the edges of your long johns blended into your skin, which was a really bizarre effect.

And your singing voice was also a big shock to me. You know, your speaking voice is pretty muted, and although I know that part of the softness is because of everything that's happened to your lungs, I kind of suspected that it had always been that way. But your singing voice was so sharp and concise, it seemed like someone else was singing out from inside your body. Robin and I talked about it later and she said that she thought you sounded like you were possessed.

I had also never seen you "pretend" before, or perform, or whatever I should call what it was you were doing. I was the most bewildered when you flipped yourself over onto all fours and acted like you were the boyfriend in the song. You pretended that you were watching over a comatose girlfriend on the ground. This was especially fucked up because the invisible person you were tending to was "lying" where you'd just been lying, so it was like you were trying to take care of your self from five seconds ago. It was really hard to watch. You were making these motions like you were trying to care for the invisible patient.

I never want to hear that song again. You started crawling along the length of the IV stand, singing to a doctor who wasn't there, wanting to know if his patient would pull through.

Then you put the IV stand into a vertical position and you grasped onto it, climbing it with your hands until you were standing up, too. Do you even remember doing any of this? It was like you were in another world. You kept the top end of your "mic" really close to your lips, and you placed the lower end of it between your thighs. And you sang straight to me.

I wanted to get up and press "stop" on the boom box and flick on the lights, but I felt paralyzed.

Toward the end of the song, you began to fold backward like you were breaking first from your neck, then your shoulders, then your spine, then your knees. Your legs started shaking from the exertion—even the shadow that you threw on the wall was shaking.

What a horrible song! Who would write lyrics like that, and why? Not "who" like "who's the artist," but what kind of person, I mean?

With your head tilted back toward the floor, all I could see was an abstract profile of your chin and moving mouth, and from that angle you looked nothing like yourself.

You sang, *"I know—It's serious."*

Finally done, you crumpled onto the floor, your hair pooled in the circle of light under the lamp. You reached out and hit the power button. I remember that the heater was the only thing left making a sound.

I think it took me at least a minute to speak. I had to wait for all these awful thoughts to pass so that I wouldn't say something I'd regret later.

"That wasn't funny" is what I ultimately said.

You propped yourself up on your elbows. The light behind your head made the top of your hair look like it was catching on fire. "Oh, come on," you said. "Yes it was."

"No." I was wringing my hands underneath the covers, where you couldn't see. "It wasn't."

"I know," you said, and I thought you were agreeing with me, apologizing to me. But then you laughed, singing, "I know—it's serious," and I realized you were just quoting the song. That night was either the beginning or end of something—whichever way you want to look at it—but it was definitely something.

CHAPTER 25

PAXIL CR • Get back to being you

Here we are. I've reached the present. First I'll say, Happy Valentine's Day. I thought about what I wanted to get you for at least a month because I didn't want it to be something dumb. Everything I thought of seemed too small. I kept getting frustrated by how impossible it is to ever make another person understand how you see him. For example, maybe there was a day when we were just lying in bed, reading, and that's how you remember it. You don't know that right then I was falling in love with you. When I think about all the moments like that, it makes me sad to grasp how separate people will always be, no matter how hard they try to be close. Every second a million things get lost. They flash through my head, but they don't get out to you. All these things that I've ever thought about you or us are stuck inside me, and I keep thinking that maybe you've really got no idea. I believe that you know I love you. You just don't know the specifics. That's not your fault or my fault. I think that if we have to place blame somewhere, it's on our bodies. They're not equipped to project thoughts outside themselves. They're not equipped to absorb outside thoughts either. This gets me down.

I think that even though it's an insurmountable job to put those thoughts on the table, I have to try. Telling stories is exhausting, and sometimes I get scared that I'll be telling the same stories for the rest of my life, trying to acquaint new people with my past until I become this factory of repetition. Sometimes I think that if I have to fill in those holes one more time, I'll never say anything worthwhile again. That's part of why this overwhelming collection of thoughts about you has been so important for me. Finally, I have something to tell you, or at least to try to tell you, that hasn't been hashed out before. I've wanted to tell you everything from the inside out. The overriding problem is that there's just too much of it.

Then last week I thought of writing you this letter. I would start at the beginning, from the very first time that I knew you existed. I would go through every moment that I could remember thinking something major, and it wouldn't even matter if you had been in the room because you hadn't been in my brain.

I remember watching this segment on the news the summer before I came here. A psychologist ran a test where he asked a group of people to watch a tape of students passing balls to each other. He asked the people to count the number of times that the balls had been passed. Even when focused on the task, they came back with a lot of different numbers. There was more, though.

The doctor had dressed up a man in a big bear suit and instructed him to walk through the middle of the game. Not a single person remembered having seeing a bear. I think he waved, too. They were shocked when the doctor played back the tape for them and told them simply to watch it without trying to count the number of passes. There was the bear, clear as day. They were horrified that they'd missed him. Their faces almost looked scared, like all of a sudden they were realizing all of the other things throughout their lives that they might have been blind to.

Here's another example: car accidents. No one ever remembers seeing the same thing. One witness says the blue car braked unexpectedly. Another says, wrong, it was the red one that accelerated for no reason. Everybody's traumatized in a different way. Everybody's operating in their own, distinct universes. We've been doing it, too, but that's just how it goes.

I know that human beings are self-absorbed because that's the way we're built. Like I said before, we literally absorb ourselves. Still, we're missing things way smaller than bears walking through our lives all the time. Smaller, but more significant because they're personal comments on us, not just our lack of decent observation skills. Even lying in the same bed, you and I are living radically different lives. It's disheartening, but true.

I didn't think that writing a letter like this would solve that distance. That wasn't what I was aiming for. I only hoped that it would help a little. Sometimes I can feel myself getting incrementally better, healthwise. Even though, overall, I'm aware that I'm still sick, that slight sensation of getting better means the world to me. I hope it's like that for us. Obviously, you're never really going to know what it's like to be me, and I'm never going to know what it's like to be you. There will always be a rift that's bigger than our best intentions. Still, I think that the simple act of trying is worth a lot. That's what I wanted to give to you for Valentine's Day.

An incomplete and naïve, but well-intentioned, account of what I've been seeing all this time. If any of it is unrecognizable to you, then the good news is that that means we're getting somewhere.

I've been writing in the hospital, in the waiting room, after you've gone to bed. One final admission: that day last week when I told you that I was working on the paper about health care in Canada, I was working on this letter. This is probably one of the biggest valentines ever, in terms of sheer length. I hope you like it more than you'd like a shirt or chocolate or whatever custom says that I'm supposed to get you. If you really want some chocolate, I'm sure I can arrange it. Just let me know, so I don't have to read your mind.

I love you. A lot. I definitely do.

—Elodie.

CHAPTER 26

From The Desk of Chester Hunter III

I felt like such a dickhead when you gave me your letter on Valentine's Day. That letter took me three days to read and I didn't know what it contained at the time. But I felt like a dickhead because you had come up with an amazing, one-of-a-kind token of your feelings, and all I had for you was a fucking bracelet.

I'd wanted to do lots and lots of candles for you, but Vivian and Sarah wouldn't let me because of that fire in that girl's room in Keeney at the beginning of the month. I guess the university sent out a "no tolerance" policy to everyone, just because of that one girl's mistake. I couldn't believe that the nurses were going to enforce the memo, since I felt and still feel that the infirmary should be considered a separate arm of the school with its own laws.

I loved that night of the fire, by the way. Watching everyone running out of the building across the street in towels and embarrassing, secret pajamas, and us kneeling in the dark, spying on all of them. It was like we knew something about human behavior that no one else did is the best way I can put it for you. I think that I haven't had that many moments in my life where I've been able just to freely watch other people without, you know, being watched myself. That night it was like we were one pair of eyes, and even though your letter argued against this idea, also one mind.

Anyway, I just wanted to tell you now that I'd envisioned lighting rows of red candles along the walls of the infirmary, and then putting white ones on the windowsills. I was going to make the infirmary look like someplace else for you, and that would have been way better than the bracelet.

When David walked in on Valentine's Day, all of a sudden I realized that I hadn't talked to or seen him in ages. Spotting him in the doorway was like being put into the Witness Protection Program, and then running into someone from my old, erased life. Like I was living in a town in the middle of nowhere and using a completely new name, and then out of the blue, David showed up in my grocery store to get some milk—that's how I felt.

When I asked him, "What are you doing here?" and he said, "I came to give you another certificate. I registered my penis in your name"—now that you've read about that first visit, you know what he was talking about.

I never showed you the star stuff, I think because it depressed me too much to even look at it. I wanted to be a fresh slate while I got to know you. But I laughed when he said he was giving me his penis, and after that joke, it was suddenly like David and I both kind of understood we'd each been ridiculous the last time we saw each other. I think at that moment, we mutually understood that we should really just toss all of that old shit to the wind.

Sarah came and told you that you had a phone call at the desk, and you left the room.

When we were alone, David told me that Marna had

dragged him to a bad party at a frat, and he'd partly left it to go get some cigarettes and partly because he just wanted to leave. On his way to the East Side Market, when he was crossing to get to the other side of Waterman, someone hit him on the head with something heavy and pretty hard. I asked him what he was hit with, he said, "I think I was clocked with medium-sized rocks in a cotton sock." And then he started laughing because that sounded like the world's worst song. So he began to dance while singing, "Med-ium sized rocks in a cott-on sock. Med-ium sized rocks in a cott-on sock."

After he got hit, he fell to the ground and cracked open his head on the concrete, and that's why he was in the infirmary that night. The ER said that he needed to be woken up every hour because of his concussion.

When David was in the hospital, the police showed up to question him, but since he'd been hit from behind, he didn't see who did it. He brought up my attack to them, and they were really interested in that connection. I couldn't think of any common enemies we might have, but David and I used to go everywhere together, so maybe there was someone who hated us both. Why, I don't know. Because while I'm not going to say that we're the best people on the planet, it's not like we're the worst either.

I was also laughing when David told me that the cops asked him if he'd gotten any hate mail or strange letters lately, and he told them, "I got an invitation from Hillel last week and I'm not Jewish." (He is Jewish.)

Then I found out that all these other people had been getting attacked after I landed in the infirmary, and I felt like

I was in some alternate universe, some Twilight Zone, because I hadn't even known.

David asked me, "Haven't you been reading the *Herald*?" And I realized that you and I had never even picked up a paper. We could have gotten one easily, asked one of the nurses to bring it in the morning with our toast. But you and I, when you think about it, really had no clue what was going on outside.

I was so confused. "Wait, why haven't any of these people passed through the infirmary?"

David told me that me, him, and that kid who got shot in the throat got the worst of it. The other people were in and out of the hospital in a few hours. Some girl was pushed into bushes, but she only got scratched up, so it wasn't that big of a deal. And there was a sophomore who passed someone wearing a hood, then felt a prick in his arm. He thought the guy had injected lethal poison into him, like that umbrella case in Russia. The doctors found a small hole where the prick was, so he wasn't lying, but they ran every test in the world and he came out clear. And then, as David puts it, "The pussy took the rest of the semester off and went home to Buffuck, Missouri." David asked me, "Doesn't anyone talk around here?" and I told him that the person I generally talked to was you, and that you wouldn't know anything more than I would, anyway.

Not one of us had gotten a good look at our attackers, so the cops didn't have any suspects.

By the time David was done telling me his whole story—and he takes a really long time telling stories because he's always talking about who he's going to sue—I was tired. So I told him I was going to sleep. You still weren't back.

And then he said, "Wait—"

And I said, "Yeah?"

Out of the blue he said, "You haven't missed me?"

I was surprised by the question. But I told him that I did miss him, which was true. I just hadn't said it out loud.

"You missed me so much you haven't called me once during the past three months?"

I tried to explain to him that absence has never made my heart fonder, and that he shouldn't take it personally. "But now that you're here, I can say to you that I've missed you," I said. "We had good times. I miss our times." I thought we were done with that, so I started to roll over and get settled under the covers, figuring that you'd be in soon.

David said, "Hold on."

"What is it?"

"Don't go to sleep. I have to get woken up every hour anyway, so the sleep isn't even worth having. That's like, crack whore sleep." He wanted to stay up and talk all night, get refamiliarized with each other's lives. First he was trying to convince me that I did the same thing every night—sleeping—and that I should try to break it up for once. Then he tried to sell me on how exciting it would be not to sleep, saying things like "We'll get that soldier feeling when the morning comes, like we've pummeled through it."

I told him that I really wanted to talk to him and catch up on everything, but I'd just had physical therapy and needed to recharge.

Again, David said, "Wait."

I was exasperated with him and completely snapped, asking what his problem was. I said, "Listen, I'm not staying up, so fucking drop it."

I guess it was me acting like that that finally made David get very intense about what he needed to say. Because his facial expression shifted, and I could see that he was done with the "Waits" and was ready to make a declaration.

"I'm going to talk about something that we can both attribute to the drugs later," he said, and he got out of his bed and squatted down on the floor next to mine (ours). He was rocking back and forth with his hands locked. He reminded me of a coach I used to have in high school, who would pull the same move when he was with us in the locker room. David would only look at his knuckles, not at me.

"What's going on?" I asked.

"I'm on hospital painkillers," David told me, taking his hands apart so he could write on the floor with his finger. I honestly can't be positive about this, but I thought he was spelling out my name. "Just like you were the last time we saw each other. Maybe I told you I felt all right a half hour ago, that I was clear-headed and in control of my memory, but maybe that was the drugs talking. You don't know. Who knows? Not me.

"If things go well during the next minute," David said, "it's all right for us to remember them. If they don't, though—" he knocked on wood, the floor—"then we'll attribute everything to the drugs, and both forget that I ever started talking like this tonight."

It was a mistake to say that to me, because as soon as he told me I might need to eventually ignore the information,

I began to make sure that I was giving him my whole attention. I told him something along those lines, and he thought I was making fun of him.

"I'm not bullshitting you. Here," he said. Then it came out.

"I'm going to tell you right now that I've had feelings for you before. When I got to this school, people talked about this air you supposedly had about you, and I was like, 'I'm going to check out this air.' No one really knew you and they were saying 'Chess is this,' and 'Chess is that,' and I encountered all of the hype before I even met you. It was as if people were making this colossal commercial for you, and I didn't even know you, but there was this image and this picture that I was given of you.

"And then when we actually came face to face I could have bought into it, but I don't operate that way, you get it? I saw the parts of you that I liked and wanted not because of your stupid, *je ne sais quoi* image, but because I was aesthetically drawn to you. And I don't mean just the outside. I mean there was something from my gut that drew me toward you. I have a very definite sense of what I like, and it cuts through the rest of everything. And my aesthetics for you were so strong that I've had this, I don't know, crush on you, not because of some loser Brown kids and the stories about what you did at this party or what you said during that history section. Who cares. Or rather, I was somewhat in love with you for a while there, and don't even try to tell me that that didn't come from the gut, because you think I *wanted* to be in love with you? I didn't. Is unrequited love ever fun for anyone? No. Never."

After the "never," which I remember distinctly, David's

mouth stayed open like there was more that was about to come out. I couldn't even imagine what more there could possibly be, because his speech covered everything, or at least it did for me. But after about thirty seconds I realized that he was at a loss for words.

Maybe I should be embarrassed to admit how I felt about his confession because I'm aware that it was a very self-absorbed reaction. But within me it produced, more than anything else, déjà vu. It wasn't that David had ever told me any of this before, but that a more nostalgic, broad-spectrum feeling of being wanted and loved came over me. Maybe I'm being an asshole to the rest of the world, David and you included, by being the kind of guy who would have this kind of reaction, but I think that I'd be an asshole to myself if I didn't.

Maybe you won't believe this at all, but I'm really doing my best to keep you from hating me. Please understand that before the attack, El, there had always been what I can only describe as an energy that sustained me from one minute to the next. There was this tension in my stratosphere that miraculously kept me assured that I was welcome in every place I showed up. To put it more clearly, it wasn't that this is what I thought, but what I just knew, and so I was never responsible for it even passing across my brain.

Basically, David's confession didn't produce shock in me. There was a positive aspect to my nonshock because it prevented me from doing something terrible like jerking back in surprise or reacting uncomfortably to the news. Because while yes, the bearer of the news was surprising, I have to admit that the content was familiar. Being around David again had taken me back to the point of missing him, but hearing that he'd had a secret crush on me took me even farther back, to a year I couldn't pinpoint if I tried.

The next thought I had was that I loved my friend, and that the last thing in the world I wanted to do was hurt him.

So I asked him something like "You're saying that your feelings for me were based on an aesthetic push?"

He seemed relieved that I was giving him an out. "Yes. Almost like the appreciation of an expert on the subject, like—" But he stopped short there and never gave me an example.

"Then how can I argue with that," I said.

We were quiet for a while because we each knew where the other stood. After some time David asked me, "Am I an idiot?"

I told him no, I didn't think so, and he wanted me to explain why not.

I said that the truth was that I was involved with you, and that I owed it to myself to see how our relationship would play out because it was an enormous, unbelievable thing. I told him that you were where I was at right then.

I remember saying, "There's this stuff—I feel stuff—that I've never felt before." And that no matter what he said that night, it wouldn't make a difference. Because there was you.

David, since he's a master at it, decided to argue his way back out of what we'd been talking about, and he made a case for the past half hour being like a quick-moving flu. He told me how when he's sick everything takes place on a different plane that resembles the normal one, except it's way more concentrated. He said, "I get this feeling like I'm operating outside of the human race. I'm on a different clock, seeing parts of the night that I usually don't, babbling about things that I usually don't, acting in ways I usually don't."

And then we were on the same plane because I knew exactly what he was talking about, having been living in the infirmary with you.

"What should we do, then?" he asked.

I said that we should go to sleep.

"I mean about the drugs I'm on," David said.

I told him that everything was fine and everything was going to stay fine, and he seemed to believe me fully. He said "okay," that he'd live with that, and he got up from the floor.

I asked him to turn out the overhead light since I was settled in bed, and while he was over at the switch, I heard Adrian, that guy who had mono and was really cranky, whisper to David, "I heard everything."

David turned off the light, then whispered back. "I could give less of a fuck what you heard. I'm not in love with you."

• • •

When I woke up early the next morning, I saw that I was in bed alone. I sat up, completely alarmed because that had never happened since we started sleeping together. The bed frame hit the wall. That woke David up.

"Elodie's not here," I said to him. "I don't know if she ever came back to the room last night."

And he told me, "I saw her last night."

"Back here?"

"No," David said. "I saw her after you went to sleep. I couldn't relax, so I went for a walk. Inside.

"I heard Elodie's voice down this hallway that's sort of

to the left if you just keep walking straight from here away from the stairs." He pointed. "So I went over there, and I looked around the corner to see if she was still on the phone or if she was talking to a nurse."

David stopped like he was nervous about telling me what was next, but I told him to keep going.

"I could barely make her out because she was sitting in the dark, but she was just there in the corner. Talking to herself. I'm saying like, a full-on conversation, Chess, with manic gesticulating and everything. It was fucking weird. Really fucking weird, you understand? It went on for a long time. There was nobody else there and there was definitely no phone."

I knew that there were people who talked to themselves, but I didn't know that you were one of them. I told David that I thought it was possible that you were working through personal issues with that technique, and if that's what you had to do, that's what you had to do.

When I was explaining this to him, you came through the door of the infirmary, looking like you were halfway to falling apart. You were all hunched over, and your hair was a big storm cloud. You looked really sick, almost shockingly, deathbed ill, and my first thought was that you had contracted something new and terrible. When you saw David and me awake, you said, "I fell asleep in the hallway."

I regarded you. And I just didn't want to know. So I said, "Okay," and that's why that was all I said.

CHAPTER 27

THE JOURNAL OF PARAPSYCHOLOGY OCTOBER 2004

In mid-February, I answered the doorbell early one morning and found E on my front step. She was slumped against the banister and looked as if she'd been beaten while walking to my house. Alarmed, I asked her if she'd walked here.

"Don't worry," she said. "I took a cab."

Once we were seated on the couch, E informed me that she was in serious pain because she'd fallen asleep leaning against a hallway wall. This had badly aggravated her fibromyalgia. When I asked her to describe the current degree of pain, E told me that she felt as if "someone gripped my neck and ankles and wrung me out."

E rarely spoke to me about her fibromyalgia, even though I knew it was a constant presence in her life. The only two other moments on record that she discusses the illness are (1) in November, when she described the sensation it produces as similar to "being covered with bruises that run seven inches deep" and (2) in January, when she referred to it, interestingly, as "moss with teeth."

I asked her why she hadn't phoned me and asked me to come to her, and she replied that after a night spent mostly awake in the infirmary, she'd wanted a morning outside of it.

"So what happened to prompt this visit?" I asked.

E reached into the pocket of her coat and produced the tape recorder that I'd purchased for her. She pressed "play." I heard her voice saying, "Come on. You? Give me a break."

For an instant, there was loud crackling on the tape. It did not sound like externally captured static, but instead like an internal default located within the recording.

Then E's voice returned, and the crackling ceased entirely. "I think you're dead, to begin with." E stopped the tape and said to me, "That crackling you hear is him talking."

"The apparition?"

"Yes."

Initially, I misunderstood. "That's what he sounds like when he speaks to you? And you are able to translate?"

"No," E said. "He doesn't sound like that when I'm next to him. He speaks good, normal English then. That crackling is what comes out when I record him."

I asked E to play the beginning of the tape again, and this time I concentrated on the variations in the crackling sound. I wanted to determine if there were any patterns within the distortion, or if I could make out any traces of a human voice beneath the static. (In recent EVP [electronic voice phenomenon] research I'd been studying, observers had been able to detect faint voices beneath static on audio recordings.) However, I detected nothing.

"So what happened exactly?" I asked E again.

"We had a long conversation," she replied.

E told me that earlier in the evening, she'd received a phone call from her father. Because it was her father on the line, she immediately knew that something was wrong, as it was always her mother who spoke first. Frantic, S told E, "Your mom is gone."

"What do you mean?" E asked. She told me that she was concerned that "gone" might be her father's synonym for "dead."

E's father proceeded to explain that her mother had encountered a man selling blue roses at a stoplight on a local street divider. Not only had A envisioned a field of blue roses, "growing like wheat," on the day that their previous oven leaked gas into their home, but this man also happened to have A's name tattooed upon his arm.

E hadn't known that her mother had been in search of the meaning of the blue roses. A had not brought that up during any of their previous conversations.

A had told S that she believed she'd been placed at that particular stoplight for a reason, and that she and the man were "key and lock." E had seen this behavior from her mother before. "Sometimes she comes across a person when she's trying to figure out a message, and she thinks she and that person are like two undercover agents. She thinks they're supposed to exchange information."

Unfortunately, the man with the roses readily played into this suspicion and invited A back to his home to explore their connection further.

"She didn't go home with him, did she?" I asked, and E told me that that was the exact question she'd asked her father.

"She's there now," S had answered. "That's where she called me from."

E confessed that for most of her life she'd avoided her

mother's premonitions and stories, and that everyone (mother and daughter included) had assumed this was because their dispositions were so opposite. Yet while on the phone with her father, E had become aware that what she'd feared most wasn't that A would derail E's life, but that A would destroy her own. She had long had the foresight, so to speak, that A's beliefs would lead A to an act of desperation. E felt that act was close at hand.

S begged E to call her mother on her (A's) cell phone. He said that because A was particularly sensitive to E's opinion, he believed that E could convince her to come home.

E wanted to know how long A planned on staying at the man's home, and S said that all he knew was that A had stated that she was not coming home until she and the man understood the sign.

E promised that she would phone A "as soon as I've figured out what to say."

Troubled by the conversation with her father, E felt that she wasn't ready to return to the infirmary. C and an old friend were in there, and E did not want to explain her distracted state to a stranger.

After the call, E had followed the main hallway down to its end, then turned the corner. At the farthest examination room, she lowered herself against the locked door and rested on the floor. The hall was completely "dark, since it doesn't have any windows." E said that she was glad for the darkness because the atmosphere was conducive to composing the talk she was going to have with A.

E had been sitting on the floor "no longer than five minutes" when the apparition in the robe came around the corner. As he had before, he was "glowing in the dark." The apparition stopped and simply said, "Hey."

At this point, E placed her recorder on my coffee table. "I'm going to let it run," she said, "and I'll do my best to fill in what the ghost said to me. Are you ready?" Checking my own recorder to make sure I had enough tape, I told her, "Yes. Please proceed."

On her tape, I recognized the same piece of speech that she'd played earlier. "Come on. You? Give me a break."

"What's wrong with me?" the present E asked, filling in for the nonpresent apparition. To avoid confusion, I will simply attribute the speech E remembered to the apparition. While enacting the apparition's end of the conversation, E maintained her regular tone and expression, as though she was in conversation with herself.

On her tape, E said, "I think you're dead, to begin with. Why don't you tell me? Tell me what you're doing here." She told me that the apparition looked thoughtful, as if he might concede to her request.

After a pause, E's voice continued. "I'd really like to know. But right now, I'm not going to help you solve whatever it is you're stuck here for. If you need me to contact someone, dig something up, I'm not going to be of much service to you. You should have taken care of it before tonight, when I wasn't feeling as distracted. Tonight, I'm the wrong girl for this. I don't have the mindset."

The apparition walked toward E. She "didn't know if he was going to leap into my body and seize it. Or put a finger on my forehead and transmit images from his life into my brain. I really had no idea what he was capable of. According to my mom, ghosts are capable of a lot." He surprised E by stopping about two feet from her and sliding down against the wall, just as she had done minutes ago. He bent his knees and hung his arms over them.

E was so close to the apparition that she could have reached out and put a hand through his chest.

"Why didn't you?" I asked later.

"Because I wanted to hear what he had to say."

While in close proximity to the apparition, E remembered the hairs at the nape of her neck lifting, "which was a first. I thought of myself as generally hairless there. Toward the bottom." She became "aware of every one of my body parts. Although it sounds strange now, I think I was the most aware of where each fingernail and each eyelash was in relation to his 'body.'" She instructed me to put the word "body" in quotations.

I reached out and paused the tape. "Was this a fearful reaction?"

"It was more the feeling of sitting next to a crush," she answered.

"You have romantic feelings for the apparition?"

"I'm not ready to say it was romantic. It was more romantic than fearful, if I have to choose one of those options."

"How do you distinguish the two?"

"I was nervous around him. I wasn't scared."

"Did you have butterflies?" I asked. I couldn't come up with a more scientific-sounding inquiry.

"I did. Yes. I did have butterflies."

"All right, then. Let's continue." I restarted the tape. There was a seventeen-second pause that had neither E's voice nor the crackling on it. Around second ten, I asked her, "What's occurring at this point?"

E told me that the apparition was looking at her, and she had held his gaze.

Then the crackling returned. E asked if she could hear her response to the apparition's speech, since during our pause, she had lost her place. Once she heard her "No," she was ready to continue. She rewound.

"The reason I'm here is probably supposed to be embarrassing," the apparition said, "but I don't feel embarrassed about it yet. You're not easily offended, are you?"

"No," E said.

"While I was in the hospital I asked one of the nurses, 'What are the odds?' and she didn't even want to guess."

"I've found out that most people in the hospital really don't like to guess," E said.

"You can tell me your opinion on the odds, okay?" the apparition suggested.

"Okay."

"The other afternoon I was reading an Internet article on fetishes. Because I like to learn as much as I can about how other people live."

"That's big of you. Sort of," said E.

"Well, that makes me sound much more innocent than I am." E remembers the apparition smiling here. "So to clear things up between you and me, I don't do all this learning because I'm a noble humanist. It's so I can find out if I share anything with anyone. Anything that maybe I didn't know about on my own."

"Oh. I follow you," said E.

"Cool. There was a section on autoerotic asphyxiation. The writer made it sound like one of those major interests that might define a person."

"Did you feel like you had a responsibility to find out if you fell into this category?"

"Yeah." Here again E remarked that the apparition smiled at her, and that he was "quick to break into a smile for someone who did not have a smiley face." By this I presume that she was referring to the natural crookedness of his mouth and the deep, dark bags beneath his eyes.

"A responsibility," he said. "That's good."

"Thanks. How'd you do it?"

"With a sheet, some thick books to stand on, and the top hook in my closet. I thought the hook was securely embedded in the wall, but it turns out that I'm no engineer. Here's where it's supposed to get really embarrassing. Are you still with me?"

"I'm fine with hearing about you masturbate," said E. "Even though I think you're dead, which is what makes it weird."

"That's fair. Back to the story. I followed the technique described in the article, but I wasn't that impressed. I felt some lightheadedness, and I saw some stars, but I can get the same effects by hanging upside down off the edge of my bed and rubbing my eyes with my knuckles." The apparition demonstrated this action to the best of his transparent ability. "So, as it turns out—I'm not a member of the club."

"Sorry," said E.

"And so was I, a little bit."

"Are you going to keep looking for things in common? Or are you too discouraged now?"

"I hope I'm an open-minded person. I hope when I get out of here, I'll keep looking. But it seems like I keep returning to what I was in the first place," the apparition said. "Can't help it. I'd bet that you keep returning, too."

"Me?"

"I can tell."

"When does the story get embarrassing?" E asked.

E told me that the apparition's "eyes were not serious at all, but he pretended to get serious with me."

"Look," he said, "This story is for you. I know what happened. I'm not telling it for my health."

"I can see right through you," E said, and then she must have realized what she had said and how absurd it sounded. "I mean, I can see right through what you just told me. You like talking to me. I can tell."

The apparition leaned closer to E. "I'm trying to connect with you. That's a pretty embarrassing thing to own up to, don't you think? Making the admission that I'm putting effort into connecting? Pretty bad. Pr-ettt-yyyy bad."

E told me that their faces were extremely close together by now. She found herself in the strange situation of both looking in and through the apparition's eyes.

"Are we really having a conversation?" asked E. "I believe that you exist. But are we in a conversation together, or is this leftover talk from back in the day? Are the moments where it seems like we're actually talking to each other coincidence?"

"To me," the apparition told E, "everything always feels like coincidence. Speaking always seems dicey."

"I know what you mean," said E.

"After I passed out and woke up in the hospital, my wrists were secured because they thought that I'd been trying to kill myself. I looked at the nurse and said, 'Wasn't trying to kill myself.' But the more I said no, the more the nurse believed that I was. The more sincere I was, the more she disbelieved."

"Yeah. I know about that, too," said E.

"She even made me draw," said the apparition.

"I've had to draw before. Hey, look, I'm even helping you connect with me."

"I know. I'm liking it. Can I show you something?" the apparition asked.

"Well, okay."

"I asked them if I could have my last picture." The apparition reached into a pocket in his robe and pantomimed pulling a rectangular object out of it. He went through the motions of unfolding the invisible paper and spreading it out on the floor in front of E.

"What do you think?" he asked.

E looked down at the linoleum, where she saw only floor. "Nothing. I don't see anything."

"Yeah," the apparition said. "I put the pen in my wrong hand and dragged it around on the paper. The doctor asked me to explain what I'd drawn, and I said, 'my interpretation of hope.' Then they let me out of the ward."

E remembers smiling at that point as well. There is another pause on the tape during which there is neither E's voice nor magnetic distortion. After exactly six seconds, the distortion returns.

"Hey," said the apparition. "A question for you."

"Mmm hmm?"

"Have you ever had tetanus?"

"No," E said. "It's one of the few diseases I haven't."

"That's what I have. It's from hitting a lower hook on the way down."

"Is that how you died?" E asked. "From the tetanus?"

"No, I'm okay. It wasn't lethal, but I'm supposed to take it easy. They've told me to lie in bed as much as I can with the lights off."

"Since you're not doing that, maybe that's why you died?" guessed Elodie.

"I'm okay."

"If you say so. Maybe it's not what I think at all, and you walked outside and got hit by a car. Maybe you had a brain aneurysm." There is a short pause on the tape. "And maybe the man with the roses could tell that my mom was the type he could pull a mean trick on. Maybe she went looking for a man with roses. Maybe she lied about the roses. Maybe she's made a mistake about the roses, and she knows it. Maybe she's right about the roses. Maybe the roses really mean something."

E noticed that the apparition appeared to be waiting on her to finish her guessing. She ceased speaking to test the interactivity between them.

"Maybe?" the apparition asked.

E reached her hand out toward the apparition's, wanting to see what would happen if she attempted to hold it. Her fingers passed through his. The apparition did not seem to notice the gesture.

E continued on the tape. "Maybe I'll talk about nothing and fill up my side of the conversation with empty talk. Maybe you can go on without me. Maybe something special will happen when I stop playing along."

"Nah, don't do that," the apparition said.

"Oh. Why not?"

"Because we have limited time before we die." For accuracy, it must be recorded that the apparition smiled again.

"Right. You would know," E nodded.

"You and me," the apparition said.

"You and me?"

"And her too."

"Who's 'her'?"

"Your mom."

Elodie wanted to take hold of the apparition's shoulder but was clearly unable to do so. "What do you know about my mom?"

"I'm looking forward to meeting her. And not in the generic way that that sounds."

E had been concentrating on the apparition's eyes, but she couldn't determine if they were focused on her or if she happened to be in a convenient spot. They glowed faintly like the rest of him, but reflected no external light. "Can I ask you something?"

The apparition's eyes darted back and forth between E's eyes.

"Does she come and talk to all of you? Do you all know her? Know about her?" E asked.

The apparition's eyes stilled. "None of that matters."

"It doesn't?"

"No."

Elodie leaned back against the wall. She remembers that her spine was beginning to hurt. "I'm too tired to find out what that means. I want to sit here for a while and think."

"Okay, then," the apparition said. "I'll sit here with you."

The last thing E remembered was sitting in the dark hallway with the apparition for at least an hour. When she woke up, it was almost seven A.M., and there was no sign of him.

E stopped the tape. "All you've got to do is check hospital records for a psych ward patient with tetanus."

"And if it's all right with you," I added, "I'd like to take the tape with me. I'm going to locate an EVP researcher and have it analyzed."

"Okay," E said, just as my doorbell rang.

"It's the ghost," she joked. "He misses me."

I excused myself to answer the door. When I saw my student, R, on the doorstep, I realized I'd forgotten our breakfast appointment. Earlier in the week, I'd held a diagnostic contest in class using a corpse, and R had won. The prize was a personal breakfast at my house and a research assistant position the following semester.

I was about to apologize to R when he said, "E." The manner in which he said her name told me that he had not meant to utter it. The front doorway offers a clear view to the living-room couch. E was in profile, but when she heard her name, turned.

"Oh, hi, R," she replied.

"You two know each other?" I asked.

"I had a collapsed lung freshman year, and we met," said R, appearing suddenly disoriented.

"We had a thing for a minute," E said.

"Why are you here?" asked R.

"Dr. Kirschling is my doctor. We were having a discussion about my health."

"You're still sick?"

"And living in the infirmary," said E.

"Jesus Christ. You're still *there*?" (A week later, E told

me that the way R had said "there" was "how I imagine they say it at high school reunions. When people who've left town gasp, 'You're still living *there*?' Which is 'here' to the people who haven't.")

"Well, you're still *there,* too," said E.

R shook his head, confused, and looking at E as though she were impaired. "No, I'm not. I have an apartment on George."

"I meant that you're also still in the same place you were when I met you. You were going to school, training to be a doctor. You still are."

"That's not the same thing, though," R argued.

I watched the two of them, fascinated. I had never before had the chance to watch E interact at length with another "civilian," so to speak.

"We're both on the same tracks we were two years ago."

"You're sick, though. That's not a normal state of existence."

"I disagree," E said. An awkward pause followed.

R turned to me. "Should I leave? Did I get the time wrong?"

"I've got to get back," said E. She asked if she could make a quick phone call in my bedroom before she left. I said yes and followed her, assuming that her request had been code-speak for her desiring to have a private discussion with me. Thus, I was surprised when she picked up my phone and dialed. She did not seem to mind my presence.

After a few seconds, E said, "Mom?" Then, "I can see ghosts now. I'm serious. Please go home. I'll call you there tomorrow and tell you all about it."

E hung up and thanked me, saying she had kept her conversation short because she did not want "to ring up a huge long-distance charge."

"Well, what did your mother say?" I asked.

"She made a really pleased sound," E told me, then walked from the bedroom to my front door. Before she stepped outside, she pressed the tape into my palm. I asked her if she needed a ride or wanted me to call a cab, but she said, "I'm going to look into the bus."

"It was nice to see you again," called out R, although he fooled neither E nor myself. Once she had left, I tried unsuccessfully to get R to speak further about his time with E. I was interested in the signs of illness she'd been exhibiting during their affair, and how he had perceived them.

I now suspected that although E's symptoms *mimicked* documented illnesses, she did not necessarily have those illnesses. This is the crux of my theory of psychic puberty.

I believe that E was going through a similar breed of transitional turmoil, as her body was preparing for a major change. It was adjusting itself to the extrasensory powers that she was acquiring. I surmised that there were two probable outcomes: (1) that once E's abilities had fully manifested themselves, her health would return, or (2) that she would continue to experience symptoms for the remainder of her life, as her body constantly readjusted itself to the outside (supernatural) forces placing demands on it.

I favor the first scenario, since both her mother and grandmother eventually reached a point where their symptoms ceased. However, E's talents already seemed to supercede those of anyone else in her family. Hence, I felt that her path to equilibrium might prove much more challenging and prolonged.

The following day I mailed the tape to an EVP specialist in Missouri. He warned me that he had projects with higher priority, but I wanted the best in the field. While I waited for results, I resumed my hunt for the apparition's hospital records. I tried every hospital within fifty miles of Providence. Not one could identify a psychiatric patient with tetanus in the last fifty years. The apparition had asked E to guess the odds of his circumstances, but now I desired an educated guess about the odds of my own. Not a single local patient during the past half century with the same identifying characteristics? Not a single lead to follow?

True to his ghostly nature, this apparition had left no traces in the tangible world. E and I had no choice but to wait on the slight physical evidence that we had in our possession—the mysterious crackling on the tape. Whether coincidence or higher intervention—at this stage in my research into the paranormal, I feel ill equipped to even venture a hypothesis—the morning I finally received the analysis of the tape was the same morning that E finally learned who and what the apparition was.

CHAPTER 28

From The Desk of Chester Hunter III

I heard guys playing Ultimate Frisbee down in the street, and as dumb as it sounds, I was pleased I could tell what they were playing even without seeing them. This was the morning of the graduation dance. Also, I remember hearing demonstrators passing by the building. They were pissed off about sweatshops. Moving in the direction of the Main Green, they were chanting, "I won't wear anything with sweat on it!" Once I read an article about blind people and how their other senses sharpen to compensate for their eyes, and it featured a kid who could ride his bike only if he made clicking sounds. Basically, he had developed bat sonar. That's what went through my mind when I was listening to all the people outside—that maybe I'd developed special powers while removed from the operational world.

You were in bed looking through the doctors' porn, and you told me that you were interested in becoming a photographer. You said that you'd be able to stare at people through the lens, and they would be so preoccupied with you looking at them that they couldn't stare back at you.

The window was open. Pieces of your hair were blowing into the air in front of you. Your aplastic anemia was back, and you had a marrow transfusion scheduled for the next week, but you seemed less nervous than I thought you should be. I was working at the desk Vivian found me downstairs, needing to pull a B-minus on my Am Civ final. My professor had given me an extension. I didn't tell you, but my grades had slipped since I moved into the infirmary.

When I looked at you, I remember thinking, "It's like we've grown old together." Not that we had become decrepit or unattractive or anything like that, but I was filled with this feeling that we'd surpassed others around us and left everyone behind. We knew about pain. And, in general, I think we just knew about more.

I remember singing to you the line *"Ain't no mountain high enough,"* and asking what you thought about that lyric.

"Are you asking about climbing real mountains?" you asked.

"I'm more curious about whether or not you believe that if two people believe in each other, there's nothing that they can't accomplish."

And you said, "I think healthwise, we're two shitty candidates. But sure."

At physical therapy, they had reiterated to me almost every hour that the mind is more powerful than the body. And obviously, the mind is what loves. I know that in the infirmary, there were definitely moments when I felt I could do anything and be anyone, and that these moments had everything to do with you.

Dr. Daly and I were discussing the dominance of the mind during one of our last sessions, and I told him, "Even though my limp's less and less noticeable to people on the outside, I'll always carry it with me."

And Dr. Daly said, "Not scars of the body, but the scars of the soul. I'm familiar with those."

• • •

While I was getting ready for the dance, you were napping. I'd forgotten what wearing slacks felt like. On the way out of the infirmary, I bent over our bed and whispered to you, "I love you, baby." Your hair smelled like a combination of rose and orange. You didn't wake up.

Sarah was at the desk eating a microwave dinner, and as soon as she saw me she rolled her chair backward and looked me up and down. She told me that I cleaned up nice.

I said, "I do, don't I?" but I wasn't saying that in a major dickhead way. It more leaked out from surprise at being reminded of information I felt like I'd misplaced. I glanced down at myself, checking out the parts that I could. I remember putting my hands in my pockets and bouncing them there because I was enjoying the feel of the fabric on my legs.

"Tonight, Sarah, I feel really great," I said.

"You've done it," she said, but not with that much excitement. She blew on a piece of pork and put it in her mouth. "Go out into the world. And please try to do something worthwhile with yourself."

"But tonight comes first before I tackle the world," I joked. "Tonight I'm going to dance." I held out my arms to show her. "I'm leaving the crutches at home."

"You think you're ready?"

"I have no doubt."

"You're going to have to be careful and take your steps slowly," Sarah said. I took a few steps forward and backward to show her I was doing all right. And then, I don't know if I was really conscious of the transition, but my steps turned into hops, and in a few seconds my arms were out and rounded like I was holding a ghost girl. I told her, "Like riding a bicycle. I'm even going to take the stairs."

"No. Just take the elevator, okay?" she said.

"I'm taking the stairs."

Sarah put down her fork and told me that if I was going to be so stubborn she wouldn't try to stop me, but she was going to help.

So I put out my hand and said, "There's no need. Look." I went down the hall to the stairs and took my first step down. Before I took another, I turned around and asked, "Are you going to be here tomorrow?"

She'd be gone by the time I came back the next day to get my stuff, so we said our good-byes then. She came over to me and put out her hand. "It's been good knowing you."

We shook. "Thanks for taking such great care of me."

"Well, it's my job," she said.

And I said, "Even so. Thanks."

I could feel her eyes on my back while I was taking those initial stairs. I was traveling carefully, step by step, but I didn't hold the rail. I kept my hands in my pockets. Downstairs the lamps were off, but the moon was huge that night, and I began this game of stepping only in squares of light on the floor. And here's a hugely dorky admission: I was pretending that I was Michael Jackson in the "Billie Jean" video, and that my feet were making every spot they touched glow.

The air outside was so vacation-like—a real kind of warm, not the heater kind of warm that we were so used to—that when I reached the front doors, I stopped to bask in it. My cab was waiting at the curb. I guess the driver thought that I was unable to go any farther, so he started to walk toward me.

"Do you need some help?" he called out.

"Do I look like I need help?" I wondered out loud. I wasn't asking that like he'd rubbed me the wrong way, but like I needed to know if a layperson could tell that I hadn't been walking for months.

Probably thinking he'd insulted me, the driver looked down and told me, "No, you look fine."

I even managed to get into the cab myself, El.

When we got to the Biltmore driveway, I saw my dad inside through the glass doors. He was sitting in a chair near the elevator. He hadn't spotted me yet, so I jogged over to the landing. I took the first five steps ducking down. Right before I put my foot on the sixth, I casually said, "Hi. Nice night, huh?"

My dad turned his head, and when I knew he'd recognized me, I took that last step. I practically jumped up it. He also jumped up and his smile was so genuine, so *rare,* and I think he didn't know what to say because all he came up with was "Welcome back!"

We hugged tightly and I asked, "Welcome back?"

"It just leaped into my mind," he told me.

"Chess!" my mom called, stepping out of the elevator. We also hugged, and afterward she held my shoulders and tilted me away from her, like she wanted to get a clear view of my knees, so she could believe they were healing. She told me I looked wonderful, and I just said thank you, thank you, thank you.

We got into another cab, and as we went up College Hill,

I felt like our moods were following that same incline. From a block away we could see the front lawn lit by hundreds of lanterns dangling from wires. The school looked like a yacht, swaying with all these carefree, euphoric people on board. The rest of the hill was dark, like it was the surrounding ocean. The music filled the car and, even though I know this is a dangerous thing to refer to, I'm just going to do it and say my soul.

The dance was so crowded that it took us thirty minutes to get from the front to the back lawn. As we made our way through the mob, my dad and mom kept turning around to make sure that I was still standing. I kept flashing them the A-OK sign.

In front of Faunce, Tyler Mandrake grabbed onto my back and yelled, "You are *it*!" He was in the Bear Necessities with me.

Tyler was really drunk, so he just kept rambling. "The guest of honor. We've all been waiting for you. I swear, I'm going to go up and tell the band that they need to play something. How about 'Tarzan Boy,' because you're a warrior, Chess, a fucking warrior." (I swear, this is the shit he was saying.) "We've missed you; no one does your part right. We tried a freshman and he sucked cock. Your legs work now, huh? You warrior. There's no one I could be more happy to see right now than you, Chess Hunter, than you." He just wouldn't stop talking, but it was nice. It was really nice.

Tyler told me that the guys were going to sing later in front of Manning, and he asked me if I'd join them.

"Yeah. I'll sing," I said. And, El, I have to admit that I was instantly, disproportionately excited, like the singing had already begun.

When my parents and I got to Lincoln Field, we saw Marna and David standing with their parents next to the statue of Marcus Aurelius. Marna's dad was trying to get her to swing dance with him, but she would only let him have her arms. David was smoking and talking with his dad, who was also smoking. David's mom was talking into Marna's mom's ear to make herself heard, and we heard David burst out, "Why don't you just nibble on her ear, Mom?"

David's mom came up from Marna's mom's ear and asked, "What'd you say, David?" in her thick Israeli accent.

"Why don't you just go ahead and eat her?"

"What are you talking about?" She pointed to Marna's mom in confusion while searching David for answers. "Janette?"

"Yes, Janette. You're standing on top of her. I'm sure she finds it very uncomfortable and weird. You've got to give people space, Mom, because people are mammals, meaning that we require air to breathe—"

"Oh, David, please," said Marna's mom, rolling her eyes but giggling, "I'm fine. Leave her alone."

Right then everyone discovered us standing behind them and their faces lit up. "Chester! Olivia!" exclaimed David's mom as soon as she saw my parents. "It's been such a long time!" My mom and dad split and joined their respective sexes, and they were like two doors swinging open, suddenly revealing me. "Hey," I said.

"Hey," Marna said.

"Hey," David said.

I don't know where you went the morning the infirmary discharged David. I think you were maybe at the hospital. Anyway, David and I had promised each other that we'd stay in better touch, but we hadn't talked since February.

That night, though, when I was reunited with my old friends, the three of us studied each other and courtesy seemed like the stupidest route to take. How do I explain it to you? Okay, it felt like time was pressing onward. Urgently. And it was erasing past disappointments and heartbreak. It was like that moment was burning so bright that everything before and after it was forced to dim, and that's as close as I can get to describing how much energy that one moment took up without taking your arm and squeezing it.

We grabbed cups of wine from the passing server and raised them to the future without verbalizing a toast. And with that gesture, I instantly felt the promise of movement. And I felt time rushing forward (like it was a solid) and taking us along with it, while everything in the past grew darker and darker behind my back.

CHAPTER 29

THE JOURNAL OF PARAPSYCHOLOGY OCTOBER 2004

The night of the campus dance, I was about to enter through the Van Wickle gates when I saw E approaching. Initially, I believed that she was an apparition born of my own psyche. I had spent so much of my time thinking about her and her case that I wondered if I was projecting her image onto another student's body. There was no reason that she would be walking down the middle of the street by herself.

As she came closer, however, I confirmed that it was, indeed, E.

She was wearing a strapless green party dress that she must have been hoarding since she arrived at school, and I noticed her collarbones immediately. Without fabric covering them, their sharpness was alarming.

She was leaning on a cane for support.

When E reached me, I asked her what she was doing outside of the infirmary, and she responded that she was going to surprise C at the dance. She refused my offer to accompany her across the lawn, saying that the cane was "help enough."

Then E proceeded to walk up to a table where a volunteer was collecting tickets. "One ticket, please," she told him.

The man patted the top of his metal cash box. "We don't sell tickets, we take them. They had to be purchased in advance."

"Please?" she asked. I watched as E stepped around to the side of the table so that the man could have a clear look at her cane. I was too fascinated by her behavior to step in and assist her in gaining entry to the dance.

The volunteer, obviously surprised to discover that this young woman was dependent on a cane, immediately softened. I believe that E, seeing this, began to make the arm that was clutching the cane shake for effect.

"I don't take up much space," she said, staring at him. I almost laughed at her performance.

"And get inside you shall!" the volunteer said, guiding E around the table and personally escorting her into the dance. Once beyond the gates, she waved and disappeared into the throngs.

The next morning the tape arrived at eight o'clock. Within a half hour, I received a phone call that set me racing back to her side.

CHAPTER 30

From The Desk of Chester Hunter III

Marna began trying to work me back into their lives. It was very sweet to watch. She touched David's thigh and said, "He has, like, three interviews with different agencies out there—"

"Four," David corrected.

"Impressive." I nodded to let them know that I was up for all of the reconnecting.

"And it's pretty much guaranteed that I'm going to be working for a nonprofit in the city," Marna continued. "They're just figuring out salary right now, but what we do is find new-looking, professional clothes for homeless people and teach them how to wear them confidently. Then we set up job interviews."

"Just tell him the name," David said.

"Okay, so it's called Person-All Style," Marna apologized. "Which I know is a stupid name, but—"

David and I laughed in unison. I mean that our actual pattern of laugh-sounds was in unison, which I found amazing, considering that there've got to be billions of different laughs in the world.

There was a group of seniors dancing in a circle near us, veering a little too close to David's sphere of personal space. A girl's elbow eventually brushed up against his back, so he turned around, basically inserting himself into the ring, and said, "If you want to dance with me, guys, you should just ask instead of trying to get me to notice you. You don't have to be so immature about it."

Everyone in that circle gaped at him and began backing up toward the left. I just remember thinking, "That's my David."

He finished his drink in one swig and then threw up his arm in exasperation. I remember watching a last drop of wine going flying through the sky. When I'm drunk—and how weird it is to realize that you've never even seen me drunk—I get fascinated by the smallest images. "No one has any integrity anymore," he said. "Hey, speaking of, did you hear that the police think they've caught the guys who did your knees and my head?"

"What do you mean? When did that happen?" I asked.

"This morning. It hasn't been released to the public yet, but they called me. They probably didn't know how to reach you. Get this—it turns out that it was a group of bullshit semiotics kids doing these attacks as part of a 'piece.' That's what they called it—'a piece.' What incredible assholes, right?"

"A piece for what?"

"They wanted to see if they could create orchestrated class warfare between Brown and the working people of East Providence. Yeah, good luck."

"But how did the police find out about them?" I asked.

"One of the geniuses turned in his senior thesis confessing *everything*. Except it was written in the third person, so it was supposed to seem fictional. But the kid's advisor turned it over to the cops."

"This is incredible," I said. "For this I spent my senior year crippled?" I was sick (not to use the word glibly, but it's the best one for the situation), discovering that I had only been a pawn in someone else's pointless game. I had been a speck in a larger whole that wasn't even a whole that represented anything important. I was so disgusted. So over it *all*.

"You know what?" I said. "Let's not talk about this anymore." And here's the most astounding thing, El. Just saying that, I felt the incident being commanded farther away. I hate to bring up my soul twice in one letter, but really, it was like the memory was lifting from my body like a separate soul. And instead of the extra soul hovering around me, it went down and burrowed itself into the ground at that dance. It stayed buried in that spot in the middle of the field, a spot capable of holding on to the phantasms of injury and death that I knew I couldn't carry around anymore.

I like to believe that it's still there.

"Tonight's for celebrating the things that are yet to come. Let's have an authentic toast," I said.

We all raised our cups, even David, whose was empty.

"To tomorrow!" I said.

"To tomorrow!" Marna and David repeated.

"So," I started, wanting to lead by example, "you two are going to San Francisco?"

Marna nodded. "Anyway, that's our plan. You're still moving home?"

"Yeah. My dad's friends with the mayor, who talked to him about this position they're trying to fill, and my name came up—"

I turned my head to glance up the lawn. That's when I saw a backlit figure moving like a grasshopper would if it could stand up straight. Every part seemed to move in accordance with different instructions. The top bobbed from side to side. The left side raised and jerked as the right side dropped. I watched as the figure approached me (and I remember grasping, *me,* that figure is approaching *me*) and all I could think was "There is something very wrong with that person."

And then I realized that it was you.

(I am sorry. I am so, so sorry.)

You came under the next row of lanterns, and they lit you up, lit up your face. You were jabbing your cane into the plywood covering the lawn, raising up your body as far as you could. And then you'd keel and lurch forward again, completing another step. I know that you could not see yourself, El.

• • •

As I was packing up in the morning, you reminded me, "Don't forget the books you were keeping in the fireplace."

"Thanks," I said. "I would have walked out of here without them." I glanced up to smile at you, and as hard as this is to own up to (I know that at least some small part of me is terrible, and I'd do anything to change it), I was alarmed by how you looked. I thought that you might be getting thinner. That was probably why you seemed stranger somehow, I guessed. And I know this is the shittiest thing to tell you, but in the spirit of total honesty, I remember thinking it was like aliens had sent you as a replacement while they took their time prodding my real girlfriend.

I only tell you these things now because I would be more terrible not to.

I zipped up my bag and then panicked for a second because I realized that I had nothing else to do with my hands. I was just standing there, lost, in the middle of the infirmary. So I said, "This is the last time I'll see this room. It's hard to believe."

"I'll send you a picture," you said.

And what I told you next was all true. I swear to God, to whatever I have to swear to. "There's a part of me that wishes I could pack up this infirmary, everything in it—" I know I looked at you. "And take it with me. On road trips I used to see trucks on the highway transporting entire houses. Have you seen that before?"

"No," you said.

I am fairly sure that I said something very stupid like "Oh."

I knew the only thing left for me to do was to pick up my bag, since that was the last action available to me. I told you I had to get going—my parents were waiting for me. That was also true.

"Okay," you said.

I kissed you on the forehead and I had trouble breaking away. I told you to take care of yourself and I fucked up the words. I hope you have the same memory of that minute because, at least in my head, it was tender.

At the door I looked back, and I'm still not sure, but I

thought that I saw some tears in the corners of your eyes. I really couldn't tell if your eyes were just tired and watering, like I'd seen before, or if you were about to cry. Like an idiot, the song that immediately popped into my head was "No Woman, No Cry," and I was going to sing that part to you. But now I know that if I was going to be a fucking, insensitive idiot and sing anything at all, it should have been the part of the song where Marley just repeats over and over again, *"Everything's gonna be all right."*

I had almost shut the door behind me when you suddenly yelled "Bye!" at the top of your lungs. It was almost a scream. And in that moment I had to decide whether I should just run out or look back in. I looked back in because I had to know.

"What was that!" I asked you.

And you said, "A proper good-bye."

You could say that this letter is mine. And maybe that's why it had to be ugly in places, because I knew you'd just be all the more disappointed in me if I didn't do it right this time. I tried to follow your example. That letter to me changed my life, you know. The tragic thing, at least to me, is that now, looking back, I've realized it changed me in a direction that led away from you. It was after I read that letter that I began to feel like I could go back outside.

What else could have been done, El?

WHAT ELSE?

I believe it had to happen. Or I should say that I have to believe that, or I'll be torturing myself forever. It's only been a week since I left, but I know instinctively the feeling would last forever.

I think of you often. I think of you with the strangest kind of love.

Sincerely,

Chess

CHAPTER 31

THE JOURNAL OF PARAPSYCHOLOGY OCTOBER 2004

On May 27th, I was the neighborhood FedEx courier's first delivery of the morning. Before I had even signed for the envelope, I was opening it and speed-reading the documents contained within. The EVP expert, Dr. Macrae, confirmed that the disruptions on the recording were the result of an outside force acting on the physical surface of the tape, and, as I suspected, were not the result of sounds laid down within the recording itself. Dr. Macrae went on to explain that he had seen this type of phenomenon before, where "spirits," as he referred to them, "left a corporeal imprint on recording (both audio and visual) materials much like the living leave footprints in mud."

Having thoroughly examined and documented the defects in the tape, Dr. Macrae concluded that they were too deliberately positioned to be coincidence. Moreover, it was his firm belief that E (and I never suspected that she had) could not have created the defects on the tape. These, he asserted, were identical to those effects produced when massive amounts of energy exert themselves upon a magnetic field, and could not be easily duplicated by human intervention. In fact, Dr. Macrae wrote that he was "pleasantly mystified that the recording device had not broken under the strain. It is truly strange that it did not."

The "bad news" came toward the close of the papers. Dr. Macrae had been able to isolate the presence of the "spirit's energy" within the defects, not the particulars of his conversation or identity. He concluded that the apparition had left no trace of his voice, thoughts, or emotions. Dr. Macrae even attempted to uncover a "track" underneath the defects, where perhaps the apparition's energy had organized itself into an urgent thought. Sadly, there was no such track.

Thus, we had our first concretized proof of supernatural activity, but it did not move us any closer toward discovering who the apparition was.

I was startled when the phone rang just as I began tucking the papers back into their envelope. After reading in depth about the apparition's imprint, I'd been left feeling as if he were in the room with me. For a split second, I believed that when I picked up the phone, I would hear an otherworldly cacophony—the apparition attempting to tell me the rest of his story.

There was a living person on the line, however. It was my old friend Dr. Wainscott, the same man who first told me about E.

He spoke. I listened. Before he'd finished, I was grabbing my car keys from the bowl in the entryway and running out the door. Later I would find out that I'd not hung up the phone, but left it on the floor.

Very uncharacteristically, I drove eighty miles per hour the entire way to Health Services. My speed only seemed to make the rest of the world move more slowly—the lights, other drivers, time itself. When I pulled up to Health Services I was giddy with anticipation, and I distinctly remember that I did not want to take the extra half second to lock my car doors. Not to place a spiritual bent on the moment, but material concerns did feel very irrelevant.

Because it was Saturday, the building's front door was locked and I had to ring the bell. I rang it more than once. When Vivian appeared, she was exasperated, and gave one of her suspicious looks, which produced déjà vu within me. I flashed back to the first day that I'd met her in the infirmary and, unwittingly, insulted her observational abilities. On the doorstep, I experienced the uncanny sensation that my own life was repeating itself.

I jogged to the top of the stairs with Vivian trailing behind, still perplexed by my behavior, and when the desk came into view, so did E. She had the phone to her ear and was facing in the opposite direction.

"E!" I called, and she spun around and called back, "Mark! I was just calling you!" Her finger was still in the process of entering my number and she lifted the phone to show me.

Vivian, trusting E's judgment and ability to fend for herself, announced that she had to go finish some work in the lab.

I placed my hands on E's shoulders, unintentionally shaking her as a result of my own raw nerves. "Listen to me," I said, "I have big news."

"I have *huge* news," E responded.

"Please, just listen to me," I continued. "Please. Ten minutes ago I received a call from Wainscott. Yesterday a patient was checked into RIH, E." I heard my voice ringing inside my head. I was hearing tones that I rarely utilize. "There was a patient admitted to the psych ward, and then diagnosed with tetanus. Wainscott found out this morning. E—"

I wanted her to seize this moment with me. While her face remained jovial, she did not seem to be grasping the magnitude of what I was telling her.

"E," I said, "the patient was recently discharged. And. He is. On his way over. To the infirmary."

"No," E said, shaking her head.

"Yes! Yes! It's difficult to grasp at first, isn't it? This changes everything!"

"No," E repeated. "He's not on his way over. He's *here*."

I remember the bottom of my stomach dropping out, and then turning around to see what or who was at my back, suddenly taken by the feeling, once again, that I was being watched. "Where?" I asked, my voice now closer to a whisper.

E motioned to the closed door of the infirmary. "In there," she said, sharing a look of astonishment with me. We stared at the closed door, barely able to ponder the answer contained within.

"But this means—" I said after two silent minutes had passed, looking back toward E.

E finished my thought. "This means that I haven't been reliving someone else's past." Her eyes grew large, locked on mine. "I've been seeing my own future."

We had been looking in the wrong direction.

Earlier that morning C had departed the infirmary, and from what I could infer, the parting had not been pleasant. E would not share much about it.

Once she was alone, E told me that she looked at the

beds, all made up except hers. Then she lingered on the impression of her body that remained pressed into the mattress. "I am a candlestick," she remembered thinking, "and that's my box I go back into." The realization that the room was hers again hit powerfully, and she claimed to have felt ownership reverting back to her. She said that she underwent a psychological transfer, becoming cognizant of every single property of the room as if she had been away on vacation and "only just came back."

Overwhelmed, she walked out of the infirmary to take a brief respite before she reclaimed her space.

Passing Vivian, E remembers noticing the nurse filling out a new patient's admissions forms, and she thought to herself, "Oh. Someone else."

E followed the main hallway down to its end, then turned the corner. At the farthest examination room, she lowered herself against the locked door and rested on the floor. She was resolved to stay there until the hallway dimmed for evening.

She estimated that almost forty-five minutes later, the apparition came around the corner. Upon seeing her, he stopped and said, "Hey."

"Come on," she said, shaking her head. She felt her eyes brimming with tears.

"You? Right now?" she accused.

"Give me a break," she begged.

It was this last sentence that struck E with recognition. She froze. They were repeating themselves.

"What's wrong with me?" asked the "apparition."

As E studied him, it became clear to her that he was no longer in ghostly form. As E put it, "It dawned on me that his head was blocking the wall behind him. It was a solid head." E understood that she was face to face with a living, breathing human being.

For the past seven months, E had been communing with a character in her imminent life who had been waiting for her to catch up. This option had not even occurred to either of us, since we had been convinced that the young man was dead.

Why hadn't we considered the option? After all, at E's birth, A had proclaimed that she would possess foresight because of her caul. I can only hazard the guess that E, fearing the development of this ability, did her best to discount it, and I subconsciously followed her lead. Although she had never been happy about the prospect of being able to see ghosts, I believe having access to the past was a less threatening alternative for her. While she might be inconvenienced by the presence (and requests) of the dead, she could still take comfort in the slight separation between their lives. To put it most simply, the relationship would be of a therapeutic nature. E would have license, just as a professional therapist does, to separate the problems of the deceased from her own.

Second sight, however, brought with it not only greater responsibility, but greater confinement. I believe that, for E, the gift of the prophecy would mean a tight cocoon of repetition, in which she would be forced to know everything before it reached her. She would be, so to speak, a ghost inside her own future.

Once, A had told E that if she should ever come into her abilities, she would fall in love with how many mysteries there were in the world. However, what E had dreaded was the opposite. She feared that when she began to see what others couldn't, there would be no mysteries left.

When she realized that the apparition was flesh and blood before her, E later reported, she had thought to herself, "My life is over." She felt instantly devastated by a locked conception of the future and confessed that the idea of suicide had flashed through her mind.

But, just as E began to feel herself in total service to inevitability, there was one detail that snapped her back to the present.

She realized she had yet to answer the new patient.

E knew that during their last meeting, she had accused him of being dead and questioned him about how he had gotten that way. Now, however, the patient was clearly very much alive, which meant that her former comments no longer made sense. The context had altered.

With this discovery, E described herself as feeling adrift. This feeling is what suddenly filled her with, in her own words, "immense gratitude." It occurred to E that no matter what she foresaw, she would never understand what her role was to be until the actual moment arrived.

Her abilities had left her a loophole: she was excised from her own visions. Within the next few months, E would confirm that this was true.

At the hallway desk, E held out her tape recorder and instructed me to listen.

I heard the patient ask, "What's wrong with me?" I felt chills hearing his voice for the first time.

Then E responded. "Nothing's wrong with you. Well, something's wrong with you because you're here in the infirmary. But here's what's wrong with me. I'm in the midst of a very bad time. My first love just left me this morning. It's become obvious that I'm not leaving here anytime soon. Painfully obvious, meaning that I have much literal pain. It's almost transfusion day again. Also, I'm under the inescapable impression that I have supernatural powers, can see the future, and knew you were coming.

"But beyond that, I don't have much to say right now. So you talk. Even if you think I'm psychotic, please talk. I think I'll be fine in awhile."

E told me that the patient appeared completely unfazed by her speech, and he walked toward her, just as he had before. Once again, he paused about two feet from where she was and slumped down, his knees bent. He hung his long arms over them.

As he stared at her and she stared back at him, E noticed the subtleties in his expression. She saw an unusual acceptance of what she had just said. She saw amusement, but not "the negative kind." She thought also that she could see a certain measure of patience.

"Please tell me a story," E said. "Tell me why you're in this hallway." She wanted to hear it all again, wanted to experience it anew.

"The reason I'm here is probably supposed to be embarrassing," the patient said, "but I don't feel embarrassed about it. Are you easily offended?"

"No."

E clicked off the recorder and looked up at me with the face of a child. "Can you believe it?" she asked. I told her no, and then I told her yes.

"Can I see him?" I asked.

"He's supposed to be resting in the dark because of his tetanus, so I finally got him to do that." E and I walked toward the infirmary door. I felt boyish again, but I suppose that all personal breakthroughs hurtle us back toward our youths, to a time when we were just beginning to figure out the nature of things. Quietly, E placed her hand on the knob and turned.

From over her shoulder I peered into the dimmed infirmary. The shades were drawn, the room shapeless. When my eyes began to adjust to the dark, I could make out a figure lying in the third bed from the left. His features became more and more defined as more seconds passed, and soon I was looking at a face that I already knew from the artist's rendering. My breath caught in my chest and felt too powerful for the cavity to hold it.

"I told him as much as I could," E said about the new patient. He turned his head toward her, now aware that we'd entered the room. I was aware of the crackling of the pillowcase—of, as E had said, "a solid head."

"Hey," the patient said, smiling in the endearing manner that E had often described.

"It is remarkable to meet you," I responded, letting the door go. I will confess my feeling upon entering that room. I am not proud of it, but it was jealousy. It was not romantic jealousy, as E and I were doctor and patient, nothing more. While I suspected that she and the patient were at the beginning of an intimate friendship, this was not what disturbed me. Instead, it was the jealousy that occurs when a secret, something shared, expands its borders to another person. E and I had been bound together under the same secret for such a long time that I could not help but feel a sense of loss when the source of that secret became independent, touchable, real outside of me.

Nonetheless, I battled my feeling and took a seat. That day, we occupied the first three beds, and we spoke until the darkness was so heavy that we could not make each other out anymore.

ACKNOWLEDGMENTS

Thank you to:

Amy Hempel, Ann Patty, the other four members of the Bennington Five (especially Hannah Pfeifle) + Kate Milliken, Cressida Connolly, David Hough, David Mead, Doug Stewart, Jodie Hockensmith, Jody Hotchkiss, the Houghtons (especially Audrey), Kay Kurashige, Kim Lash, John Nguyen, the Litwacks, my family, Nick Dalton, Philo Farnsworth, Sean Daily, Sheila Kohler, Sloane Miller, and Spack.